THE PICKLEBALL MURDER

A LISA MARCH MYSTERY

BY HARVEY S. CARAS

The Pickleball Murder

A Lisa March Mystery

ISBN 978-0-578-79435-8

First Printing, November 2020

Cover design by Carasmatic Design

Published by YM Press

Printed in the United States of America

To Joanne, the love of my life, who inspires me to sit down and write, and to get up and play Pickleball.

To my children, Jonathan, Rachel, and Michael, to whom I told many stories in their youth.

To Sarah, Dan, and Leah, and to all of my gorgeous grandkids.

To all of our Pickleball friends at PGA Verano.

CHAPTER 1

JULY 9, 2018, 4:00 P.M.

"Hello, this is Brian Reagan in the TV 12 newsroom. We just received word that the jury has reached a verdict in the trial of Dr. Leonard Bates. For more on this breaking news let's go to Mary McCambridge, live at the court house in Fort Pierce."

"That's right, Brian. I'm here in front of the St. Lucie County court house, where we have just been notified that a verdict was reached after four days of deliberation in this, the highest profile trial ever to hit the Treasure Coast. Many people have dubbed this The Pickleball Murder Trial because the Riverside Estates community, where the murder occurred, is well known as the Pickleball capital of south Florida."

"Twice the jury had told judge Jose Velez that they were deadlocked, but both times he refused to accept a hung jury and forced them back into deliberation."

"Doctor Leonard Bates was accused of planning the murder of his wife, Diane Bates, in February of this year. The tumultuous trial lasted three weeks before it was handed over to the jury, and soon we will learn whether this sixty-nine year old retired doctor will go home, or spend the rest of his life behind bars."

"You can see behind me that many people are now entering the courthouse and we expect to hear the verdict read within the hour."

"Thanks Mary. As soon as the verdict is announced we'll break into our regularly scheduled programming to bring you back to Mary at the courthouse."

• • • • •

That verdict would mark the end of a case that shook an exclusive Pickleball community in Port St. Lucie, Florida. Or would it?

CHAPTER 2

FEBRUARY 15, 2018, 3:15 P.M.
POLICE HEADQUARTERS
PORT ST. LUCIE, FLORIDA

Detective Lisa March was seated at her desk when she heard the booming voice of Captain Davis.

"March! Torres! Get your asses in here, now!"

At age fifty-seven, and a five time grandfather, Captain Robert Davis was a rugged thirty year veteran of the Port St. Lucie Police force. He had worked his way up through the ranks and, after having been passed over several times, finally made captain in 2014. He was well respected among the rank and file as well as the top brass.

Within seconds, Lisa and her partner, Dan Torres, were in the captain's private office. Davis closed the door behind them.

"We just got a 911 call from a man named Len Bates in Riverside Estates." Davis said sternly. "He says his wife was murdered. Listen to this."

Female voice: "911 operator, how can I help you?"

Male voice (calmly): "Ah, yes, ah, my name is Doctor Leonard Bates. My wife has been murdered. We need the police and a coroner to come and check out the crime scene."

Female voice: "Excuse me sir, did you just say that your wife was murdered?"

Male voice (calmly): "Yes, she was bludgeoned to death. I found her here a few minutes ago and I checked her pulse. She's dead. It appears that she was killed about three to four hours ago."

The captain reached into his desk and handed Lisa a slip of paper.

"Here's the address. I need you guys to get over there right now."

Lisa looked at the address and said, "Riverside Estates, that's a pretty swank neighborhood!"

"Yup," Davis replied. "it's by far the most exclusive community in Port St. Lucie. I think it's where the mayor lives, so we need to get all over this case fast."

"Forensics?" she asked.

"Already there, with the coroner and several uni's to keep the gawkers away. But apparently the husband is driving them all crazy."

Lisa felt an adrenalin rush. "We're on our way, boss!" she said with confidence.

As Lisa and Dan headed for the door she heard Captain Davis say, "Don't fuck it up!"

"Thanks for the vote of confidence, boss!" Lisa replied with a grin, as she and Torres made their way out of the precinct to their awaiting car.

This was an assignment Lisa March had dreamed about. At forty-three, she was an eighteen year veteran of the Port St. Lucie police department, She stood barely five feet tall and weighed less that 100 pounds, but everybody knew that Lisa March was the toughest and best detective in the department.

Her partner, Dan Torres, was much less experienced, but in his two years as a detective he had proven himself to be a valuable team member. At thirty-one, handsome, and single, he was the most talked about man by the women of the Port St. Lucie police department.

Within minutes, Lisa and Dan arrived at Riverside Estates. As they drove up to the guard house they were met by a spectacular display of water fountains and palm trees.

“This place is amazing!” Dan said, “nothing I could ever afford.”

“Who knows, Danny. Maybe someday. Just keep buying those Powerball tickets.”

The two detectives flashed their badges and drove past the guard house and then followed their GPS to the crime scene at 1520 River street. They parked the car and forced their way through the crowd while ignoring the questions that were fired at them. They ducked under the yellow crime scene tape and made their way to the front door.

You just don’t expect to find a dead body in a house like this, unless it’s from a heart attack or an accident, certainly not a murder, Lisa thought. As they made their way up to the front door they were met by Ron Hazelton, from the fire department.

“Hey, Ronnie,” Lisa said, “I heard you’re the new battalion chief?”

“Ye,” Ron said, blushing.

“I couldn’t think of anyone more deserving, Ronnie.”

“Thanks, Lise.”

“So, what’s going on in there?”

“No need for us,” Ron said, “it’s a murder scene now.”

“Okay, thanks,” Lisa replied. “send my love to Patty.”

Lisa and Dan walked inside the house and were greeted by a huge window and a spectacular view of the St. Lucie River. In the back of the house was a large stone swimming pool with a rock waterfall. Behind the house was an empty boat dock. The sun was beating on the river and a few sailboats were passing by.

“They say this river is dirty, but you’d never know it from here,” Dan said, “this place musta cost a fortune.”

Lisa walked into the master bedroom and saw that Stephanie Rogers, the county coroner, was examining the body. The forensics team was busy doing their jobs.

Next to Stephanie were two uniforms and a strange man. He was wearing shorts, a tee shirt and hat, and a pair of tennis shoes. He was a little pudgy with gray hair peaking out from under his cap. It only took a glance for Lisa to realize that this was the husband and the victim was his wife.

The husband was hovering over Stephanie's shoulder and Lisa could see Steph didn't like it. She walked up to him and thrust out her hand.

"Hi, sir, can we go talk in the kitchen?"

The husband stared at Lisa and said, "my wife is dead."

Lisa noticed that Len Bates was as cold as the victim, not his body but his demeanor. He just didn't seem like a man whose wife was lying dead. But then again, who knows how I would react if it were my husband lying there, she thought. Yes I do, she figured. I'd be crying like a baby if anything like that happen to my husband.

Lisa walked out of the bedroom into the living room, hoping the husband would follow. He did. They sat down in chairs opposite each other and Lisa switched on her recording device.

"I'm detective Lisa March of the Port St. Lucie police department," she said softly, "and you are?"

"Leonard Bates. That's my wife lying dead in the bedroom."

"First, let me say Mr. Bates. that I'm very sorry for your loss," Lisa began, wondering if that would evoke any emotion.

"Thank you," was his calm and cold answer. "and it's Doctor Bates."

Lisa noticed his strong Boston accent. The word doctor sounded like 'Doctah' when it came from his lips.

"Of course, Doctor Bates. I'm recording our conversation so we'll have a record of it."

"I know. I was a coroner for thirty years in Boston, so I know the routine."

"Good. So you also know that it's important that we search your house. Do you have any objection to us doing that?"

"Of course not," Bates replied.

She asked Dan to look for any forced entry into the house and make sure that all the rooms were clear. Then she turned her attention to Doctor Bates.

"You were the one that found her?"

"Yes."

"What time did you leave the house this morning?"

"I left here at 9:00 to play Pickleball. The games usually start around that time."

"And when did you finish playing?"

"Around 11:00. After Pickleball I went to brunch with a group of friends."

"And where did you have brunch?"

"At our club. I called Diane to invite her to join us but she didn't answer."

"Okay. I'll need a list of everyone that you had brunch with."

"There was a whole crowd, probably ten people. We do it all the time."

"And what time did you finish brunch?"

"I guess around 12:15."

"And you came home then?"

"No. Then I went to Home Depot to buy some boxes, And after that I stopped at CVS, then I got a haircut."

"Where was that?"

"At Super Clips, in the Saint Lucie Shopping Center."

"So then, what time did you finally get home?"

"It was just about 3:00 when I got home."

"Okay, now," she said, "you said you found her. How exactly did that come about?"

"I saw that Diane's car was in the garage. I called her name when I got in the house but she didn't answer. I figured she was at a neighbor's house or something so I went to take a shower. When I walked into the bedroom I saw her there. She was lying in bed face down with the covers over her."

"Was that an unusual thing for her?"

"No, she always sleeps like that. She sometimes takes a nap during the afternoon so I went to wake her. That's when I saw that she'd been beaten to death."

Still no emotion from Bates.

“How did you know she was dead?” Lisa asked.

“Young lady,” he said, puffing out his chest. “I told you I spent thirty years as a medical examiner. I think that qualifies me to determine when someone is dead!”

“I understand, sir. But I just wanted to know if you touched her body,” Lisa said.

Lisa could see that the doctor was getting annoyed by the fact that she would question him. “Of course I touched the body!” he said, with obvious derision in his voice.

“I checked her pulse first, and I looked for signs of breathing,” he continued, totally emotionless. “Once I removed the blanket, I could see that her head was badly bruised. Based on my estimate of her body temperature, and taking into account the fact that she was under a blanket, I determined the time of death to be between ten and noon.”

“Okay, that’s fine,” Lisa replied. “Now, we’re gonna need you to give us the clothes you’re wearing.”

“You can have them!” Bates shouted. “But I didn’t kill my wife, for God’s sake!”

“Does your wife also play Pickleball, Doctor Bates?”

“Yes, she does quite often, but today she was expecting a FaceTime call at 10:30 from her daughter and grandkids in Boston, so she decided to skip Pickleball.”

“So, are you certain that Diane was alive when you left, sir?” Lisa asked. “ Did you speak to her before you left?”

“What kind of question is that?” Bates answered with derision. “I certainly would have known if there was a dead body in my bed!”

“Yes, I see, but, just for the record, did you speak with your wife before you left the house?”

“No, she was sleeping. I didn’t want to wake her.”

“She was in the bed?”

“Of course she was! That’s where she is now and I didn’t move her.”

“Did you happen to notice anything missing when you got home? Jewelry, or anything valuable?”

"I didn't look for that," Bates replied. "I was concentrating only on trying to help my wife."

"Did you and your wife have dinner together last night?" Lisa asked.

"Yes, we did."

"And what time did you finish eating?"

"Around seven, I guess."

"About what time did she go to bed?"

"She always goes to bed at 11:00."

"And you?"

"I stayed up and watched the news, so I went to bed at 11:30."

"Did your wife snack at all between dinner and bedtime?"

"No," Bates replied, "why are you asking this?"

"Because this will help the coroner determine the time of death."

Bates was irate. "Young lady, I am a coroner and I just told you the time of death!"

Lisa could feel the tension mount. It was clear that Bates didn't like the idea that he was being questioned.

"Look, Len," she said

"Doctor Bates!" he shot back, obviously letting her know that his status was above hers.

Lisa wasn't buying it.

"Okay, Doctor Bates," she said calmly, "as a former coroner you certainly understand that the police need to get all the information from the crime scene as soon as possible."

"Uh huh."

"And that is exactly what I'm doing, and I truly appreciate your cooperation."

Bates seemed to calm down a bit after that.

"Okay, okay," he said.

"Doctor Bates, did your wife take any medications before she went to sleep last night?"

"She always takes an Ambien before bed."

"Okay," Lisa said, "Doctor Bates, can you think of anyone who would want to harm your wife?"

"No, not really," he answered quickly. She was surprised that he gave her question such little thought.

Just then Dan Torres appeared and said, "the house is clear, and no signs of forced entry, but the back sliders are unlocked. Forensics is dusting it for prints."

"Thanks, Dan." Lisa said, and returned her attention to Doctor Bates, "sir, do you normally keep your doors locked when you leave the house?"

"No, not really," he answered, "we lock up when we go to bed at night but during the day we don't lock our doors. Sometimes we even forget to lock up at night. This is a safe neighborhood. We've got a guardhouse so nobody can get in here without permission."

"I understand," Lisa said, thinking about the irony of what he had just said.

She asked Dan to check with the security guard and get a list of everyone who came into the community today.

"How long have you and your wife been married?"

"We just celebrated our eighth anniversary last Christmas."

"Kids?"

"She has two daughters from a previous marriage. I have one son."

Lisa gave Bates her business card and said, "thank you. I'll certainly have more questions as the investigation continues. In the meantime if you think of anything that could help us please let me know."

Len Bates examined the card and grunted.

"As you know this house is now a crime scene so we need you to move out until further notice," Lisa said, "do you have a place to stay for a few days?"

"My son lives in Jupiter."

"Okay," Lisa added, "do you plan to inform your wife's daughters about what happened today"

"No I'm not planning to do that. We don't communicate."

"Oh, uh. Okay then. I'll let them know."

Lisa asked Dan to stay with Doctor Bates while he changed clothes and she gave him a bag to collect them. She instructed the officer to escort him to his car and see that he left the house. Then she walked back into the bedroom and was greeted by Stephanie Rogers.

At six foot-one, Stephanie towered over Lisa, and over most men too. With over thirty years on the job she was the most experienced coroner in the department

By now a hearse from the coroners office had arrived and was preparing to take the body away.

"She was hit three times on the back of her head with a blunt object," Stephanie said, "we'll know more after the autopsy."

"Okay, thanks. Did you happen to find her cell phone?"

"It was right next to her on the night stand. I'll bag the phone for you."

Lisa left the house to be met by a crowd of onlookers, most of them neighbors who were curious to find out what had happened. A uniformed officer approached her with a hysterical young woman.

"This is Mrs. Bates' daughter," he said, "her name is Jennifer Messenger. She wants to see her mother."

Lisa was moved by the sight of the frantic daughter. She walked with her to the side of the house, out of view from the gawking crowd.

"I'm so sorry," she said quietly, "but I can't let you in there."

The young woman cried frantically, "But that's my mother in there. I have to see her! Is she gonna make it?"

Lisa shook her head and said, "I'm sorry to tell you, your mother has died."

"No!" Jennifer cried. "I have to go in there!"

"I understand how you feel, Mrs. Messenger," she said, "but this is a crime scene and we just can't let anyone in there." She held Jennifer's hand and kept her from entering the house.

"He killed her, didn't he!"

"Huh?"

"Her husband! He killed her! She said he would kill her, and he did!"

"I'm sorry, ma'am," Lisa responded, "I know how painful this must be for you. I'll come to your house and talk to you about it tomorrow. And I can assure you that we're gonna do everything in our power to find out who killed your mother and bring that person to justice."

With that Lisa asked Dan to escort the daughter back to her house.

As she left the scene, Lisa asked if anyone in the assembled crowd had seen someone enter or leave the Bates house between 9:00 and 3:00. Nobody had seen anything. She took all of their names, addresses, and phone numbers and gave each of them her business card.

As she entered the car, she called Captain Davis.

"Hey, boss, we're gonna need a team for this," she said, "tell everyone to get a good night's sleep, because tomorrow's gonna be a busy day."

CHAPTER 3

FEBRUARY 16, 2018, 9:00 A.M.

PORT ST. LUCIE POLICE HEADQUARTERS

Captain Davis addressed the group that had gathered in the precinct conference room. The room was filled with twelve detectives, including Lisa March and Dan Torres. Also present was prosecutor Megan Harris.

"As you all know," Davis began, "yesterday there was a murder in the Riverside Estates. Because it's the mayor's neighborhood, we consider this a high profile case. There's no doubt that the press and the mayor will be all over us to solve this crime quickly. Chief Sales already asked me to keep him abreast of everything we find out."

Several small conversations ensued.

"Alright," Captain Davis shouted, "settle down."

"Lisa March will be the lead detective on this case so I want you all to help her with anything she needs. This is priority number one. Everybody got that?"

All heads nodded.

"Lisa, why don't you give them a rundown on what we know so far."

Lisa stood up to speak. As she reached her feet Detective Lonny Carter shouted "Stand up, Lisa!" A few chuckles followed.

“Alright, asshole,” Lisa shot back at Carter, “I admit I’m short but why don’t you admit where you don’t measure up?” She held her thumb and forefinger two inches apart as the room erupted in laughter. Carter grinned but sat stoically after that.

“As I was saying, before I was so rudely interrupted,” Lisa began, “a fifty-nine year old woman named Diane Bates was found bludgeoned to death in her bed yesterday at 3:00 p.m. by her husband. His name is Doctor Leonard Bates, sixty-nine, a retired coroner from Boston.”

“Stephanie is doing the autopsy this morning, so we should have more details on the cause of death later today. And we can expect the complete forensics report the next day.”

“Doctor Bates says that he was playing Pickleball at the time his wife was murdered and that she was alive when he left her at 9:00 a.m. and dead when he returned at 3:00 p.m..

“Lonny, I need you to make yourself useful. You and Danelo head over to Riverside and interview everyone who plays Pickleball. Let’s find out if the husband’s alibi holds up.”

Dan Torres chimed in, “and you should also ask if there is anyone else they know of that might have a reason to kill Diane Bates.”

Detective Carter and his partner Beth Danelo both nodded.

“Eddie,” Lisa said, in the direction of detective Ed Coppola.

“That’s me!” Coppola answered with a smile.

“I want you to find out everything there is to know about Diane Bates. From the time she was born to the time she died. I wanna know everything she did in her life, family, friends, business, affairs, Pickleball, whatever. I want to know what’s in her bank account, what’s in her will, and what life insurance she has, Who benefits from her death.”

“I’m all over it, Lisa,” came Eddie’s quick reply, “if she took a shit in the woods I’ll find it.”

“Good,” Lisa replied, “and Joseph,” she said to detective Joe O’Hara, “I need you to do the same thing to the good Doctor.”

By now Lisa was in total control of the room.

“Yes ma’am,” Joe said.

"Based on what we know now, Len Bates was the last person to see the victim alive, and the first person to see her dead, so you know what that makes him."

"He's our number one suspect," Joe responded quickly.

"It's always the husband!" Lonny shouted. "I watch Dateline, and it's always the husband!"

"If you had a date once in a while, Carter, you wouldn't be home watching Dateline every night!" Detective JoJo Worthington joked. She was among the many who loved to tease Lonny Carter. Lonny just had a way of making himself the target.

The laughter subsided when Lisa continued.

She pointed to detective Sheila Feeney.

"Sheila," she said.

Sheila Feeney was an attractive red head. At thirty-seven, she was an eleven year veteran of the Port St. Lucie police force, and for the past five years she had been a detective specializing in surveillance and computer technology. People said that there was no code Sheila Feeney couldn't break, no password she couldn't hack.

"Forensics has the victim's cell phone, Sheila," Lisa continued.

"As soon as they release it I need you to go through it with a fine toothed comb. Let's find out who she talked to, who she texted with, what apps she used, what photos she had. You can use that to help Eddie, okay?"

Megan Harris added this, "And if anybody needs a warrant for anything just let me know. I've got a judge on speed dial."

"The husband said his wife was expecting a FaceTime call at 10:30," Lisa continued, "I want to know if that call ever happened."

"Ten-four," was Sheila's reply, "I might be bugging you for a lot of warrants, before this case is over, Megan!"

"No problem," Megan replied, "I know what you do, and I'm here for you. Let's just make sure we do things the right way."

"It's the only way I do it, Megan," Sheila answered.

"Andy," Lisa said.

"Yes sir!" Andy replied

Lisa chuckled. She and Andy Spears had been partners for four years, ending when Dan Torres became her partner in 2016. Andy always called her 'sir'.

"Danny has a list of everyone who came through the guardhouse before three that day. I need you to follow up and find out what every one of them did once they got past the guard."

"I'm all over it sir!"

"And finally," Lisa said, "I need Doug and JoJo to canvas the street and see if anyone saw or heard anything that might help us find the killer. Anybody who came or went between 9:00 and 3:00 is a person of interest, for sure."

The two acknowledged their assignment.

"Also," Lisa continued, "I need you to go to the homes on the other side of the river. It's a different neighborhood, I'm not sure of the name. But it's possible that someone over there saw a boat approaching the Bates house that morning. Okay?"

"Got it,"JoJo replied, and that ended the initial assignments for the case.

"Danny and I are gonna focus on Len Bates. We'll bring him in for questioning."

"I'm afraid you won't be doing that," came the quick retort from Megan Harris.

"Huh?"

"Bates lawyered up. I got a call this morning from JD Treem."

"JD Treem?" Captain Davis asked.

"The one and only JD Treem," Megan replied. "He says that he now represents Leonard Bates and that all future communication should come through him."

John David Treem was well known throughout South Florida as the premier criminal defense attorney. Whenever a wealthy person was charged in a high profile case JD Treem was the man. JD was a grizzled veteran of forty years whose reputation was that he would do anything to win a case, regardless of whether it was ethical or not.

JD was a small man, no more than five foot-four, with a large crop of curly white hair. His signature dress in the courtroom was a suit with suspenders and a big bow tie. Over the course of his career JD had defended wealthy socialites, politicians, TV stars, and even a United States Congressman. Any prosecutor who faced JD Treem in court would have to work harder and smarter than they ever had before, and most of them failed to live up to the task.

"Does that also include the son in Jupiter? I was gonna talk to him too."

"Treem didn't specifically say so but my guess is he'll want to keep you away from the son too."

"That sucks. But I can assure you guys that if Bates is the guy we're gonna nail his ass for this. Right now, I like him for it."

She paused for a moment and spoke again to Megan.

"Okay then, Bates is off limits, but Danny and I will track every move he made that day. We'll see if he told me the truth about his whereabouts. And we'll talk with Diane's two daughters. One lives in Boston but the other one lives right there in the Riverside neighborhood. I've got an appointment to visit her this afternoon."

"One more thing," Megan added. "JD Treem will exploit any mistakes we make in this case. We all have to do our absolute best. Everything by the book, no shortcuts."

Megan Harris had never lost a case. In her four years as St. Lucie County prosecutor every case she had handled had been either pled out or the defendant had been found guilty in court. Megan was an attractive young woman but she always dressed down in court, never wanting to let the jury focus on her looks, but instead on the words that she and her witnesses were saying.

She relished the thought of taking on the "old master" JD Treem in what would certainly become the highest profile case ever to hit the Treasure Coast.

"Okay," Lisa replied. "We get that."

"Every possible lead has to be explored," Megan continued, "and every possible suspect has to be cleared before we can charge anyone, especially Leonard Bates."

“All I ask is that you respect that,” Megan concluded, “and please keep me updated on what your investigation finds.”

“Will do,” Lisa replied to Megan. And then to the entire group, she added, “Now let’s go find a killer!”

CHAPTER 4

FEBRUARY 16, 2018, 9:00 A.M.

RIVERSIDE PICKLEBALL CLUB

Lonny and Beth pulled their car up to the parking lot of the Riverside Pickleball club.

"Ever played this game before?" Lonny asked as they walked towards the courts.

"Never," Beth said, "I played a lot of tennis in my younger days but I never even heard of Pickleball until a couple of years ago when they started building courts in town."

"I never played either," Lonny said, "I heard it's like tennis, but for old farts to play!"

"Better keep that to yourself when we talk to these people," Beth said, as she surveyed the scene in front of her.

There were several miniature tennis courts, and each court was filled with four people, two on each side of the net. In between the rows of courts were chairs under a covered canvas roof, and several players were sitting and chatting between games.

"This place is awesome!" she said as they walked up to the courts, "if they had clubs like this when I was young I might have played this game."

"My family could never afford a place like this," Lonny said.

"Mine either," his partner replied.

Lonny surveyed the players in their tennis outfits and sneakers. Then he looked at Beth in her black slacks, gray top, and black shoes.

"You think they'll notice us?" he said with a grin.

"Yeah, you blend!" Beth replied in her best New York accent.

"Just like my cousin Vinny!" Lonny joked, "great movie!"

Beth and Lonny sat down in two of the sideline chairs and watched one match. It seemed like the players were having a lot of fun, joking and teasing as they smacked a plastic ball back and forth with what looked like overgrown ping pong paddles.

"What's the score?" one player asked.

"I can't remember!" her opponent replied.

"Whose serve is it?"

"Mine, I think."

"Didn't you just serve?"

"Yeah, you're right."

"Confused?" came a question from behind Beth. She turned around to be met by a handsome gentleman dressed in tennis clothes. He thrust out his hand and said, "Hi, I'm Bob Benson."

"Hi, Bob," Beth replied, "this is a confusing game, isn't it?"

"Actually, it's pretty simple," Bob responded, "we just make it look complicated!"

"Oh."

"Are you two thinking of moving to Riverside?"

"Actually…" Beth tried to respond before she was interrupted.

"Because I'm the number one realtor here in the Estates." He handed Beth a card that said Benson Realtors. "There's never been a better time to buy than right now! A lot of couples like yourselves move here just because of this fabulous Pickleball Club."

That's when Lonny decided to show his police badge.

“Actually we’re not a couple,” he said, “and we’re not here to buy a house.”

“We’re here investigating the murder of Diane Bates.”

“Oh,” Benson replied coldly, “tragic, wasn’t it?”

“Do us a favor, will you?” Lonny said, “please let everyone know that nobody should leave this club until we’ve had a chance to talk with them.”

“If anyone needs to go soon we’ll talk to them first,” Beth added.

For the next three hours Lonny and Beth methodically interviewed thirty-three Pickleball players. Each one was asked what they knew about Diane Bates, her husband Len Bates, and who they thought would have a reason to want to see Diane dead.

Exhausted, they left Riverside.

“Is that the most hated woman you ever heard of?” Lonny asked his partner.

“Absolutely!” Beth replied.

“And how about that Benson guy?” Lonny said, “the number one realtor!”

“He said there’s never been a better time to buy!” Beth joked. “What do you say partner, you ready to buy?”

“Oh yeah,” Lonny replied, “have you ever heard a realtor say it’s a bad time to buy?”

The two partners laughed as they headed back to the station, anxious to tell Lisa what they had learned

CHAPTER 5

FEBRUARY 16, 2018, 1:30 P.M.
THE HOME OF JENNIFER MESSENGER
RIVERSIDE ESTATES

Lisa and Dan drove up to the house at 1212 Panama Way. It was a nice house, but modest compared to the mansion occupied by Len and Diane Bates. They were greeted at the door by Jennifer Messenger, her eyes still red from crying over the loss of her mother.

"When can I see my mother?" Jennifer asked as Lisa and Dan entered the house.

"As soon as the coroner releases her body you'll be able to see her and make funeral arrangements," Lisa replied.

"Okay," Jennifer said, "I really need to tell her I love her and I need to say goodbye. My sister's flying down from Boston tonight"

"I understand," Lisa said, "and we'll certainly make sure you both have that opportunity to say goodbye to your mom."

Dan interjected, "Today we'd like to learn everything we can about your mother, her marriage, family, friends…"

"Anything you can tell us that will help us find out who did this to your mother," Lisa added. She turned on her recording device and said, "we'll be recording this for future use."

Jennifer took a deep breath as she sat on the sofa opposite Dan and Lisa.

"My mother was a wonderful woman," she began, "she was strong and was never afraid to speak her mind."

"That is very admirable," Lisa replied. She had learned over the years that showing compassion for the victim's family was very important in a murder case.

"You said something to me yesterday at your mother's house about her husband," Lisa said softly, "would you care to elaborate on that for us?"

"He did it! Plain and simple," Jennifer said, "there's no doubt in my mind that he did it."

"What makes you think that?" Dan asked.

"Because she told me he would!" Jennifer responded, "she said, if I ever end up dead, it was my husband that did it."

"Why do you think she believed that he would kill her?"

"Money. It was all about money?"

"Can you elaborate on that for us, Jennifer?"

"My real dad was a wealthy man," Jennifer began, "after he died we moved to Boston and soon my mom began dating. We were very concerned that she might meet a man who was after her money."

"How did she meet Doctor Bates?"

"She met him through an online dating service that catered to wealthy people"

"Really!" Lisa replied, "I've never heard of such a thing."

"It's called Millionaire Match," Jennifer continued, "so, when she met Len Bates, he said he was a doctor, and he acted like he was very rich. He wined and dined my mother and charmed her, and soon they got engaged."

"So, he wasn't rich?" Dan asked.

"Far from it," Jennifer answered, "he was almost broke. My sister and I checked him out. He never had a private practice of his own. He only worked for the city of Boston as a coroner."

"And you told this to your mother?"

"We begged her not to marry him. He was a phony and we knew he was after her for her money."

"But they got married anyway?"

"Yes, they did."

"Did she have a will?"

"Yes, she did, but my sister and I made sure he wasn't the beneficiary. We even hired a lawyer to make him sign a prenup."

"So, what are the provisions of the prenup?"

"I can't remember everything, but basically it said if they got divorced he wasn't entitled to any of her money, and that her will could never be changed without the consent of her daughters."

"And he signed the prenup?"

"Yes, he did. But right after they got married he took out a two million dollar life insurance policy on my mom."

"Okay," Lisa responded, "so how did the marriage go?"

"At first it went pretty well. They moved to Florida and they both liked it. They started playing Pickleball, and they made a lot of friends. My husband and I moved here a year later."

"So, when did the marriage start to go downhill?" Dan asked.

"At first they were Pickleball partners, and they were the best team at the club," Jennifer said, "but then they started losing games, and Len started complaining that mom wasn't good enough. He always picked on her, so she quit being his partner. It didn't take long for him to find another partner."

"What was her name?" Dan asked.

"Abby," Jennifer answered quickly, "Abby Jenkins. She was a lot younger than him, and I guess she thought he was a rich guy, so she played with him. It didn't take long before they started having an affair."

"When did all this take place?"

"Last year, around June, I think."

"So your mother found out about the affair?"

"Yes. We suspected that he was cheating with Abby, but we didn't have any proof. Then one day he told mom he was going up to Boston for a retirement party of an old colleague. My sister Becca lives in Boston so we had her follow him and see what he was up to. Sure enough, she caught him and Abby going into his hotel room together."

"So, what happened after that?" Lisa asked.

"Becca and I begged mom to divorce Len, but she said she didn't want to face the embarrassment of everyone gossiping about them. Len begged for another chance so she gave it to him. Abby even moved out of Riverside."

"When was that? When did Abby move away?"

"Just after Thanksgiving last year, I think."

Lisa adjusted her chair slightly and asked, "Jennifer, you told me that your mother knew that Len was going to kill her. Tell me exactly why you think she believed that."

"Well, in the past few months they weren't getting along at all. Mom suspected that Len was having another affair, but he denied it and she couldn't prove it. But she started resenting him more and more every day."

"Okay, but what made her think that he wanted to kill her? That's a pretty drastic thing to do."

"She said he really wanted to divorce her but then he wouldn't get anything. She owned the house so he would be forced to leave Riverside with nothing."

"Uh huh, but murder? Where did that idea come from?"

"Mom said Len was obsessed with TV shows like 20/20 and Dateline. And he would always comment about how dumb the husbands were that murdered their wives and got caught."

"And that's it?"

"No. She also sneaked a peak at his cellphone one morning while he was playing Pickleball and she checked out the websites he visited."

"And what did she find?"

"It was all these sites about how to get away with murder!"

"Okay," Lisa responded, "we'll definitely take a look at his cell phone."

"Jennifer," Dan interjected, "I know that you firmly believe that Len killed your mother. But can you think of anyone else that would have a reason to kill her?"

"Absolutely not!" Jennifer shot back. "It was Len Bates! Doctor Leonard Bates!"

"Okay, thank you, Jennifer," Lisa said, "I need to ask you one final question so we can eliminate you from suspicion. Where were you between the hours of 9:00 and 3:00 yesterday?"

"I was at my daughter's nursery school," Jennifer replied, "I'm a volunteer mom, and yesterday was my day to help out."

"What time did you arrive?"

"I drove Emma to school at 8:15 and I stayed there until school ended at 3:00. When I got home around 3:15, my neighbor told me something was happening at my mom's house, so I went over there."

"Thank you, Jennifer," Lisa said, "you've been a big help."

She handed Jennifer her card. "If you think of anything please don't hesitate to call."

"When can I see mom?"

"We'll definitely let you know as soon as we can."

Lisa and Dan walked out of Jennifer's house.

As they entered their car, Dan said, "if Len Bates was studying how to get away with murdering his wife he sure did a lousy job!"

"My thoughts exactly," Lisa replied.

CHAPTER 6

FEBRUARY 20 2018, 6:00 A.M.

PORT ST. LUCIE POLICE HEADQUARTERS

Lisa met with Coroner Stephanie Rogers in her lab in the basement of the police station. She was surprised to see Prosecutor Megan Harris there.

The body of Diane Bates was lying face-down on the autopsy table, partially covered with a sheet. Every dead body was creepy to Lisa, and it always amazed her how clinical and matter of fact the coroners were when they talked about the dead.

"I just wanted to see for myself," Megan said, as Stephanie lifted the sheet to uncover the deceased's face. "and I'm curious about the cause and time of death."

Stephanie pointed to the back of the victim's head. "As you can see she was hit with three fierce blows to the back of heard while she was sleeping in her bed."

"The first blow probably did enough damage to kill her, but then the killer hit her two more times."

"Brutal," Lisa said.

"Yes, it was," Stephanie replied, "she had a massive hematoma in her brain which resulted in her death. There was a little external bleeding as we found dried blood in her hair."

"Was she raped?"

"We found no signs of sexual assault, and the lab is working on DNA. We should get those results in a few days."

"How was it done?" Megan asked.

"It appears that she was asleep in the bed, face down, when the killer jumped on top of her. He bludgeoned her to death very quickly," Stephanie replied, "the whole thing took only a few seconds. She had no chance to fight back and she was dead within a few minutes."

"Sounds like she hardly knew what hit her," Lisa said.

"True. And we found Ambien in her system, a very heavy dose, and also Valium. She must have been out like a light."

"Any evidence that she was drugged by someone else?" Megan asked.

"Are you thinking maybe the killer drugged her to make it easier to kill her?" Stephanie replied.

"That's exactly what I'm thinking," Lisa said, "she couldn't fight back because she was drugged."

"Forensics found the prescription bottles. Her prescription was to take one, 10 milligram Ambien before going to bed but she had taken at least three that night, along with a 10 milligram Valium. That alone could have killed her, but she was clearly bludgeoned. It's likely that she was sound asleep right up until the time she was murdered."

"Any chance she was already dead when she was hit?"

"No. She was out like a light, but still alive."

"But, there's no way to tell if she took the pills herself or if somebody else gave them to her." Lisa said, "any DNA on the pill container?"

"I'm sure they'll find hers and also her husband's."

"So the husband's DNA could be on her meds?" Lisa said, "that could be huge!"

"Yes, but, in all honesty, that's pretty common. He could be using them too."

"How about fibers?"

"We found fibers from the husband's clothing on the blanket, but he was all over her when we got there, so that was expected."

"And the murder weapon?" Megan asked.

"We found traces of polymer in her hair and the wounds are about three quarters of an inch wide," Stephane replied, "it's not something I've seen before, but we're working on identifying the murder weapon."

"Could it be a Pickleball paddle?" Megan asked.

"I've never seen one before, but I'll get a few different paddles down here and see if one of them matches up to the wounds."

"Did they find a Pickleball paddle in the house?"

"Well," Stephanie replied, "forensics went through the entire house with a fine toothed comb, they even went through the trash cans in the garage. They found nothing like that."

"Did they check the cars?"

"Both of them, his and hers. They found one Pickleball paddle in his trunk but it was still in its case and was clearly not the murder weapon. He must have been using it when he played that morning."

"They only found one paddle?" Lisa asked.

"Yes."

"Bates said that both he and his wife played Pickleball," Lisa said, "so that means there should have been at least two paddles in the house or in the garage."

"So where did her paddle go?" Megan asked.

"I guess only the killer knows that," Stephanie said calmly.

Lisa grabbed her cell phone and quickly called her partner, Dan Torres. The phone rang several times before a groggy Dan answered.

"Danny?" she said, "sorry to wake you, partner."

"It's okay," Dan replied, "I was gonna get up in a few minutes anyway. What's up?"

"I need you to get right on something big."

"What's that?"

"I need you to contact the property manager for the St.Lucie Shopping Center, " Lisa said, "make sure that none of their dumpsters get emptied until we release them. And do the same for every dumpster in or near that shopping center."

"Go it, Lisa."

"And then I need you to assemble a team to search every one of those dumpsters."

"Dumpster diving?" Dan joked, "my favorite sport! So what are we looking for?"

"We're looking for anything that came from the murder scene, but especially we're looking for a Pickleball paddle that was used to kill Diane Bates."

"A Pickleball paddle in a dumpster," Dan replied, "that's gonna be a fun job."

"Get a bunch of rookies to do it," Lisa said, "but make sure they all wear gloves and bag anything they find, even if it seems insignificant."

"I'm on it right now, partner."

"Thanks, Danny," Lisa said, "I owe you lunch."

"Hmmm," Dan replied, "that makes, what now, twenty-three lunches you owe me?"

Lisa laughed, ended the call, and returned her attention to the coroner.

"Let's talk about time of death," Stephanie continued, "based on the stomach contents, rigor mortis, and body temp, I can safely say that she was killed between 10:00 a.m. and noon."

"Okay, so maybe that clears the husband," Megan said.

"Only if his alibi stands up," Lisa corrected her, "he said he was playing Pickleball from 9:00 a.m. to 11:00 a.m., brunch after that, and shopping until he got home at 3:00 p.m."

"Okay."

"We're gonna check all of that out," Lisa continued, "it's possible that he could have slipped into the house sometime between 10:00 a.m. and noon."

“His house is only a couple of minutes from the club,” Megan added, “and, like you said, it only took a few seconds to kill her.”

“It pisses me off that the husband was right about the time of death,” Stephanie said with a grin.

“Me too,” Lisa said, “he’s a smart guy, but that doesn’t mean he’s not a murderer too.”

“And, by the way,” Stephanie added, “the forensic boys grabbed a water bottle from the husbands car so we’ve got his prints and DNA.”

“I could kiss you right now!” Lisa said with a grin.

• • • • •

Megan returned to her office to find a missed call from JD Treem. As soon as she sat down at her desk she picked up the phone and dialed the office of Treem and Associates. She asked to speak to JD Treem and was placed on hold for what seemed like an eternity. As she listened to the obnoxious “on hold” music she thought about hanging up, but, just as she was about to do, so she heard the booming voice of JD Treem.

“How are you today Mrs. Harris?”

“Just fine, Mr. Treem. What can I do for you?”

“I just wanted you to know that I also represent Jefferey Bates.”

“Len Bates’ son?”

“Yes, that’s him. So any questions you have for Jeffrey need to come through me. Okay?”

“That’s fine,” Megan replied, “I didn’t realize that Jeffrey Bates was a person of interest in this case, but I’ll let the detectives know that you represent him as well as his father. As long as I have you on the phone, is there anyone else that you represent that we should know about?”

Treem chuckled, “well, my firm has over 600 clients, so I’ll let you know if any of them are involved in your case.”

“That’s very thoughtful of you, Mr. Treem,” Megan said sarcastically.

“Come on now, Mrs. Harris,” Treem replied. “you don’t have to be so formal with me. You can call me JD. May I call you Megan?”

"Sure, JD, call me Megan. And by the way, I was going to call you today because I have a warrant for Doctor Bates' cell phone. Shall I send an officer to pick it up or would you prefer to deliver it to us?"

"Oh, what a shame!" Treem replied.

"Shame?"

"Doctor Bates misplaced his phone in his haste to comply with the detective's order to leave his house. He can't find it."

"How convenient," Megan replied sarcastically, "so I guess we need to look for it in the house." She knew that the cell phone would never be found.

"Yes, you do that Megan, and can I tell you one more thing?"

"Sure, what's that?"

"I know you probably think that Len Bates killed his wife. I just want you to know that he didn't. So, the sooner you clear him, the sooner you can get around to finding the real killer."

"That certainly makes sense, JD, I'd be happy to clear your client. Why don't you bring him to the station tomorrow for a full interview?"

JD chuckled, "oh you're good, Megan. I heard that about you. The interview isn't gonna happen. But if you tell the detectives to submit a written list of questions, I'll gladly review them with my client, and we might even answer some of them."

"Okay, JD. I think we're done for now."

"Let's keep in touch, Megan."

As Megan Harris hung up the phone she realized why JD Treem was the best criminal defense lawyer in Florida.

CHAPTER 7

FEBRUARY 20, 2018, 9:00 A.M.

PORT ST. LUCIE POLICE HEADQUARTERS

The team was assembled once again in the precinct conference room. Both Megan Harris, the prosecutor, and Stephanie Rogers, the coroner, were also present at the meeting.

Captain Davis started the meeting.

"We're here again investigating the murder of Diane Bates," he said, "the Chief called me first thing this morning and he wants a briefing this afternoon. Lisa, what do we have so far?"

Lisa stood in front of a large white board. The name DIANE BATES was written in large letters across the top of the board. A straight line from that name connected to the name LEN BATES.

"Yesterday," Lisa began, "Dan and I met with Diane's daughter, Jennifer Messenger. She's one hundred percent convinced that Len Bates killed her mother. There's no doubt that Bates had motive and opportunity, but we're gonna need a lot more than that before we can charge him."

Lisa placed a large circle around the name of LEN BATES on the white board.

"Eddie, what did you find out about Diane Bates?"

Ed Coppola stood and looked at his notes. "It's the strangest thing I ever heard," he said, "Diane Bates didn't exist before 2007!"

A rumbling from the room began, and it got progressively louder as the detectives pondered what Ed had just told them. The noise was interrupted by prosecutor Megan Harris.

"That's no surprise," she began, as she looked carefully at her notepad.

"I got a call from the FBI last night," she continued. "It seems our victim had quite a background."

"What?" Lonny Carter asked, "was she in the CIA or something?"

"Not quite, Lonny," Megan replied, as she walked toward the white board to address the group.

"Diane Bates was born in San Diego in 1958. Her name was Janice Foster."

"Janice?" Lisa asked.

"Yes. And in 1981 she married Donald Whitson, an attorney whose office was in San Diego. Together they had two daughters, Denice, who was born in 1983, and Rachel, in 1985."

"Wait a minute!" Lisa shouted, "I met one daughter, and her name was Jennifer, and she said her sister was named Becca!"

"This gets better and better," Megan replied, "so, let me continue. Donald Whitson had a very successful law practice, and that made him a very wealthy man. But that all came crashing down in October of 1997 when he was indicted for laundering money for a Mexican drug cartel."

Megan took a sip of water and continued.

"Janice Whitson was the bookkeeper for the firm so she was also up to her eyeballs in the money laundering."

"Then what?" Lisa asked.

"Then Donald Whitson agreed to turn states evidence and testify against five top members of the cartel. In exchange for his testimony, his indictment was dropped, and he and his family were placed in the witness protection program."

"Wow!" Captain Davis shouted.

"Wait, it gets better!" Megan responded, as she once again consulted her notes.

"All five drug men were convicted and each was sentenced to twenty years in Federal prison."

"And what happened to the Whitsons?"Lisa asked.

"In 1998 the Whitsons were moved to Boise, Idaho, where they became the Melon family. So, Janice Whitson became Amy Melon, and her husband became Henry Melon. And the rumor is that he had a lot of money hidden in Swiss bank accounts."

"Okay, then what?" Ed Coppola asked.

"I though you'd never ask!" Megan replied with a grin, "In 2005 Henry Melon was shot to death while he sat in his car in front of a restaurant in Boise. That murder was never solved, but there's little doubt that it was a revenge hit ordered by the cartel."

"This is fascinating," Captain Davis said, "so then what?"

"So then," Megan continued, "Amy Mellon and her daughters were relocated again. This time they moved to Medford, Massachusetts, and they became the Frank family, Diane, Jennifer, and Rebecca Frank."

"Wow!" Eddie said, "this is freakin' amazing!"

"I'm surprised they could keep even track of who they were!" Lonny Carter shouted, as everyone chuckled.

"Shortly after that, all three women got married," Megan continued, "my FBI friend said they believe that the women all set out to find husbands just to get new last names. Harder for the cartel to track them, I guess."

"So that explains why I couldn't find anything about Diane Bates!" Eddie said.

"And it might also explain why she married Len Bates," Lisa added.

"Yes, that's true," Megan responded, "but it also creates someone else with a motive to kill Diane Bates."

"You think the cartel found her and killed her?" Dan asked.

“No, I don’t believe that,” Megan responded quickly, “I think Len Bates killed her. But I can assure you that Bates’ lawyer will try to exploit this to create reasonable doubt.”

“So how do we clear the cartel?’ Lisa asked.

“I’ll work with the FBI on that,” Megan replied, “you guys keep working the local angles”

Once again the room was buzzing.

“Okay, settle down!” Captain Davis shouted, “let’s keep going, March.”

Lisa once again took control of the meeting, “Eddie, were you able to find out about the will?”

“The will leaves everything to her two daughters and their husbands.”

“So, how much are we talking about?”

“We’ve got warrants to check all of her accounts. The banks aren’t willing to give us any information without the warrants.”

Sheila Feeney jumped in, “I think I can help with that.”

“We’re all ears, Shiela,” Lisa said.

“Diane Bates had a St. Lucie Bank app on her phone that allowed her to monitor her investment portfolio,” Sheila said, “I was able to hack into it.”

“You’re amazing,” Captain Davis said, “how’d you do it?”

“Most people use a password that will be easy to remember, like the names of family members and important dates.”

“Okay.”

“Diane’s granddaughter is named Emma and she was born in 2014. So the first we password I tried was emma2014. Bingo!”

“Holy shit!” Captain Davis decried, “I’m gonna change all my passwords tonight!”

“How much does she have, Sheila?” Lisa asked.

“This account had 21.7 million dollars. All of it had been transferred from the Swiss Bank account in 2010.”

The group of detectives began to mumble.

“Who did you say gets that money now that she’s dead?” Lisa asked.

“The will leaves everything to her two daughters and their husbands, split four ways.”

“And the house?”

“The house is appraised at 1.9 million. No mortgage. It’s in Diane’s name only so it goes to the daughters and their spouses too.” Ed Coppola said.

“So that’s puts the estate at what?” Megan asked.

“With investments, cars, jewelry, and other assorted shit, we figure it’s well over 25 million.”

“Don’t the Feds want a piece of that, Megan?” Captain Davis asked.

“I’m sure they would love to get their hands on it,” Megan replied, “but part of the deal they made with Diane and her first husband was that they could keep their money.”

“And Doctor Bates gets nothing from the estate?” Lisa asked.

“Well, if you call a two million dollar life insurance payout nothing, then I guess he gets nothing!” Ed replied.

“Those daughters were pretty smart about keeping their mother’s money away from Len,” Lisa said, “but two million is certainly enough for a motive.”

“Well, they weren’t that smart,” Ed said.

“How’s that, Eddie?” Lisa asked.

“They allowed their husbands to be named as beneficiaries in the will,” Ed replied.

“I wonder, why would Diane Bates have done that?” Lisa said.

“I have no idea,” Ed replied, “that’s a question only the daughters can answer.”

“Wow!” Lisa said, “this just keeps getting better and better!”

“So, they added the husbands to the will,” Megan said, “does this mean that each of the son-in-laws gets the same amount as the daughters?”

“Yes, but here’s the sad part,” Ed said, “Jennifer’s in the process of getting divorced from her husband.”

“And they never changed the will?” Lisa asked.

"Nope," Ed added, "even when then husband moved out, the will was never changed."

"I bet Jennifer's not happy about that now!"

"But the son-in-law must be really happy!" Dan Torres said.

"I wonder if he even knows about it?" Lisa added.

"The husband's name is David Messenger," Lonny said, "he was also one of the Pickleball players."

"People say he was the best Pickleball player in the club," Beth added, "he and a few other guys would play from 8:00 to 10:00 every morning and then he would leave to go open his restaurant in Jensen Beach in time for the lunch crowd."

"But, like you said," Lonny continued, "Dave and his wife split up two months ago."

"Strange, she never mentioned any of that to me." Lisa said.

"According to the Pickleball players the divorce was really nasty," Lonny continued, "lots of fights about money, who kept the house, who got custody of their daughter. You know, the usual stuff."

"You know all about nasty divorces, don't you Lonny?"came a comment from detective Joe O'Hara, "how many times have you been divorced now, Carter?"

Most in the group laughed when Lonny answered back, "I lost count, Joey!"

Beth broke the laughter when she continued with her narrative, "David Messenger moved out of his house right before Christmas, but because he was still a homeowner he continued to play Pickleball at the Riverside club almost every day."

"But, here's the juicy part," Lonny said, "apparently, his mother-in-law was accusing him of some bad shit."

"Like what?" Lisa asked

"Like molesting their three year old daughter," Beth said.

"That's despicable!' Lisa responded.

"We heard from several of the Pickleball players that Diane was telling everybody that Dave was a child molester," Lonny said, "it got so bad that Dave had to quit playing Pickleball."

"And, it gets even worse," Beth added, "one day Diane walked into Dave's restaurant and announce to his staff and to the patrons that Dave was a child molester. She wouldn't leave until the cops came and ushered her out."

"Wow!" Lisa said, "that would make me want to kill her!"

"I think inheriting one fourth of her estate would motivate me even more!"

"Me too!" came the mumbling from the group.

"If Diane Bates hated her son-in-law so much why would she leave him one fourth of her estate? It doesn't make sense!" Megan said.

"I'm not sure she even knew about it," Ed Coppola answered, "the will was drafted by her daughter's lawyer and Diane might not even have read it before she signed it."

"I guess we'll never know that," Lisa said.

"I bet the lawyer knows," Dan replied.

"Sheila," Lisa said, "let's get a copy of that will, and I want to talk with the lawyer who drew it up."

"Will do," Sheila replied.

"Andy, can we put Dave Messenger in the Riverside neighborhood that morning?" Lisa asked.

For the first time detective Andy Spears spoke up.

"I checked the gate logs for every visitor that came into Riverside that morning," he said, "Dave Messenger's name wasn't on the list"

"Yeah, but wait," Dan Torres replied, "wasn't Messenger still considered a homeowner?"

"You're right!" Andy shouted, "so that means he wouldn't have come through the visitors gate. He could have just come in the homeowners gate."

"Find out if he still had one of those gate thingees," Lisa said.

"Gate thingee?" Andy chuckled, "you mean one of the stickers on the windshield that opens the gate?"

"I think it's called a transponder," Captain Davis offered.

"Yeah, that thingee!" Lisa said, "I never lived in a gated community, so I never got one of those …"

"Gate thingees!" every detectives shouted in unison.

"Okay I'll check with security," Andy said, "and I'll find out if there's any way to tell if he came in, and what time."

"Captain, can you get some uni's to pick up Dave Messenger and bring him in for questioning?"

"Consider it done," The Captain replied as he walked into his office to make a phone call.

"Lonny, I'll handle this interview," Lisa whispered, "the wife was so adamant that Bates killed her mother but she never said a word about her husband. Strange!"

"Be my guest," Lonny replied.

Lisa wrote the name DAVE MESSENGER on the white board.

"Any reason to suspect the daughters?" Megan asked Lisa.

"I don't think so," Lisa responded, "one daughter lives in Boston and I talked to the local daughter. She has an air tight alibi that checks out."

"Lonny, you and Danelo are up," she said firmly, "what did you find out from the Pickleball crowd?

Lonny stood up, relishing in the fact that everyone in the room was paying attention to him. His partner Beth Danelo sat quietly by his side.

"We interviewed thirty-three Pickleball players," he began, "and the one universal thing we learned is that everybody hates Diane Bates. And I mean everybody!"

"Not one person had a nice thing to say about her," Beth added, "she was loud, rude, and confrontational. She hated to lose and always blamed her partner."

"And she cheated at Pickleball!" Lonny added, prompting several chuckles in the room.

"Cheated at Pickleball?" Captain Davis asked, "how the hell do you do that?"

"Easy," Lonny replied, "in Pickleball, each team calls the other team's shots in or out."

"Same as tennis," JoJo offered.

"Apparently, Diane had a habit of making bad calls in her own favor," Beth added.

"And we heard that she always whined about the game whenever she lost," Lonny added, "she would criticize the other team for not playing fair. People didn't like that."

"Okay, so she's a cheater and a big baby," Lisa said, "I can't believe anybody would kill her for that!"

"Wait, there's more," Lonny said, "it looks like she wasn't just cheating at Pickleball, she was also cheating on her husband."

"We found out that she was having an extramarital affair," Beth added.

"Do you have a name?"

"Yep, Bobby James."

"Bobby James what?" Captain Davis asked.

"Just Bobby James," Lonny replied, "his last name is James."

"He's a handyman that takes care of a lot of the houses in Riverside," Beth said.

"Apparently, he takes care of several of the wives too!" Lonny added.

"So, you think there could be a jealousy angle here?" Lisa asked.

"Dunno," Lonny answered, "but we're bringing the handyman in this afternoon."

Prosecutor Megan Harris spoke up.

"Let me know the time of his interview, please," she said, "I want to watch him because, if he didn't kill Diane, we have to clear him before we can arrest the husband."

"Gotcha," Lonny said.

"Anything on Doctor Bates' alibi?" Lisa asked.

"Lots of people saw him at the Pickleball courts," Beth replied, "nobody remembers him leaving until a bunch of them went to brunch around 11:00."

"And he didn't leave the clubhouse during brunch?"

"Well, he did go outside shortly after they arrived to make a phone call," Beth said.

Megan stood up and said, "sorry to interrupt you, Beth, but I have to ask Stephanie. Any chance you guys came across the husband's cell phone at the house?"

"No!" came Stephanie's quick reply.

"Thought so," Megan replied.

"Bates said he was calling his wife to see if she wanted to join them at brunch," Beth continued, "most people estimate he was gone for about fifteen minutes."

"That's a long time for one phone call," Lonny said, "they all had to wait for him to return before they ordered, and a few of them were pissed off."

"I don't think he had enough time to go home and kill his wife," Beth said, "and then come back to the clubhouse in fifteen minutes."

"Well," Lisa said, "let's test it out. Stephanie, you said it only took a few seconds to kill her, right?'

"Yes that's right," Coroner Stephanie Rogers replied, "it was fast."

"So, the question is," Lisa said, "could the doctor have left the clubhouse, ostensibly to make a phone call, then drove home, killed his wife, and made it back to the clubhouse in fifteen minutes?"

"Highly doubtful," Lonny said.

"But not impossible," Lisa shot back.

"What about the murder weapon?" Lonny asked

"He could have dumped that when he went shopping," Dan replied, "that might be the reason he went shopping, just to get rid of the murder weapon."

"We've got a bunch of rookies out there dumpster diving for it now," Lisa said.

"Okay," he responded, "but do we have an eyeball on him back at the house just after 11:00?"

"Doug and JoJo," Lisa said, "what did you guys find out?"

"No luck at all, Lisa," JoJo replied, "we visited every house on River street."

"And even the ones across the river, like you said," Doug added.

"We got nothing," JoJo said, "nada, bupkis."

"Nobody saw anybody go into that house?" Dan asked.

"Nope," JoJo replied. "But it wasn't like anybody was sitting there watching. Most of them weren't even home."

"So, it is possible that Bates drove into the garage and killed his wife just after 11:00. That fits within the time of death window," Lisa said.

"Possible? Yes," Doug said, "but can we prove it? Not yet."

"Did you guys learn anything else?" Lisa asked.

"It's interesting that Lonny heard about the handyman," JoJo said, "because we have an eyewitness that saw his truck parked on River street that morning."

"How did they know it was his truck?" Lisa asked.

"Apparently, everybody knows that truck," JoJo said.

"It's a white F-150 with a confederate flag painted on both sides," Doug added, "pretty hard to miss it."

Lisa added the name BOBBY JAMES to her whiteboard.

Lonny spoke up, "we're sure as hell gonna ask Bobby James about that."

"Okay good," Lisa said, "Beth, what did you learn about Bates' little shopping trip after brunch?"

"We checked the security cameras at Home Depot and CVS," Beth said, "and they both confirmed that he was there when he said he was."

"What about Super Clips?"

"Bates checked in at 1:45 and got his hair cut, so he's telling the truth about that too."

Lisa was disappointed by what she was hearing. "Any cameras by any of the dumpsters?"

"No," Lonny laughed, "I guess they don't care if anybody steals their garbage!"

"Anybody need a bio break?" Lisa asked the group.

Several hands went up.

"Okay, let's take fifteen. Then I want to hear from forensics."

As the group was leaving, Lisa turned to her partner. "How's the dumpster dive going Danny?"

"We were able to stop all collection of the dumpsters."

"Good. How many are there?"

"Believe it or not there are 22 dumpsters in and around that shopping center." But we got lucky 'cause they weren't scheduled to be picked up this week."

"And you got a crew out there searching?"

"Yep," Dan replied, "we've got five rookies diving right in!"

"So I can assume they haven't found anything yet?"

"So far, nothing," Dan replied, "but they've only finished four."

"And hating you, I bet!" Lisa joked.

"Not me, Lisa," came Dan's retort, "I told them this was your project so it's you they all hate!"

Lisa laughed, pondered a moment, and said, "you know, Danny, the daughter told us that Bates was having an affair with a woman named ah.."

"Jenkins," Dan replied, "Abby Jenkins. But she said they broke it off a while ago, and she moved away."

"That might be true," Lisa said, "but it might not be true."

"Okay."

"So see if you can find this Abby lady and bring in for questioning."

"Okay, I'll get O'Hara working on it tomorrow."

"Good. I wanna know if Bates had a reason to see his wife dead, other than just for money."

CHAPTER 8

FEBRUARY 20, 2018, 11:05 A.M.

PORT ST. LUCIE POLICE HEADQUARTERS

The group gathered back in the conference room, all seated in exactly the same chairs they had been in before the break.

Lisa once again started the meeting.

"I think we've made good progress today," Lisa looked toward Sheila Feeney. "Did you find anything else worth knowing on her cell phone?"

"I did," Sheila replied, "very interesting!"

"Len Bates left a voice message at 11:03."

Sheila pressed a button and the message played.

"Hi, Di. It's me. Everyone missed you at Pickleball today. Hope your call with Becca and the kids went well. Listen, we're all having brunch at the club, so if you want to join us let me know and I'll order for you."

"He could have made that call to see if she was still sleeping," Beth Danelo said.

"He called two more times and left messages," Sheila added, "once at 12:38 and again at 2:41 to say he was on his way home."

"Sounds to me like Bates was shoring up his alibi," Lisa quipped.

"How about that 10:30 FaceTime call she was expecting?"

"Never happened. No FaceTime call was made to her phone that day."

"So, the good doctor was lying about why Diane skipped Pickleball. It wasn't because she was expecting a call. It was because she was drugged, right Stephanie?"

Coroner Stephanie Rogers stood up. "We found a near lethal mixture of Ambien and Valium in her system," she said, "it wasn't enough to kill her but it certainly knocked her out cold for a long time."

"Makes it easier to kill her, I suppose," Lisa added.

"But why bludgeon her to death and leave a mess?" Megan asked, "why not just give her a little more Ambien and kill her that way?"

"Because that points right to the husband," Lisa replied, "he's the only one who could have poisoned her, but anybody could have beaten her to death."

"Very true." Megan replied.

"What else, Sheila?"

"We found several text messages to the handyman, Bobby James," Sheila continued, "and a few…shall I say..ahh. revealing selfies from Bobby to Diane."

"You mean dick pix?" Lonny shouted, as the room erupted in laughter.

"Lonny wants to see them!" JoJo shouted.

"No," Lonny shot back, "but I bet you do!"

Lisa stood up. "Okay children, settle down," she said, "Sheila, anything else you can you tell us about the phone?"

"There was a series of strange texts from Diane to Bobby," Sheila explained, "It looks like he was ah, "servicing" a woman named Deborah and Diane didn't like it."

"Deborah?" Lonny said, "I bet that's Deborah Cooper. She's part of the Pickleball crowd. She's the hot number that all the guys like."

"And it was obvious that she hated Diane's guts!" Beth added, "she's the one who told me about the handyman. She said it was disgusting that Diane paid him for sex. She said she never paid a man for sex in her life."

"Now that I think about it, she was the Pickleball player that refused to give us her prints and DNA sample."

"Hmm," Lisa said, "was she part of the brunch gang?"

"Nope," Lonny replied, "she told everyone she had errands to run."

"Oh well," Lisa said, "it looks like we've got another person of interest." She then wrote DEBORAH COOPER on the white board.

"That board is really filling up!" Captain Davis quipped.

"That's true," Lisa said, "but I still like Doctor Bates for it."

"You all realize," Megan said sternly, "that before we can charge anyone for this crime we have to eliminate all of the other suspects."

"Got it," Lisa responded, "O'Hara, what can you tell us about Bates?"

Joe O'Hara stood up and addressed the room. A twelve year veteran of the force, O'Hara had been a detective for the past three years.

"Doctor Leonard Bates has quite a background," he began. "He was born in1949 in Lexington, Mass and got his medical degree from Tufts. He did his internship at Mass General Hospital, and his residency at Brigham and Women."

"In 1979 Bates joined a private practice in Lexington Mass, but he had a major malpractice suit against him in 1982. After that he was let go by the group."

"Soon after that, Bates was hired by the coroners office of the Boston Police Department, and he stayed there until his retirement in 2014."

"What about his family life?" Lisa asked.

"He married a woman named Justine Miler in 1988, and they had a son named Jeffrey in '89. Justine was a Boston police officer, but she was killed in the line of duty in 1991."

"So, Bates has had two wives that were killed," Lisa said.

"No, actually it was three," O'Hara replied, "in 1997 he married Donna Pratt, a nurse. Three years later she died in a house fire."

"House fire?" Captain Davis asked, "so, where the hell was he?"

"Apparently, Bates and his son were on some kind of Boy Scout camping trip when the fire started."

"Any chance they were camping in their own back yard?" Lonny shouted, "toasting marshmallows?"

"Any more wives?" Lisa asked, ignoring Lonny completely.

"Just Diane," O'Hara replied, "he met Diane on a dating website in 2007 and they were married in 2009."

"She wins the prize," Captain Davis said, "she lasted eight years!"

"Three wives, three dead wives," Lisa said, "he's either the unluckiest man on earth..."

"Or he's a murderer," Megan added.

"We'll find out soon," Lisa said, "Stephanie, what did forensics find?"

Stephanie stood up to address the group.

"We've got Bates' prints and DNA from a water bottle he left in his car. Of course, we expect his prints and DNA to be all over the crime scene because he was there. But we're particularly interested that his prints are on the prescription bottles of Ambien and Valium."

"Anybody else show up?" Captain Davis asked.

"We've got prints and DNA from at least two other people who were in that bedroom. So far no matches are in the system but we hope to get one after we bring in all the suspects."

"Was there any sign of burglary?" Lisa asked.

"Not likely," Stephanie answered, "the victim's purse was sitting on the nightstand and her jewelry drawer was never opened. She had some expensive stuff in there and it was not taken."

"So that means whoever entered that bedroom had one goal and only one goal, to kill Diane Bates."

"Okay, everyone," Lisa barked, "I think we found our killer. Now let's make sure we arrest the right one!"

CHAPTER 9

FEBRUARY 20, 2018, 2:30 P.M.

PORT ST. LUCIE POLICE HEADQUARTERS

INTERVIEW ROOM 1

Lonny Carter escorted Bobby James into the interview room, where Beth Danelo was waiting. Gone was the wise cracking office clown, as Carter transformed into the serious detective that everybody knew he could be.

At six foot four, Lonny towered over the much shorter Bobby James. James was wearing a white sleeveless tee shirt and jeans. He was about five foot four, and his muscular arms were covered with tattoos. James took a seat on one side of a small table with Lonny and Beth seated opposite him.

Watching and listening on the other side of a two way glass were Lisa March and Megan Harris. If anyone ever fit the profile of a potential killer, Bobby James certainly did, Lisa thought.

Lonny switched on the recording device and said, "thank you for coming here today. As I told you, we're investigating an incident that took place on February 15th at the home of Doctor and Mrs. Leonard Bates."

"I know," Bobby said, "the wife was murdered."

"As you can see," Beth continued, "this interview is being taped for future use."

"It is important for you to know that you're here as a possible witness and you are not under arrest," Lonny said calmly, "so, it's also important that you acknowledge that you're here of your own volition and that you can choose to end this interview and leave at any time."

"I acknowledge that," Bobby replied.

"I'm detective Lonny Carter, and this is my partner, Beth Danelo. Please give us your full name and address."

"My name is Bobby James and I live at 477 Martin Luther King Street, in Fort Pierce, Florida."

"Is that your full name sir? Bobby? "

"Yep, it's Bobby, not Robert. Just Bobby."

"Do you have a middle name?" Beth asked.

"No," Bobby replied, as he placed his hands behind his neck and stretched.

"May we call you Bobby?" Beth asked.

"That's what everybody calls me. Sure."

Lonny signaled for a lab technician to enter the room.

"Bobby," he said, "this is Steven Oppenheim. He works in our lab."

"Hello, sir," Oppenheim said.

"Bobby," Beth explained. "we have no reason to believe that you were involved in this case. We would like to take your fingerprints and a DNA sample so that we can formally eliminate you from the list of people that are suspects. That way we can focus only on finding the person who committed the murder of Mrs. Bates."

"Uh huh."

"Do you have any objection to giving us your prints and a DNA sample?"

"No, it's okay," Bobby said.

As the lab tech processed the prints and took a saliva sample Lisa commented in the observation room "Nice move, Lonny. Best to get them to give it up before they think they're a suspect."

After the lab tech left the room Beth began the formal questioning. "Bobby, do you have any information you can share with us that will help us find out who killed Mrs. Bates?"

Bobby thought for a few seconds and said, "nope."

Lonny took over, "Bobby we understand that you often do handyman work for residents of the Riverside Estates. Is that true?"

"Yep."

"And have you ever done handyman work for Doctor or Mrs. Bates?"

Bobby hesitated and then said, "dunno, what's the address?"

"They live at 1520 River Street in Riverside Estates. Have you ever been inside that house for any reason?"

"Can't say as I have."

"Does that mean you have never been there or that you don't remember being there?"

"Both, I guess."

Sitting in the observation room, Lisa turned to Beth and said, "this guy's not gonna give up anything. It's like pulling teeth."

Back in the room, Lonny remained composed and asked, "Bobby, do you drive a white F-150 pickup truck with confederate flags on the sides?"

"I sure do," Bobby smiled. "Sweet ride!"

Beth pounced, "Bobby if I told you that your truck was seen parked on River Street the same morning that Diane Bates was murdered how would you explain that?"

"I'd explain that I was working there."

"Where were you working?"

"I was working at Mrs. Goldman's house."

Lonny checked his notes. "The Goldman's live it 1526, three houses down from Mr. and Mrs. Bates. Is that where you were?"

"Yep."

"And what were you doing at 1526 that day?"

"I was power washing their pool deck."

"Were the Goldman's home?"

"No they're up north somewhere. New York, I think."

"You have a key to their house?"

"No, I just walk around back and through the screen door."

"Did the Goldman's pay you for this?"

"Not yet. They always take care of me when they get back."

"Well, did they ask you to power wash their deck?"

"I do it twice a year and they pay me $200 each time."

Lonny was very skeptical. "So, let me get this straight. If we were to call the Goldmans, they would tell us that they didn't know you would be power washing their deck on February 15th. Is that right."

"I guess you could say that."

Back in the observation room Lisa said, "he just happened to power wash the deck two doors away, on the same day that the lady he was having sex with got murdered?"

"Okay," Beth asked, " what time did you get to the Goldman's house?"

"I guess about 10:30."

"And what time did you leave?'

"Around noon."

"So, while you were power washing the Goldman's deck, did you see anyone enter the Bate's house?"

"No."

Beth opened her cell phone and showed Bobby the photo that had been retrieved from Diane Bates' cell phone. "Bobby do you recognize this?"

Bobby was startled to see a clear photo of his own penis. He looked carefully at the photo and said, "no, can't say as I do."

"Well, Bobby," Lonny said, "what if I told you this photo came from a text message that was sent from your phone to Diane Bates' phone? How would you explain that?"

"I dunno."

Lab technician Steven Oppenheim walked into the interview room and whispered something in Lonny's ear. Lonny nodded and waited for Oppenheim to leave the room.

"What if I told you a clean set of finger prints were taken from the sliding door to the Bates' home that perfectly match the prints we took from you today," Lonny said, stoically, "how would you explain that, Bobby?"

Bobby leaned back in his chair. He was clearly rattled. "Look," he said, "Mrs. B was a nice lady."

"Nice?" Beth said, "how nice?"

"Sometimes she would give me a few extra bucks to spend a little quality time with her. You know what I mean."

"And did you spend a little quality time with her on February 15th?" Beth asked.

"We were planning on it. That's why I did the power wash job, so I could sneak into her bedroom. She even left the sliding door unlocked for me."

"And what time were you supposed to meet her?"

"We were supposed to meet at 10:30, while her husband was playing Pickleball."

"Did you go over to her house at 10:30?" Beth asked.

"I went there and tapped on her bedroom window. That's always been my signal. But I thought I heard talking in the room and I knew it wasn't her voice so I figured there was someone else in the room with her."

"So, then what?" Lonny asked.

"Then I waited until 11:00 and tried again. Same thing. Somebody talking.

"So you waited again?"

"I waited and came back at 11:20. This time I went into the house."

"So you went into her bedroom, right?"

"Right, but when I got there she was dead! I swear it, she was dead!"

"And just how did you know that she was dead?" Beth asked.

"I could see she was lying face down in the bed with the covers over her. I called her name and she didn't answer. So I lifted the covers and I could see her head was bashed in. I got scared, so I put the covers back and ran out of the house."

"What time was that?"

"About 11:30, I guess."

"Did you touch her body?" Lonny asked.

"I don't remember," Bobby said, "it all happened so fast. I mean, I saw her lying in the bed, and it looked like she wasn't breathing. I called her name and she didn't answer."

"You never touched her?" Beth asked.

"No I never touched her!"

"So you found a woman dead in her bed and what did you do, Bobby?" Lonny asked rhetorically, "did you call 911? No! You just hauled your ass out of there and told nobody. I don't believe a word of that story Bobby!"

"I..."

"Bobby, you killed Diane Bates," Lonny shouted, "we know it, and you know it. Now the best thing for you to do is to come clean and tell us what really happed in that bedroom!"

"Nothing happened!" Bobby pleaded, "I didn't kill her!"

"Maybe it was an accident, Bobby." Beth said calmly, "maybe you didn't mean to kill her."

"No!"

"Bobby," Beth said, "we can help you. But you gotta tell us what happened."

"I told you what happened!"

"You killed her, Bobby." Lonny shouted.

"No!"

Lonny stood up, took his handcuffs out from his belt, and said, "Bobby James, you are under arrest for the murder of Diane Bates."

As Lonny secured the cuffs Bobby cried, "I didn't kill her! I swear I didn't!"

"You have the right to remain silent," Beth read from a card, "anything you say can be used against you in court. You have the right to talk to a lawyer for advice before we ask you any more questions. You have the right to have a lawyer with you during questioning. If you cannot afford a lawyer, one will be appointed for you before any further questioning if you wish. If you decide to answer more questions now without a lawyer present, you have the right to stop answering at any time."

Back in the observation room Lisa said, "wow, I didn't think it would be over this fast!"

"I'm not sure it is," Megan replied, "I'll get you a search warrant for Bobby's place. We've gotta find that murder weapon."

CHAPTER 10

FEBRUARY 20, 2018, 6:00 P.M.

THE HOME OF LISA AND RICK MARCH

Lisa waked through the front door of her new home in St. Lucie West. She and her husband, Rick, were both proud of this, their very first new house. Although it was modest by the standards of the mansions in Riverside Estates, this house fit perfectly in with the other homes in their Coventry community.

As she entered the house, she heard the warm voice of her husband, Rick March."Hi gorgeous, are you ready for a glass?"

Lisa entered the kitchen to be met by Rick, who was holding a large wine glass filled with chardonnay, her favorite wine.

"Kendalll Jackson?" She asked as she took a sip.

"Sorry, babe, we ran out of KJ so I had to give you Simi."

"Okay, I'll forgive you this time," she joked.

Rick approached his wife and hugged her from behind "Simi for my police girl." he said with a grin, "are you sure you don't want to put me in handcuffs?'

"Maybe later," She snapped back, "right now I'm starving!"

"I thought you might be, so I slaved over dinner for you. I made your favorite, pizza!"

Rick then revealed a box filled with pizza that had been delivered a few minutes earlier.

“Pizza again?” Lisa asked playfully, “that’s four days in a row!”

“I know,” Rick replied sheepishly, “I sort of messed up the dinner I was trying to make for us.”

Rick was a very handsome man and, even after twenty years of marriage, he still gave Lisa goosebumps every time she saw him. He was only five foot-six but that was the prefect height for Lisa.

Lisa and Rick had met at the police academy back in 1995, and while she graduated and went on to a stellar career in law enforcement, Rick was diagnosed with a heart defect that disqualified him from serving on the force. Instead, he had gone back to Florida State to complete his law degree, and eventually landed a job at the Simmons Law Firm in Fort Pierce.

They married in 1997, and their only child, Alexis, was born in 1998. Just eleven weeks ago Rick had undergone open heart surgery and he was still under doctor’s orders to work part time only. During his hiatus from work Rick had decided to take up cooking, a decision both he and Lisa would soon come to regret.

As they sat at the kitchen table Lisa asked, “did you hear from Lexie?”

“Oh yeah, she called me today. You know what that means.”

“She needs money!”

“You guessed it, some kind of sorority thing. I put three hundred in her account.”

“I hope she makes a lot of money in her career because she sure loves to spend it!” Lisa said with a smile.

“Or maybe,” Rick said, “once she stops spending our money and has to spend her own money she’ll think twice about throwing money away.”

“I seriously doubt it.” Lisa said matter of factly, as she sipped her wine.

“So how did it go today, babe?” Rick asked, “any luck on the big murder case?”

“Actually, yes,” Lisa replied, “we arrested someone today.”

“You caught the killer?”

"We think so."

"Did he confess?'

"Almost. He confessed to being in the lady's bedroom on the morning she was killed."

"But?' Rick said, "I'm sensing a but, here."

"But, are you ready for this? He says she was already dead when he got there."

Rick walked to the refrigerator and returned with a cold beer. "So he went in the room to kill the lady but somebody beat him to it?"

"Not exactly. He says he went in the bedroom to have sex with her."

"Oh, this just keeps getting better and better! And who is this guy?"

"The handyman."

"The handyman?" Rick laughed, "the handyman? Really? This sounds like a bad porn movie!"

"And how would you know about bad porn movies, Rick March?" Lisa joked.

"The guys at work tell me honey, they're all pigs!"

They both laughed.

"We've still got a lot of work to do on this case."

"What've you got so far?"

"He gave us prints and DNA," Lisa said, "and we were able to match his prints to a set of prints on the sliding door to the house. We still have to prove that the handyman actually killed the woman. We have to find the murder weapon to place it in his hands."

"He gave up his prints and DNA voluntarily?" Rick asked, "why the hell would he do that if he knew they would put him at the crime scene?"

"Obviously not the brightest bulb on the tree, hon."

"I thought you said you were gonna nail the husband for this."

"Well, we haven't ruled him out just yet. Not until we have evidence that the handyman killed the victim."

"What's the motive?" Rick asked.

"Huh?" Lisa replied.

"The motive," Rick responded quickly, "you always say there has to be a reason people kill. So what's the handyman's reason?"

"Good question, honey," Lisa pondered for a moment, "that's a very good question that we're gonna have to answer."

"You always told me that people kill other people for one of three reasons, passion, money, or revenge."

"That's true, hon. That's very true."

"So which one is it?"

Lisa began to think about why Bobby James would want to kill Diane Bates. She was giving him money and sex and there didn't seem to be any revenge factor here. So what would he have to gain from her death?

Maybe he was telling the truth.

CHAPTER 11

FEBRUARY 21, 2018, 8:30 A.M.

PORT ST. LUCIE POLICE HEADQUARTERS

As soon as Lisa walked into the office she was met by detective Andy Spears. He was very excited.

"Hey boss, I've got something to show you."

Lisa walked over to Andy's desk and sat in a chair next to his.

"I met with the Riverside property manager yesterday," he began, "I asked if there is any way to find out if someone came into the community through the resident's gate."

"Do they record that?"

"No, they don't," Andy replied, "so there's no way to know when Dave Messenger came into Riverside through the resident gate that morning."

"So, we're screwed."

"No, we're not, boss!" Andy replied with excitement, "you see, the speed limit in the community is 25 miles per hour. They have signs posted everywhere."

"So?"

"So, they have two radar devices on the main entrance road. One is for speeders coming into the development and one is for cars going out."

"I think I know where this is going."

"Yep," Andy said, "the radar device records the license plate of speeding cars and sends that data to the property manager. If someone speeds more that once they get a warning. After three warnings they get their gate pass suspended."

"Did they nail Dave Messenger?"

Andy showed Lisa a sheet of paper. "This came from the property manager. You can see that on the morning of February 15th Dave Messenger was clocked at 42 miles per hour leaving the neighborhood at 11:33."

"Bingo!" Lisa replied, "he's coming in today, and I'll be sure to find out what he was doing in Riverside at the very time his mother-in-law was murdered."

Lisa stood up and continued, "that's really nice work, Andy. Messenger will be here in less than an hour and this gives us a lot to talk about!"

As Lisa sat down to prepare for her interview with Dave Messenger, Captain Davis summoned her into his office. He closed the door.

"Just got a call from the chief," he said, "we have a meeting at 2:30 today with the mayor."

"We?" Lisa asked.

"Yes, we!" Davis replied, "she wants a complete rundown on what we've done so far. So please be prepared to tell her."

"Gotcha, Captain," Lisa replied, "I wonder if she can help us."

"What makes you ask that?"

"Well, Lonny met with Bobby James in his cell last night and Bobby gave him a list of all the houses he did handyman work for."

"So?"

"So, guess who's house is on that list?"

"No!"

"Yes!"

"Wait a minute. You're telling me that our perp worked for the mayor?"

"That's what he says."

"Holy shit!"

"You gonna mention that to the mayor today, boss?"

"Not a chance, Lisa," he replied, "for now let's just keep that information between us."

"Okay, but you better sit down with Lonny," Lisa said, "you know he sometimes talks too much."

As Lisa walked out of the captain's office she heard him shout, "Carter! Get your ass in here now!"

CHAPTER 12

FEBRUARY 21, 2018, 9:30 A.M.
PORT ST. LUCIE POLICE HEADQUARTERS
INTERVIEW ROOM 1

Lisa was seated at the table as Dan Torres escorted Dave Messenger into the room. She was taken aback by how striking Messenger was. Tall, dark, and handsome fit him to a tee.

Messenger sat down across from Lisa and Dan sat next to her.

"Good morning, Mr. Messenger," Lisa began, "my name is Detective Lisa March and you've already met my partner, Dan Torres."

"Yes," Messenger replied.

"Mr. Messenger," Lisa continued, "we truly appreciate you coming here today. I know you are busy and it was very kind of you to take the time to help us."

"No problem."

"As you can see, Mr. Messenger…would you prefer that we call you that?"

"Dave's fine."

"Okay, Dave. And we're Lisa and Dan."

"Fine."

As you can see, Dave, this interview is being recorded. You're here of your own volition and you can terminate this interview at any time. Do you understand that, Dave?"

"Yes."

"Good. Now for the record, would you please state your full name and address."

"My name is David Gary Messenger. I live at 232 Ocean Street in Jensen Beach."

"Okay then let's get started. Detective Torres and I are investigating the murder of Diane Bates and we're hoping that you can provide us with information that will help us catch the killer."

Dave adjusted himself in his seat. "I heard you already got the guy."

"We do have a suspect in custody," Lisa replied, "but we're still looking to find out everything we can."

"Gotcha."

Lab technician Steve Oppenheim walked into the room.

"Dave," Dan said, "this is Steven Oppenheim. He works in our lab."

"Hello, sir," Oppenheim said.

"Dave," Lisa explained, "we have no reason the believe that you were involved in this case. We would like to take your fingerprints and a DNA sample so that we can formally eliminate you from the list of people who are suspects. That way we can focus only on prosecuting the person who committed the murder of Mrs. Bates."

"Okay."

"Do you have any objection to giving us your prints and a DNA sample?"

"Be my guest," Dave said.

Steve Oppenheim completed his task quickly and left the room.

Lisa chose a little small talk to start the interview.

"Dave," she said with a smile, "two of our detectives interviewed several of the Riverside residents, and they learned that you're the best Pickleball player at the club."

Dave grinned. “There’s a few others,” he said, “but I guess I’m the best!”

“How did you get to be that good?”

“I’m not sure. I used to play a lot of tennis, so Pickleball just came naturally to me.”

“I’d like to try that game some day,” Lisa said.

“Let me know when you want to start,” Dave replied, “I’d be happy to teach you.”

“I might take you up on that offer,” Lisa said, “Dave, can you tell us what your relationship is to Diane Bates?”

“She was my mother-in-law.”

“So, you’re married to her daughter?”

“Yes, Jennifer is my wife.”

“But you no longer live with Jennifer? Is that correct?”

“Correct. We’re separated.”

“Separated, but not yet divorced. Is that correct?”

“Yes,” Dave replied, “I’m expecting the divorce to be finalized in a couple of months.”

“What can you tell us about your personal relationship with Diane Bates?”

Dave appeared uncomfortable, He squirmed in his seat and paused while he pondered how to answer Lisa’s question. Finally he spoke.

“The truth is that we hated each other,” he said, “she hated me and I hated her.”

“Can you elaborate on that for us, Dave?”

“When I first started dating Jennifer, Diane really liked me,” Dave said quietly, “she said I was a good match for Jennifer.”

“Really?”

“Yes. In the first couple of years she was great to Jennifer and me,” Dave explained, “she paid for a big wedding for us. She helped me buy my restaurant, and she even gave us the downpayment for our house.”

“So, when did things change, Dave?” Dan asked.

"As soon as Emma, our daughter, was born, everything changed," Dave replied, "from that moment on our relationship went down hill!"

"How so?"

"Diane tried to bully us into letting her control everything about the baby," Dave said, "she told us what pediatrician to use, what baby food to feed her, even what diapers to buy. Everything we did was wrong. She even hired a nanny without asking us. She wouldn't let us raise our own child!"

"How did Jennifer react to all that, Dave?"

"Jennifer was intimidated by her mother, so she never pushed back."

"But you did?" Lisa asked.

"I did," Dave said, "we fought constantly. I wasn't gonna let her run our lives and raise our child."

"And that eventually led to the breakup of your marriage?" Lisa asked.

"Not entirely," Dave replied, "but she was a big part of it, that's for sure."

"Dave," Dan said, "do you know of anyone who would want to see Mrs. Bates dead?"

"Do I?" Dave chuckled, "about half the people in Riverside would like to see that…" he caught himself and then stopped.

"Why do you think that is?" Lisa asked.

"Because Diane Bates is, or was, the most unpleasant and nasty woman on the planet. Everyone hated her. That's why!" Dave said, "she tried to intimidate everybody just like she tried with Jennifer and me!"

Lisa knew that there was more to this story so she dug deeper.

"Dave," she said calmly, "we learned that there was an incident recently involving Diane Bates that caused you to stop playing Pickleball at Riverside. Could you tell us about that?"

Dave was clearly uncomfortable. "She was telling lies about me," he said, "turning my friends against me."

"Were these lies about Emma?"

Tears welled up in Dave Messenger's eyes.

“She told people that I was molesting my daughter. It was all lies! Totally made up!”

“Why do you think she would do that, Dave?”

Dave took a deep breath and tried to compose himself. He paused and then replied.

“Like I said, it all had to do with her trying to control us. Jennifer and I were working things out between us but Diane was having none of that. She told me that she didn’t want me to have joint custody of my daughter.”

“Why do you think she felt that way?”

“She said I would find another wife, and Emma would then have a step mother, and that would ruin her. It was all bullshit! She really just wanted to punish me for leaving her daughter, or for marrying her daughter in the first place. I don’t know!”

“So you believe she made up the molestation accusation to keep you from having joint custody of your daughter?”

“Absolutely. Even Jennifer knew I wasn’t hurting Emma. I would never do anything like that. I adore my daughter! And social services cleared me completely.”

“So you were cleared of the charges?”

“Yes, I was, but it was too late. The damage was already done at Riverside. I couldn’t stand all the gossip so I stopped playing Pickleball there. I had to give up all my friends too.”

“Do you play somewhere else?”

“Yes, at the public courts at Memorial Park.”

“Okay, thanks Dave,” Lisa said calmly, “I know this has been difficult for you to talk about and I appreciate your honesty.”

“It is difficult.”

“I have to ask you, however, about an incident that took place at your restaurant involving Diane Bates. What can you tell us about that?”

Once again, Dave Messenger paused to arrange his words carefully.

“It happened just after the new year,” Dave said, “Diane came in to the restaurant and stood at the bar. The place was packed with people, and in a loud voice she started accusing me of molesting her granddaughter.”

"She did?" Lisa responded.

"I asked her to leave, but she wouldn't. She just kept yelling."

"How did it end?"

"I had to call the police and have her escorted out of the restaurant. And then I had to get a restraining order to keep her from coming back."

"Did you ever work things out between the two of you?" Lisa asked.

"Never."

"So, how are things now between you and Jennifer?"

"They're actually not bad. We talk. We're civil to each other. I go there and pick up Emma every other weekend. We've had no issues."

"Okay," Lisa said, "thanks for being so candid with us."

"No problem."

"Just a couple more things."

"Sure."

"Can you tell us if you were in Riverside the morning Diane Bates was murdered?"

"Yes, I was."

"What time did you arrive and what time did you leave?"

Dave pondered for a moment. "Let's see, I think I got to Riverside around 10:00 and I left around 11:30. And I suppose you want know what I was doing there?"

"My next question," Lisa replied.

"I went to the gym first," Dave said, "I guess I was there for about an hour."

"Anybody else in there at the same time?" Dan asked.

"Lots of people," Dave replied, "the place was packed, and I talked to a lot of people."

"So, you left the gym at around 11:00. What did you do then?"

"I went over to my house, err, Jennifer's house now, but I still own half of it."

"And what was the reason you went there?"

“I needed to pick up my toolbox from the garage. I needed it to hang some things up in my new apartment.”

“And how did you get into the garage?”

“I know the code. It’s 2014. The year my daughter was born.”

Lisa looked at Dan and smiled.

“Dave,” Lisa continued, “when was the last time you were in Diane Bates’ house?”

“Oh gosh. It’s been at least six months.”

“Okay then. Just one last question.”

“Sure.”

“Are you aware of the provisions of Diane Bates’ will?”

Dave looked puzzled by the question.

“No,” he smiled, “but I’m sure she didn’t leave a penny to me!”

“Okay, thank you very much, Dave,” Lisa concluded, as she handed her card to him, “if you think of anything else that could help us please give me a call.”

“You bet,” Dave said as he stood up and left the interview room.

After the door closed Lisa said, “Danny, either this guy is innocent or he’s the world’s best liar!”

“I’ll check out everything he told us.” Dan replied.

CHAPTER 13

FEBRUARY 21, 2018, 2:30 P.M.
PORT ST. LUCIE CITY HALL
THE OFFICE OF MAYOR CANDACE WILSON

Lisa was nervous. This was the first time she had ever been inside the mayor's office. She was pleased that both Captain Davis and Megan Harris were there so she wouldn't have to bear the brunt of the mayor's questions. She remembered that Lexie had dated the mayor's son, Andrew, for a few months in high school, but she chose not to mention it to the mayor. After all, it was Lexie who dumped Andrew.

As they walked into the office also waiting was Police Chief Warren Sales. Sales was a very large man, well over three hundred pounds, Lisa guessed. He was a thirty-five year veteran of the St. Lucie police department. Sales had been the third African American to make Sergeant, the second to make Captain, and the first to be named Chief back in 2011.

Lisa, Captain Davis, and Megan Harris joined Chief Sales in seats around a large conference table. In a few minutes a young gentleman entered the room. He was dressed in a three piece suit, something Lisa hadn't seen on a man in years.

"Hello everyone," the young man said, "my name is Troy Edison. I'm an aide to Mayor Wilson. She'll be here shortly. Can I get anyone coffee?"

In unison all four shook their heads no.

Lisa was pleasantly surprised to see a man doing a task that was commonly given to women.

One minute later the door opened and in walked Mayor Candace Wilson. She was not a large woman but in many ways she was bigger than life. At forty-two, the mayor was a stately and attractive woman. As soon as she entered the room everyone seated at the table stood up.

Mayor Wilson had been a shocking winner of the 2012 mayoral campaign, easily defeating the three term mayor, John Haslett. She had run on a platform of reforming the Port St. Lucie government and being more responsive to the needs of the people. Port St. Lucie was one of the fastest growing cities in Florida, and Candace Wilson was viewed by many as the right person at the right time to lead the city to greatness. Smart, savvy, and tough as nails, that was the image she had carefully crafted.

The mayor was re-elected in a landslide in 2016 and now, in 2018, she was running as the party favorite in the Democratic primary for governor. The party elites were excited, and there was no limit to the potential political future for Candace Wilson. For her, all roads would eventually lead to the White House, at least that was the scuttlebutt among party insiders.

"Good afternoon ladies and gentlemen," Mayor Wilson said with a big smile. "Troy, did you offer our guests coffee?" she said sternly.

"No takers, ma'am" Troy replied.

"Okay then," The mayor said, "that will be all, Troy."

Troy knew that his cue to leave room.

Mayor Wilson sat down at the conference table and immediately everyone else sat.

"Okay, I know three of you but who is this young lady?" Mayor Wilson asked as she pointed directly at Lisa.

Captain Davis spoke next. "Mayor Wilson, this is Lisa March. She is one of our best and most experienced detectives, and she's the lead detective on the Diane Bates murder case."

"Pleased to meet you, Detective March," Mayor Wilson said, "and as a good detective, I'm sure you've learned that I live in Riverside Estates."

"Yes ma'am, we have learned that."

"Then why am I just meeting you now, Detective March?" The mayor said sharply.

Lisa cleared her throat, She waited to see if anyone was going to help her, but nobody at the table stepped up.

"Well ma'am," she said, "I certainly did plan to give you a full briefing on the status of the case, but I didn't want to bother you until we had something meaningful to report."

"Well, I understand that you've arrested a suspect."

"Yes, ma'am, we have."

"Well, I certainly think that was significant enough for you to brief me." She paused."Or would you rather I read about it in the St. Lucie News?"

Lisa was dumbfounded. She hadn't anticipated this attack and she could see that everyone was hanging her out to dry.

"I'm sorry, Mayor Wilson," Lisa said, "it was never my intention to keep you in the dark. Quite honestly, I made the judgment that you might not want to get involved in the case at all, and that you would signal us if you did."

"Well, consider yourself signaled," Wilson replied, "so tell me where you are."

Finally, Megan relieved Lisa of the burden to do all the talking.

"Mayor Wilson," she began, "we have a gentleman named Bobby James in custody. Right now we have proof that he was at the Bates' home and in their bedroom within the time that the coroner says Mrs. Bates was murdered."

"Okay, so what's the problem?"

Captain Davis spoke up. "He says the victim was already dead when he got there. We're trying to locate the murder weapon so we can link it to James, but so far we haven't been able to find it."

"Okay," the mayor said, "and what do you know about this handyman?"

Lisa looked at Captain Davis, hoping he would be the one to lie to the mayor. Since neither of them spoke, it created an uncomfortable pause that Lisa felt the need to break.

"At this point we have a lot to learn about him," she said, "we're continuing to question him but now he has a court appointed lawyer."

"What else are you doing?" the mayor asked.

Lisa then launched into a long winded presentation. She told the mayor about every one of the suspects they were investigating… the husband, the son-in-law, and even the drug cartel.

By the time she had finished, Lisa felt that she had left little doubt in the minds of the mayor and the police chief that she was more than up to the task.

"Okay then," Mayor Wilson said, "that's it for now. But don't make me chase you guys down again. This is a very high profile case and I don't want any surprises. Got it?"

"Got it," all said in unison.

After they left the Mayor's office, Chief Sales stopped Lisa in the hallway.

"That was very impressive, young lady," he said.

"Thank you sir," Lisa replied.

"Just one more thing I want to make clear," he continued.

"What's that, sir?" Captain Davis asked.

"You don't say anything to the mayor that you haven't said to me first. Are we clear about that?"

"Yes sir."

"Are we clear?" he said louder.

"Crystal." Captain Davis replied.

This sounds like a scene from *A Few Good Men*, Lisa thought. But she wisely chose not to say so.

CHAPTER 14

FEBRUARY 21, 2018, 6:30 P.M.

THE HOME OF LISA AND RICK MARCH

Lisa walked through her front door and smiled when she saw Rick standing in the kitchen wearing two oven mitts. Since his work was only part time, Rick had decided to learn to cook, a decision both of them often regretted.

"Hungry?" Rick asked with a smile.

"Starved!" Lisa replied, "what'd you make tonight?"

"Pizza," Rick said, "sausage and mushrooms, your favorite."

Rick opened the oven door and removed a pizza box. He gently placed it on the countertop.

"Pizza Delight?" Lisa asked.

"Your favorite delivery place!" Rick replied, as he placed two paper plates next to the pizza box.

"Okay then, let's eat," Lisa said, "but we need to turn on the TV."

"What's up?" Rick asked.

"I heard that the famous lawyer representing Doctor Bates made a statement in front of city hall this afternoon. I wanna watch the news and see it."

With that, Rick turned on the TV and used the remote to select the local news station. A commercial was playing. He switched to another station and there was the scene in front of Police Headquarters.

JD Treem, dressed in his signature suit and bowtie, was addressing the media. Standing next to him was none other than Len Bates.

"Today," Treem began, "is a very good day for the people of Port St. Lucie."

"He's a pompous ass, isn't he?" Rick whispered.

"Shhh," Lisa scolded, "I wanna hear this."

Treem continued, "last night the Port St. Lucie police arrested the man that they believe murdered Mrs. Diane Bates."

"He's full of himself…"

"Shhh!"

"Now that the suspect is in custody, the people of Port St. Lucie can rest more comfortably without fear that the same fate could befall them, or a loved one."

"You're shitting me!"

"Hush!"

"On behalf of Doctor Leonard Bates and the entire Bates family, I would like to thank the Port St. Lucie police department for the excellent work they have done. We pledge our full support to them as they pursue justice for the family of Diane Bates."

"That's it, I guess," Lisa said as the screen faded back to the newsroom, "he's so smooth."

"They say he's the best," Rick replied.

A male reporter in the newsroom spoke.

"Our sources within the Port St. Lucie police department tell us the man arrested was Bobby James, a handyman, who did work for many of the residents of the Riverside Estates community where Diane Bates lived."

"And here's an interesting twist," his female partner added, "our sources tell us that James, the handyman, even did jobs for none other than our mayor, Candace Wilson. She apparently lives in Riverside Estates and hired Bobby James several times."

"I bet the mayor will have more than a passing interest in this case," the man added, "now let's look at the weather forecast for the Treasure Coast."

• • • • •

Lisa was stunned by what she had just heard. "Holy shit!" she bellowed.

Within seconds Lisa's cell phone rang.

"Danny? Yes, I just watched it. I have no idea how they got that information, do you? I know I never said anything. Of course I know it wasn't you."

Immediately Lisa received another call, this one from Captain Davis.

She listened for a moment as the captain raged about the leak.

"I'll be there at eight. Yes sir."

As she hung up the phone she was still in shock.

"What the hell is going on, babe?" Rick asked.

"Rick, we knew about the handyman and the mayor but we decided not to say anything to her about it this afternoon."

"Oh shit," Rick said, "so now she sees it on the news."

"This could cost me my job, Rick!"

Rick hugged his wife and said, "I don't think so, babe. You're the best detective they have and you certainly didn't leak this to the news."

"I'll tell you one thing," Lisa replied, "Captain Davis is gonna find out who did, and he's gonna hand that person's head to the mayor on a silver platter."

CHAPTER 15

FEBRUARY 22, 2018, 8:00 A.M.

PORT ST. LUCIE POLICE DEPARTMENT

Captain Davis was enraged like Lisa had never seen before. The veins in his neck were sticking out.

He stood in front of the assembled group of detectives and immediately noticed that one of them was missing.

"Where the fuck is Carter?" he bellowed.

No response from the crowd.

"Anybody seen him?"

Again no response.

"Well then, I think my question has been answered. Anybody know what my fucking question is?"

Silence engulfed the room until Lisa spoke up.

"Last night on the news it was reported that our suspect, Bobby James, was employed by Mayor Wilson." Lisa said calmly, hoping this would cause the captain to calm down as well.

She failed.

"I wanna know who the fucking asshole was that leaked this tidbit to the press, and we're not leaving here until I find out!" Captain Davis bellowed.

"Does anybody have an idea who it was?" Lisa added.

Beth Danelo spoke up about her long time partner.

"Lonny called me last night," she said, "he was very upset."

"So, he doesn't have the balls to come here and talk for himself?" Captain Davis shouted, "he sent you to speak for him?"

Beth continued, "Lonny told me, after he spoke to Bobby James and heard about the mayor, he mentioned it to a friend at the bar."

"I told him not to say anything!" Captain Davis shouted.

Beth took a deep breath and continued.

"That's true, Captain," she uttered, "but he says that was the next morning, after he had already told someone about it the night before.

"He never said a fucking word to me about that!" Davis yelled, "if he had told me we probably would have changed what we said to the Mayor yesterday!"

"He knows that, sir," Beth replied.

She reached into her purse and removed a badge. "And that's why he gave me this, and asked me to give it to you."

Beth handed the badge to Captain Davis, who was still furious.

"That's not all he's gonna lose!" he screamed, "everybody get back to work1'

The captain retreated to his office, followed closely by Lisa.

"Lonny made a mistake," she said.

"Mistake?" Davis yelled, "that's not a mistake. Forgetting to sign paperwork is a mistake. Walking into the wrong meeting is a fucking mistake!"

"What are we gonna say to the mayor?"

"I'm gonna talk to the Chief first and see how he wants to handle it."

"Do you want my help on this, boss?" Lisa said.

She could see that Captain Davis' anger had morphed to anxiety. Maybe he was worried about losing his badge too, she thought.

"No Lisa," Davis said, more calmly, "I'm the Captain and I have to handle it. Thanks for the offer though."

"And what should we do about Lonny?" she asked.

"He's done, Lisa. That's a given."

"He's been on the force for twenty-two years, Captain," Lisa pleaded, "this job is all he has. He's got no family, very few friends. His badge is what he lives for!"

"That son of a bitch always had a big mouth," Captain Davis replied, "he's had reprimands for this in the past, Lisa, and this time it cost him his job, plain and simple. If he's lucky he'll be walking a beat!"

Lisa walked out of the office deflated. She was worried about how Lonny would deal with losing his detective job.

As soon as she left the Captain's office, she dialed Lonny's cell phone. It went right to voice mail.

"Hello there, person," came Lonny's voice, *"If you don't know who this is, then you got the wrong number. If you do know who I am, then leave me a message. But make it short because I got a very short attention span!"*

Classic Lonny, Lisa thought. I hope he can handle this.

CHAPTER 16

FEBRUARY 22, 2018, 1:30 P.M.
THE LAW OFFICE OF BAKER AND BREEM
STUART, FLORIDA

Lisa and Dan walked into the lobby of the large office building and immediately headed for the reader board in the lobby.

"Third floor," Dan said after perusing the board.

The two partners stepped off the elevator on the third floor and were immediately met by a young lady who said, "are you from the police department?"

Lisa nodded and the young lady said, "please follow me. Mr. Droter is expecting you."

The two detectives were ushered into a small conference room. Waiting for them were a short man and a very attractive woman. He was middle aged, bald, overweight, very unattractive. She, on the other hand, was young, blonde, and had the looks of a super model.

No way they're a couple, Lisa thought.

"Welcome," the man said, "I'm Henry Droter, and this is my assistant, Kelly Knowles."

"I'm detective Lisa March, and this is my partner, Dan Torres."

All four then sat down around a small conference table.

"Yes, we were expecting you," Droter said, as he grasped a thick legal folder. "I believe we have everything requested in your warrant, right here."

"Thanks," Lisa said, "as you know, we're investigating the murder of your client, Diane Bates."

"I heard you arrested the man that killed her," Kelly said.

Lisa ignored the comment and continued.

"We're here to discuss Mrs. Bates' will."

"It's all here," Droter said, as he placed the folder in the middle of the table, "do you have any specific questions about it?"

"Yes, we do," Lisa began, "we were told that the will was written in 2013. Is that correct?'

Droter looked at his assistant. She nodded.

"Yes, that's correct," he said.

"And we also understand that there are four beneficiaries on the will."

"Again, Droter glanced at his assistant. She nodded and he said, "correct."

"And her husband, Doctor Leonard Bates, was not one of the beneficiaries?"

Another glance, a nod and an affirmative answer.

"So the four beneficiaries were Diane's' daughter, Jennifer Messenger, her son-in-law, David Messenger, her daughter, Rebecca Still, and her son-in-law, James Still. Is that correct?"

Glance, nod, "yes."

"Can you explain to us why Diane chose to have four beneficiaries and didn't just leave the estate to her two daughters."

Finally, Mr. Droter spoke for himself.

"I remember. It was her daughter, Rebecca's idea," he said, "she said that her husband was like a son to Diane Bates, the son she never had, and that he was just as important to her as her daughters were."

"He must be one helluva guy!" Lisa said.

"Apparently," Kelly Knowles added, "and when Jennifer Messenger learned about what her sister was doing she asked to do the same thing for her husband."

"Where can I find a wife like that?" Dan interjected.

"Was this something that your firm recommended?" Lisa asked.

"Just the opposite. We were vehemently opposed to that arrangement,"

Droter replied, "but, in the end, we can only advise."

"Both daughters insisted that the will be written that way," Kelly added.

"When the will was first written to include the two son-in-laws, was Mrs. Bates aware of this and approved it?" Lisa asked.

"Of course," Kelly replied, "I brought the will to her myself. She read it from cover to cover and signed it. And I notarized her signature."

"Diane Bates went along with her daughters' requests," Droter said, "but she insisted that the will state that the son-in-laws must be married to her daughters at the time of her death in order to qualify for their inheritance."

"Separated was okay?" Dan asked.

"She didn't anticipated that, I'm sure," Droter replied.

"I guess not," Dan said.

"The truth is that it really didn't matter whose name was in the will," Droter continued, "once they received the inheritance and deposited it in a joint account it would become the joint property of the husband and the wife anyway."

"How much are we talking about here?" Lisa asked.

Kelly Knowles looked at the file. "The estate is valued at approximately twenty-six million dollars," she said, "after estate taxes are paid each of the four beneficiaries should receive close to five million dollars."

"When Jennifer and David Messenger separated, did Mrs. Bates ask you to change the will?" Lisa asked.

"Actually, it was Jennifer who requested the change."

"When was that?" Dan asked.

Kelly Knowles opened the folder again and examined several pages before she responded.

"Let me see, ah, we got the request to change the will from Jennifer Messenger on January 19th."

"That was four weeks before Diane died," Lisa said, "so, was the will changed before she died?"

"I'm afraid not," Droter responded.

"Why was that?" Dan asked.

The file was again opened and Kelly reviewed several documents before she responded.

"Okay," she said, "here is the sequence of events. The request for a change came to our office, as I said, on January 19th. I logged it into my desk when I received it on January 25th."

"Why the delay?" Dan asked.

"It wasn't really a delay," Kelly replied calmly, "that's usually how long it takes for a request to be logged into the system."

"Uh huh," Lisa replied, "then what?"

"Then I typed the change removing David Messenger from the will and sent it over to Mr. Droter."

"Okay, so what happened next?"

Henry Droter checked his calendar and spoke up. "I reviewed the change to the will on January 31st."

"Another delay," Lisa said, "okay, then what?"

"Then I noticed that the year of the will had not been changed from 2013 to 2018," Droter said, "so I sent it back to Kelly to make the correction."

"And, when was that done?" Dan asked.

"I made the correction on February 5th," Kelly replied, "but, then I was wondering if the other daughter, Rebecca, also wanted to remove her husband from the will. Jennifer had only asked about removing her husband, not both."

"Why were you concerned about that?" Lisa asked.

"Well, I thought if Rebecca learned what her sister had done and she wanted to do the same thing, then we would have to revise the will again. I figured it was better to do it all at one time."

"Okay, so what happened then?"

"I called Rebecca to ask about the will. She didn't answer, so I left her a voice message to call me."

"Did she call you back?"

"Not right away," Kelly replied, "I left two or three messages before she finally called me back on February 8th."

"And, did she want the change?"

"No, she insisted that we keep her husband as a beneficiary."

"So you completed the new will, when?"

Kelly once again checked her files. "I completed the will on February 12th and sent it back to Mr. Droter for review."

"I reviewed the will on February 14th," Droter added, "and then I gave it back to Kelly to have Mrs Bates sign it."

"I went to her house after work on the 15th," Kelly said, "but when I arrived at the house the police told me I couldn't go in. There was yellow crime scene tape all around the house."

"Yes," Lisa replied calmly, "we know."

"I found out from the neighbors that she was dead."

"We're gonna need copies of all of these documents, please." Dan said.

Kelly handed him the folder. "Everything you requested is in here," she said.

Lisa and Dan left the building and returned to their car. As they sat down Dan said, "they sure dragged their feet on that will change."

"Maybe," Lisa replied, "but I think that's pretty typical of the way large law firms operate. They're not in a big hurry unless they have to be, and the longer it takes the more billable hours they rack up. My Rick has told me a number of horror stories about his firm losing papers and delaying things for months."

"I guess so," Dan responded, "and it's not like they knew she was gonna die on February 15th!"

They both chuckled at that thought.

CHAPTER 17

FEBRUARY 23, 2018, 11:30 A.M.
PORT ST. LUCIE POLICE HEADQUARTERS
INTERVIEW ROOM 2

Dan Torres walked into the interview room with Deborah Cooper. Deborah was a truly stunning woman. She was not too flashy, but perfectly dressed in a pink dress with matching pink shoes and purse. Her head was adorned with a white hat with a pink flower.

As Lisa looked down at the gray blouse, black slacks, and white tennis shoes she was wearing she couldn't help but compare her outfit to Deborah Cooper's. I guess I'm in the wrong line of work, she mused.

Dan pulled out a chair at the table and held it for Deborah to sit. Then he sat next to Lisa on the opposite side.

I've never seen Dan do that for any other witness, Lisa thought. This should be interesting!

"Good morning, Ms. Cooper," Lisa began, "my name is Detective Lisa March, and you have already met my partner, Dan Torres."

"Yes," Deborah replied.

"Ms. Cooper," Lisa continued.

"It's Mrs. Cooper."

"Okay, thanks, misses Cooper. We truly appreciate your taking the time to visit with us today. It was very kind of you to come in and help us."

"My pleasure," Deborah replied, flashing a big smile at Danny.

Lisa looked over at her partner smiling back at the witness. She hadn't often taken the time to notice, but Dan Torres was very handsome man. He was tall, with a nice face and a tight muscular body. All the women at the office stared when Danny walked away.

"As you can see, Mrs. Cooper…would you prefer that we call you that?"

"You can call me Debbie. Everyone else does."

"Okay, Debbie. We're Lisa and Dan."

"Nice to meet you, Dan," Deborah said as she once again batted her false eyelashes. Lisa wanted to reach out and smack her partner across the back of his head, but she resisted the temptation.

"As you can see, Debbie, this interview is being recorded. You are here of your own volition and you can terminate this interview at any time. Do you understand that Debbie?"

"Of course."

"Good. Now for the record would you please state your full name and address."

"My name is Deborah Jill Cooper. I live at 10075 Viacount Way in Port St. Lucie, Florida."

"And that is in Riverside Estates?" Lisa asked

"Yes, it is."

"Okay then, let's get started. Detective Torres and I are investigating the murder of Diane Bates, and we're hoping that you can provide information that will help us find the killer."

"I thought you caught him already?"

"We have a suspect in custody," Lisa replied, "but we still have a lot more investigating to do."

"Anything I can do to help," Deborah replied, "Diane was a friend of mine. We played Pickleball together a lot."

Technician Steve Oppenheim walked into the room. Dan remembered that Deborah had refused to give samples to Lonny and Beth.

"Debbie," Dan said, "this is Steven Oppenheim. He works in our lab."

"Hello ma'am," Oppenheim said.

"Debbie," Lisa explained, "we have no reason to believe that you were involved in this case. We would like to take your fingerprints and a DNA sample so that we can formally eliminate you from the list of people that are suspects. That way we can focus only on prosecuting the person who committed the murder of Mrs. Bates."

"No way!" Deborah replied.

"It is certainly your right to refuse," Lisa said, "but, may I ask why you object to giving us your prints and a DNA sample?"

Deborah smiled and said, "look, I did not kill Diane Bates. As a matter of fact, I've never even been in her house."

"But..." Lisa started to say. Deborah interrupted her.

"There's no reason in the world for you take my fingerprints and DNA, because I didn't do anything. But, once you have that stuff it goes into your 'system', and I don't want to be in your 'system.' You understand, don't you Danny?"

Dan nodded agreement and he began to speak until Lisa kicked him in the shins under the table.

"Okay, Mrs. Cooper," Lisa said sternly, "we will note that you refused to give a sample. That certainly is your right." She then motioned to Steve Oppenheim to leave the room.

"Good," Deborah replied, "I assume we're done now."

"Can you tell us about your relationship with Diane Bates, please?" Lisa asked.

"Like I said, she was a friend of mine," Deborah replied, "we payed Pickleball together almost every day."

"How did Diane get along with the other Pickleball players?"

"She was fine," Deborah said, "look, some people took offense to her strong personality. You know what I mean. She said what was on her mind. She never held back."

"And this rubbed some people the wrong way?" Dan asked.

"Yes, Danny. Some people are sensitive, but not me," she said, "I can handle the rough stuff!"

Lisa watched as Danny sat mesmerized by this woman.

"How did Diane get along with her husband?"

"I guess they hated each other," Deborah said, "like most married couples."

"Hated each other?" Lisa asked.

"Well, maybe hate is the wrong word. They just argued a lot on the Pickleball court, and I heard they argued a lot at home too."

"Oh, can you give us an example of their fights?"

"Sure," Deborah said, "they used to be doubles partners, but whenever they lost a game, or even if one of them made a bad shot, they screamed at each other. It was very uncomfortable for the other team. They fought so much they had to find other partners."

"And what other partners did they find?"

"Diane tried a lot of partners, but she could never keep one," Deborah said, "she was pretty strong, and I guess most men don't like it when the woman is a better player than they are. You know, it's an ego thing, I guess."

"And Len?"

"Oh, he hooked up with Abby Jenkins, little Miss Cutie Pie!"

"Cutie Pie?"

"That's what he called her all the time. She's a lot younger than most of us."

"Do you have any more information about Doctor Bates' relationship with Abby?"

"Only rumors," Deborah replied

"And the rumors were, what?" Dan asked.

Deborah smiled at Dan. "Honey, we all knew that Abby and the doctor were practicing a lot more than just Pickleball, if you know what I mean."

"Okay then, what can you tell us about Bobby James?" Lisa asked.

"Bobby?" Deborah replied, "he's a loser…a real loser."

"What makes you say that, Debbie?" Lisa asked.

"Look, by now I'm sure you know all about Bobby James. He would screw any woman on the planet, no matter how old or how ugly she was!"

"How do you know that, Debbie?"

"Cause he told me, that's why! He screwed every single woman that he did a job for. Every single one he told me. No exceptions!"

"Did Bobby James work as a handyman for you?' Dan asked.

"A few times, Danny."

"And did you have a sexual relationship with him?" Lisa added.

"Just one time," Deborah answered, "he just didn't measure up. If you know what I mean," She looked at Dan. "I like a man that brings the right tools to work!"

Lisa ignored that remark. "Deborah," she continued, "if I were to tell you that we found a text message from Diane Bates to Bobby James telling him to stop seeing you, how would you respond to that?"

"I would say Diane could keep him. That's how I would respond!"

"Where were you on February 15th between the hours of ten and noon?"

"Let's see," she replied, "I played Pickleball from 9:00 to 11:00 that day and then I went to my hairdresser."

"What time was your hairdresser appointment?'

"It was 11:30 at Toby's salon. You can check it out. I was there until one."

"Yes, we will check it out," Lisa replied, "Is there anything else you can tell us that will help us with our investigation?"

"Nope," Deborah replied, "I think you got the right man."

"Okay, thank you Mrs. Cooper," Lisa said, "here's my card. If you think of anything else please give me a call."

"Sure," Deborah said as she accepted the card. Then she turned toward Dan Torres.

"Don't you have a card for me, Danny?"

Dan fumbled in his wallet and pulled out a card. He gave it to Deborah as she smiled and left the room.

"You want a cigarette, Danny?" Lisa asked after Deborah left.

"Huh?"

"Come on Dannnniieee," she said sarcastically, trying to imitate Deborah's voice. "It looked like you and Debbie were gonna do it right on this table. It's a damn good thing I was here!"

Dan blushed.

"I think she's clean, don't you?" Lisa said.

"I'll check her alibi but I think she's not a suspect," Danny replied, "but I'm afraid to say so, cause you'll be all over me about it!"

"Come on, partner," Lisa laughed, "if I couldn't tease you what fun would life be for me?"

"Oh, I think you'd find someone else to tease," Danny laughed.

"By the way," Lisa said, "did you catch it when Deborah said that Bobby had sex with every woman he did work for?"

"I didn't, but I remember it now."

"Did you see the way she said 'no exceptions'?"

"Uh huh."

"If that's true then you know what it means?"

"I sure do," Dan replied, "I sure do."

"By the way," Lisa asked, quickly changing the subject. "How are the rookies doing with their dumpster dive job?"

"They're about half way through. Still no signs of a Pickleball paddle."

"And still hating me, I presume?"

"More and more every minute, partner!"

"Good!" Lisa replied, "keep them on it all weekend. I'll get the captain to authorize the overtime."

CHAPTER 18

FEBRUARY 23, 2018, 6:00 P.M.

THE HOME OF LISA AND RICK MARCH

Lisa walked into the house, to be met immediately by the smiling face of her husband Rick.

"I did something really good today!" Rick grinned.

"Well, it's about time," Lisa shot back with a grin. She loved the fact that they could tease each other. "And what is that good something, another pizza for dinner?"

"Nope," Rick replied, "much better. Let's go in the bedroom."

"Rick, I've had a long day!"

"Not that!" Rick said, "well, maybe that, but not right now."

As they walked into the bedroom Lisa saw a red dress lying on the bed.

"What's up, Rick?"

"Madam, your bath awaits you, and my favorite dress."

"Okay, why?"

"Because tonight I'm taking my favorite girl out for dinner at Parelli's."

"Am I invited?" Lisa joked.

"We've got a reservation at seven," Rick laughed, "so, go ahead and get yourself all dolled up, and I'll be waiting to take you whenever you're ready."

"Okay!" Lisa said as she walked into the bathroom and saw the tub filled with water, "just give me ten minutes."

Lisa stepped into the warm tub and relaxed. These past several days had been very stressful for her, so a nice night out with her husband was just what the doctor ordered. The upcoming weekend would, hopefully, give her some needed rest and renewed energy.

Just as Lisa stepped out of the tub and began to towel off, she heard Rick's voice.

"Honey come out here quick. You gotta see this!"

Lisa wrapped herself in the towel and ran to the family room. On the television was Mayor Candace Wilson.

"Can you rewind it Rick? I don't want to miss a word she says."

Rick grabbed the remote and reversed the show until Mayor Wilson was just stepping up to the microphone. She was standing in front of City hall and a small group of reporters had gathered around her.

"As you all know our city suffered a tragic loss last week with the murder of Diane Bates in Riverside Estates. Diane was a neighbor of mine and, although I didn't know her well, I was as shocked as everyone to learn about the brutality of her murder.

"Here comes damage control," Lisa said.

"As soon as I learned of the brutal murder I spoke with Police Chief Warren Sales and told him that I wanted him to put a team together to solve this terrible crime."

"That's bullshit."

"Chief Sales assured me that he would personally manage the investigation and that I would be briefed on a regular basis, which I have been."

"More bullshit!"

"When the name of the arrested man was revealed, my husband reminded me that he had once hired the man to assemble storage cabinets in our garage."

"Once??"

"And, knowing what we know now, I'm relieved to report that the work was completed without incident."

"She is so smooth!"

"My heart goes out to Doctor Bates and the entire family, and I pledge the full efforts of this city to ensure that justice is served in this case."

With those words Mayor Wilson walked away from the microphone, as a few reporters shouted questions that she ignored.

"You're looking at our next governor," Rick said, as the segment ended, "she can make chicken salad out of chicken shit!"

"I'm not so sure, honey," Lisa replied as she walked back toward the bedroom.

Rick grabbed her towel and yanked it to the ground. She looked back at him with a grin and kept walking toward the bed with Rick in pursuit.

They were late for dinner.

CHAPTER 19

FEBRUARY 24, 2018, 10:00 A.M.

THE HOME OF LISA AND RICK MARCH

Lisa woke up and looked at the clock on her nightstand. It was 10 a.m. This was the latest she had slept since high school. She checked the other side of the king sized bed, and was not surprised to see Rick gone. Most likely out for a walk, she thought.

Last night had been perfect, everything about it was wonderful, and she woke up this morning refreshed and happy.

Until her cell phone rang.

It was Captain Davis. "Lisa, I need you to do something for me right away."

"Sure, Captain, anything," she replied.

"I need you to come to Lonny Carter's apartment, do you know where he lives?"

"I do. Why? What's going on, Captain?"

"I'm just pulling into the parking lot now," Captain Davis replied, "I'll see you when you get here." With that he abruptly ended the call.

Lisa jumped out of bed and threw on a pair of jeans and a blouse. She washed her face and threw on a light coat of make up. A baseball cap hid the mess her curly hair had become during the night.

Fifteen minutes later Lisa arrived at the apartment building where Lonny Carter lived. She saw Captain Davis outside of one building talking to several uniformed police. A crowd had gathered outside, and Lisa could easily guess what this all meant.

Lisa parked her car, flashed her badge at the onlookers so they would step aside and let her pass through. By the look on Captain Davis' face she knew what had happened here.

"Is it Lonny?" she said to Captain Davis. He replied with a grim nod.

"Do you need me to go in?"

"Yes, please," was all the captain said.

Lisa walked hesitantly up to the door of Lonny Carter's first floor apartment. She entered the apartment and found coroner Stephanie Rogers on her knees examining the body. It was a gruesome sight, completely unrecognizable.

"Lonny Carter?" Lisa asked grimly.

"Yes," Stephanie replied. "single gunshot wound through the mouth and into the brain."

"Suicide?"

"For sure," Stephanie said, pointing to the gun that was lying next to the body. "It's his gun, and I'm certain we're only gonna find his prints on it. She pointed to the right hand of the dead body. "It's clear that he shot himself and the residue test will certainly confirm it."

"This is so sad," Lisa said.

Captain Davis entered the apartment.

"He has a sister in Miami, that's the only relative I know of."

"I know he's got a couple of ex-wives," Lisa replied, "but I don't know anything about them, other than the jokes he always told about them."

"I'll ask the sister," Captain Davis said, "hopefully she'll take care of the funeral."

"Did he leave a note?" Lisa asked.

"They haven't found one yet," The captain replied, "but I think we all know why he did it. We have to wait for Stephanie to make it official and rule the death a suicide. Then we can release the body."

"Oh, my," Lisa said, "I better call Danelo."

"I took care of that already," The captain replied.

"How'd she take it?"

"She wasn't surprised, but she was still devastated."

"They've been partners a long time."

"Almost five years. But she's a strong woman, and I know she can handle it."

Lisa nodded. "Monday is gonna be a rough day for all of us."

"Yes, I get that."

"Hey boss," she asked, "I hate to change the subject at a time like this, but did you see the mayor on TV last night?"

"Sure did," Captain Davis replied.

"She's really good."

"Yes, she is," Davis replied, "she handled the revelation about the handyman so smooth."

"Rick says she's gonna be our next governor."

"I think that's what she's going for."

"I guess what Lonny did turned out to be not such a big deal, after all, huh boss?" Lisa asked quietly.

"Oh no, Lisa," Captain Davis replied, "it was a big deal, a very big deal. Almost cost me and you our jobs!"

"Really?"

"Oh yes," the captain said, "the mayor was ready to can you and me both but the Chief talked her out of it."

"Chief Sales stood up for us?"

"He was amazing. He threw Lonny Carter under the bus, and painted him as a rogue cop with a big mouth. But he really protected you and me. He told her we knew nothing about it, and he said the department would fall apart without us."

"And she bought it, huh?

"Yes, but it wasn't easy. You see, there's two versions of Candace Wilson, the one the public sees and the one we see."

Lisa pondered for a moment. "Boss, is there anyway we can pay tribute to Lonny at the station on Monday?"

"Let me think about it Lisa," Captain Davis replied, "under the circumstances I'm not sure if that's a good idea."

"Alright then, let me arrange something at the Three Nines Monday night," Lisa replied, "we can make it an unofficial thing and you won't even have to know about it."

Lisa walked away from the apartment and headed for her car. Just as she sat down to drive back home her cell phone rang.

"Danny..."

"I heard about Lonny," Dan said, "anything I can do?"

"No Danny, they're just buttoning things up here and I'm heading home to my husband."

"I've got something that might cheer you up," Dan said.

"Sorry partner, I don't think there's anything that could cheer me up today, except maybe a good stiff drink. Make that several stiff drinks!"

"Well, at least let me try."

"Okay, what is it?"

"We found the murder weapon."

"Get out! No you didn't!"

"Yes we did. Just like you said, it's a Pickleball paddle. It's called a Head Gravity Light Paddle."

"Where was it?"

"You won't believe it," Dan said, "the team looked through every dumpster in the parking lot and they found nothing. When they finished that last one they decided to have lunch at The Irish Pub. It's not exactly in the shopping center but real close to it. It's behind the shopping center and not really part of it."

"So?"

"So, when they got there they saw another dumpster."

"And?"

"One of the rookies, Jerry Lewis…"

"That's his name?' Lisa interrupted, "Jerry Lewis? Really"

"Yep."

"I bet his parents had a sense of humor!"

"I guess," Dan replied, and quickly returned to his story, "so any way, Lewis sees the dumpster sitting right in front of the Irish Pub. He puts on his gloves, yells 'Geronimo' and jumps in. They were all a little nutty after all those dumpsters."

"Did he get hurt?"

"Nope. You won't believe it. He comes up with a shitty grin and a Pickleball paddle in his hand! I'm on my way to the lab for prints and DNA."

"Danny, I owe you…"

"I know Lisa, you owe me another lunch, right?"

"This one deserves a dinner, partner!"

CHAPTER 20

FEBRUARY 26, 2018, 8:00 A.M.

PORT ST. LUCIE POLICE HEADQUARTERS

The detective group was assembled around the table in their usual seats. There was, of course, one empty chair, and not a word was spoken by anyone. The usual banter, teasing, and stories of weekend escapades was replaced by stone cold silence, which was broken only by the entrance of Captain Davis.

Davis took a deep breath and spoke softly, his normal booming voice was nowhere to be found.

"I'm sure all of you know that this past Friday Detective Lonny Carter took his own life." He paused, as all heads nodded.

"There was no note left at the scene, but there's no doubt that the events of last week contributed greatly to his decision to kill himself."

"I spoke with Lonny's sister in Miami," he continued, "although she and Lonny were estranged she has agreed to handle the funeral arrangements for her brother."

"Beth Danelo has asked if she could say a few words."

Beth stood up and walked to the head of the table. Beth was a twelve year veteran of the police force, and for the past five years she had been Lonny Carter's partner on the detective team.

"You all knew Lonny, and I'm sure everyone has formed an opinion about him," she began, "but I just want to take a minute to tell you about the Lonny Carter I knew."

"Lonny was a very complex man," she continued, "he was quick with a joke. He loved to tease people but he loved it just as much when they teased him right back."

"He acted like a clown sometimes, and he could annoy the hell out of me. But when it really mattered, Lonny was a real pro. I always knew that he had my back, and I had his."

"He had trouble in his personal life, and he often confided in me," she said, "those talks will remain with me, but I want you all to know that he was like a brother to me, and I'll miss him forever."

With that, Beth broke down, and several of her colleagues stood up to comfort her. After a moment she composed herself, held up her coffee mug, and said "To Lonny!"

"To Lonny!" The crowd roared as they all raised their coffee cups.

"Now, let's get to work and finish this case," Beth said, "that's what Lonny would have wanted us to do!"

Lisa paused to let the emotion of Beth's speech subside. Then she stood up in front of the white board and spoke.

"I put together a time line of events that will help us wrap up the case," she said, pointing toward the white board, "this is what we know."

"At 11:00 p.m. on February 14th, Diane Bates took three Ambien tablets and one Valium and went to bed. She never woke up"

"At 11:30, Len Bates went to the same bed."

"At 9:00 a.m., Len Bates left the house to play Pickleball."

"At 10:00, Dave Messenger arrived at Riverside."

"We know that Diane Bates was killed some time between 10:00 and noon."

"At 10:30, Bobby James tapped on the bedroom window to signal Diane that he was ready for sex, but he says he heard a voice in the room with her."

"At 11:00, Bobby James tried again and again he heard the voice."

"Also at 11:00, Len Bates finished Pickleball at the club and joined a group for lunch, but he excused himself ostensibly to call his wife to invite her to come to the club for brunch."

"At 11:03, Len Bates left a voice message for Diane asking her to come to brunch."

"At 11:20, Bobby James entered the Bates house through an unlocked sliding door and proceeded into the master bedroom. When he got there he claims that Mrs. Bates was already dead. Rather than call 911, he ran out of the house and left Riverside."

"At 11:33, Dave Messenger was caught speeding out of Riverside."

"At 12:30, Len Bates left the clubhouse and went shopping."

"At 12:38, Len left another voice message on Diane's phone, this time telling her that he was going shopping and would be home later."

"At 2:41, he left a final voice message to say he was on his way home."

"And finally, at 3:00, Len Bates arrived home and found his wife dead in their bed."

"That's it," Lisa said, "so all three of these men had the opportunity to kill Diane Bates."

"And the good news," Dan Torres added, "is that we found what we believe to be the murder weapon in a dumpster that's located near the shopping center where Len Bates was seen shopping."

"Any prints yet?" JoJo asked.

"We just got word from the lab," Stephanie Rogers replied, "they found Diane Bates' DNA on the edge of the paddle, so it definitely is hers and most likely it's the murder weapon."

"That's great news!" Lisa replied, "but how about the handle of the paddle?"

"They found a mixture of four DNA samples on the paddle- Diane Bates, Len Bates, Bobby James, and someone named Michael Studdard."

"Who the hell is Michael Studdard?" Captain Davis asked.

"He's the head pro at the Pickleball club," Beth replied, "we interviewed him last week. Real smooth talker, everything was wonderful at the club. Everybody got along great. Blah blah blah."

"Sounds like you need to talk to him again," Lisa said.

"I'll do it," Beth replied.

"It looks like we can eliminate Dave Messenger as a suspect," Megan Harris said, "his alibi checked out."

"I think you're right," Lisa responded, "so that narrows the field down to the husband and the handyman."

"And don't forget the Pickleball pro," Beth added.

"Oh yeah, him too." Lisa replied.

"The husband and the handyman," Joe O'Hara mused, "Lonny woulda had a field day with that one!"

"Megan," Lisa asked, "do we have enough to arrest Len Bates?"

Megan thought for a moment and replied, "no Lisa. The fact that his DNA is on his wife's Pickleball paddle is hardly enough evidence. JD Treem would make mincemeat out of that one."

"Okay," Lisa said.

"We need to place him at the scene of the crime between ten and noon. And so far the only one we can say that for certain about is Bobby James."

"Sheila," Lisa asked as she turned toward Sheila Feeney, "did you get a chance to go through Bobby James' cell phone?'

"Oh yes!" Sheila replied with a grin, "very interesting!"

"Don't keep us in suspense."

"I found several calls made and received from the cell phones of women in Riverside Estates," Sheila said, "it seems that our handyman was very popular with Pickleball ladies."

"I think we knew that, Sheila," Lisa replied, "but it's good to make it official."

"Any other … ahh… special photos sent to women?"

"Oh yes!" Sheila replied with a grin, "our handyman apparently loved to show off his equipment to the ladies!"

"What a piece of work!" Lisa said, "anything else significant on his phone?"

"Actually there is," Sheila answered, "we found several calls made from a burner phone, you know the kind you buy at Walmart."

"That's interesting," Megan said, "When were these calls made?"

“The first one was made on January 27th,” Sheila said as she checked her notes.

“Then there were a number of calls back and forth between January 28th and February 9th.”

“Any more after that?” Lisa asked.

“Yes there were series of calls on February 14th.”

“The day before the murder,” Captain Davis interjected.

“Uh huh,” Sheila continued, “and then there were two calls on February 15th, one at 8:52 and one at 11:02.”

“Any way we can find out who was on the other end of those calls?” Lisa asked

“Not exactly,” Sheila replied, “we can force the phone company to give us tracking data so we know where the phone was purchased and where it was used. But that can’t tell us who was actually holding the phone and talking into it.”

“Okay then, let’s get whatever we can,” Megan added, “I’ll prepare the warrant for you, Sheila.”

“I guess I’ll just have to ask Mister Bobby James about that burner phone!” Lisa concluded, “okay everyone, thanks again for all your help.”

“Bobby James will have his court appointed lawyer with him,” Megan said, “so I’ll join you, Lisa.”

“Okay, I’m gonna talk to Bobby at the jail at 1:30 today,” Lisa replied.

Sheila Feeney waited for everyone to leave the room before she approached Lisa.

“Hey, Lisa,” she said in a quiet tone.

“What?”

“I didn’t want to say this in front of the group,” Sheila said, as she looked around to make sure nobody else was within earshot. “when I went through all the calls on Bobby’s phone I found a few calls from the mayor’s private cell phone.”

“I thought you might,” Lisa replied, “let’s keep that between us for now.”

CHAPTER 21

FEBRUARY 26, 2018, 1:30 P.M.

ST. LUCIE COUNTY JAIL

Lisa and Megan entered the jail and were met at the security checkpoint by Don Gantz, a large grizzled man in uniform.

"Hey Shorty!" Don joked, as he greeted Lisa, "did they finally catch up with you?"

"No Donnie," Lisa responded quickly with a laugh, "just visiting today, buddy."

"Nice of you to add a little class to this place today. Come on in and join us."

As the two women were escorted into the private interview room, Megan spoke up.

"You know that guy?"

"Sure do," Lisa replied, "he was my training officer when I was a rookie. He taught men everything I know!"

"Looks like they put him out to pasture," Megan said.

"Yeah, sort of," Lisa replied, "it was a medical thing."

Within one minute they arrived at the interview room. Bobby James was seated at a table and a young court appointed lawyer was seated next to him.

“Hi. I’m detective Lisa March and this is prosecutor Megan Harris.”

“Yes, Ms. Harris and I have talked on the phone,” the lawyer said, “I’m Keith Schwartz.”

“Okay Mr. Schwartz,” Lisa began, “as you know your client is under arrest for the murder of Diane Bates. I understand that his bail was denied.”

“Yes,” Schwartz replied, “we’re appealing that.”

“Well, good luck with that,” Lisa responded sarcastically, “I have a few questions to ask your client.

“Go right ahead.”

“Okay Bobby, our forensics team went through your phone and they found a series of calls made from a number that turned out to be a burner phone. Are you familiar with a burner phone?”

“I heard that’s a phone that can’t be traced,” Bobby said, “but I never had one.”

“Well, not exactly,” Lisa said, “we’re in the process of tracing it now and we’ll soon find out who owned it. But I thought you could speed things up by telling me.”

Bobby looked at his lawyer. After he received an affirmative nod he responded.

“I don’t remember.”

“You don’t remember?” Lisa said with a grin, “now, Bobby, you know that we don’t believe that. It might help you if you tell us who it was before we find out.”

Schwartz intervened. “Asked and answered!” he said stoically, “anything else?”

“Why yes,” Lisa replied, “as a matter of fact there is.”

“Do you have another question for my client?”

“Bobby, we were able to locate the murder weapon and we found your DNA on it.” Lisa said, “would you care to explain that?”

Bobby was about to speak when his lawyer interrupted. “Okay, this interview is over.”

“Megan Harris spoke for the first time, “you have my number, Mr. Schwartz, and I want you to know that we will be seeking the death penalty for your client.”

The two women left the interview room. They were escorted back through the security checkpoint where Lisa said goodbye to her friend, Don.

As they exited the building Megan said, “I’ll be expecting a call from Mr. Schwartz very soon.”

CHAPTER 22

FEBRUARY 26, 2018, 6:30 P.M.

THE HOME OF LISA AND RICK MARCH

Lisa walked through the front door, kicked off her shoes, and grabbed the mail that was waiting on the desk in the foyer. The first thing she noticed was the Visa bill for $1866.33.

"Rick!" she yelled, "did you see this bill?"

"I did, honey," Rick replied, as he met his wife walking into the kitchen. He immediately handed her a glass of Kendall Jackson chardonnay, "here, take this, it'll calm you down."

"Why should I calm down?" Lisa shouted, "I told you not to give her a credit card!"

"I spoke to Lexie just a few minutes ago. She said she knew this bill would be high, but she promised it would never happen again. She needed clothes for the spring."

"She's got more clothes than you and me combined, Rick," Lisa yelled. She took a sip of her wine and sat down on the living room sofa.

"That's true, Lise," Rick replied, "but now Lexie knows that this is her last chance. One more bill like this and she loses the card completely."

"You're always the soft one, Rickey March, you know that, don't you?"

"Yep," Rick said with a grin, "and that's why our daughter likes her father better than her mother."

"Oh, that's great."

"But don't worry, honey," he continued, "I can assure you that'll all change when she settles down and has kids of her own. That's when she'll be wanting her mommy again.

"Her penniless mommy, you mean. What's for dinner, babe?"

"Your favorite."

"You say that every night! So what's my favorite tonight?"

Rick opened the oven, placed a pair of oven mitts on his hands, and gently removed a casserole dish."

"You made that?" Lisa said incredulously.

"Well, not exactly," her husband replied.

"What do you mean, not exactly?" Lisa asked with a grin.

"Your mother stopped by and left this for us," Rick said, "I heated it up."

"What is it?"

"It's tuna casserole. She said it was your favorite."

"My favorite? She said that?" Lisa replied, "tell me, Rick, in all the years we've been together, have you ever seen me make tuna casserole, or even eat tuna casserole?"

"No, but your mom said you used to love it."

"I love my mom but she's getting really forgetful in her old age," Lisa said, "it was my sister Carol that loved her tuna casserole. The rest of us hated it!"

"Okay then, I'll give it to the cat."

"When did we get a cat?"

"I'll borrow one."

Lisa's cell phone chirped. She noticed that the call was from Prosecutor Megan Harris.

"Hey, Megan, how are you doing?"

"Just got a call from the Bobby James' lawyer,"

"Oh, really!"

"He wants to talk."

"Talk?"

"He wants to make a deal."

"Deal, what kind of deal?"

"We'll both find out tomorrow," Megan replied, "can you come to my office at 9:00?"

"Wouldn't miss it for the world!"

Lisa ended the call as her husband asked, "what's up, Lisa?"

"Honey, I think we just put this case to bed!"

"I ordered a pizza." Rick replied.

CHAPTER 23

FEBRUARY 27, 2018, 9:00 A.M.

THE OFFICE OF PROSECUTOR MEGAN HARRIS

This is a pretty tiny office for a prosecutor, Lisa thought, as she parked herself in one of the two chairs opposite Megan Harris' chair. There was barely enough room for the young lawyer to join them.

Just as she sat down, Keith Schwartz, the public defender assigned to Bobby James, entered the room. To Lisa, Keith Schwartz looked more like a high school freshman than a full fledged lawyer. He was wearing a suit that looked like it came from Walmart, with a crooked tie, and old shoes. He was carrying an old worn briefcase.

He politely shook hands with both women, and began to make small talk about the weather. Megan was having no part of it.

"Okay Mr. Schwartz," Megan said sternly, "you asked for this meeting, so what did you want to talk about?"

Schwartz opened his briefcase and removed a few papers. He looked at them for a few seconds and then began.

"I spoke with my client last night..."

"Bobby James?" Megan interrupted.

"Yes, Mr. Bobby James."

"And?" Megan asked. It was clear to Lisa that Megan was establishing dominance over Schwartz. Maybe it's lawyer thing, she thought.

"Mr. James would be willing to plead guilty..."

"Oh, he would?"

"Yes, um, he would be willing to plead guilty to a lesser charge."

Megan saw her opening and pounced. "So, Bobby James admits that he killed Diane Bates?"

"As I said, "Schwartz continued, "my client is willing to plead guilty if he is charged with manslaughter."

"Manslaughter?" Megan laughed, "Mr. Schwartz, your client walked into Mrs. Bates' bedroom while she was asleep and bludgeoned her in the head three times until she was dead. That is not manslaughter!"

It was then that Lisa noticed a change in Mr. Schwartz' demeanor.

"He was paid to kill her."

Lisa was shocked. She couldn't help but shout, "by who?"

Schwartz puffed out his chest. "That is something he will reveal only when he has a deal."

Megan was not taking the bait. "Look, Mr. Schwartz. You asked for this meeting and I gave it to you. But you've got a lot of nerve coming in here and trying to play hardball with me."

She continued with her rant. "We have enough evidence on your client to put him in the electric chair and you know it," she said, "so if you want some kind of deal you'd better not play games with me. You understand?"

This was a side of Megan Harris that Lisa had never seen before, and she loved it.

Just as Megan stood up and appeared to be ready to ask him to leave, Schwartzspoke again.

"Ms. Harris," he said quietly and calmly, "the one thing I admire most about you is that you have a reputation for seeking the truth."

"So?"

“So, there’s a person out there right now who planned and paid for the murder of Diane Bates, and this person will get away with murder unless my client testifies.”

“Uh huh.”

“We are willing to spare you a trial in the case of my client and hand you the real culprit on a silver platter,” Schwartz said with growing strength, “and all we ask in return is some consideration on your part of the charge my client pleads to. It’s hard for me to believe that you would turn down an offer like this and let a murderer go free.”

Wow, Lisa thought, where did that come from?

“I’ll get back to you,” Megan said firmly. “but I can guarantee you it won’t be manslaughter.”

“Thank you ma’am,” Schwartz said calmly, “our offer is on the table, We eagerly await your counter offer, and I thank you for your time.”

Schwartz assembled his papers, closed his briefcase, stood up, shook hands with Lisa and Megan, and calmly walked out the door.

“Geez,” Lisa said, “is it me or did that guy just grow a pair in front of our eyes?”

“He’s got a lot to offer us.” Megan replied.

“Bates?”

“That’s my guess.”

“So, what’s the next move?”

“I’ll talk to the D.A.,” Megan replied, “but I’m not sure he’ll go for it.”

“Why not?” Lisa asked.

“Because we could never convict Len Bates solely on the testimony of Bobby James. He’s lied so many times it’s ridiculous. JD Treem would eat him for breakfast!”

“Right now we only have circumstantial evidence to pin the crime on Len Bates. He and his wife didn’t get along, he had an affair, she was sleeping with the handyman, and she predicted he would kill her.”

“And don’t forget the two million dollar life insurance policy,” Lisa said.

"Okay, so how's this for a working theory?" Megan asked, "Bates calls Bobby from a burner phone and offers him money to kill Diane. Bobby arranges to have sex with Diane on the 15th because he knows the neighbors are away that day."

"The night before, Len gives his wife a huge dose of pills, not enough to kill her just enough to make her an easy mark for Bobby. He leaves her Pickleball paddle in the bedroom so Bobby can use it to kill her."

"Shortly before he leaves for Pickleball, Bates calls Bobby to make sure all systems are go."

"Bobby is supposed to do the deed at 10:30, so Len has a perfect alibi. But when he arrives at the bedroom and sees Diane sleeping there he gets cold feet and he backs off."

"He tries again at 11:00, but he still can't bring himself to kill Diane."

"Bates calls him shortly after 11:00 and finds out the deed isn't done yet. Bobby tells Bates that he changed his mind and he doesn't want to do it. Bates gets mad and tells Bobby to get the job done now, or else. So Bobby finally enters the bedroom and finishes her off at 11:20.

"Then Bobby leaves the estates, stops for lunch at the Irish Pub, and tosses the paddle into a dumpster."

"That's quite a story," Lisa said.

"Yes, now all we gotta do is prove it."

• • • • •

Lisa returned to her desk at the police station and saw a note from Sheila Feeney.

"I've got some info on the burner phone."

Within seconds Lisa had made her way over to Sheila's desk.

"Got some good news for me, Sheels?"

"Maybe good, maybe not so good," Sheila replied, "I was able to trace the burner phone. It was purchased from a place called Larry's Barber Shop in The Villages and activated on January 27th."

"From a barber shop?"

"Yep," Sheila said, "this guy Larry is a well known reseller of burner phones. You see, he buys them legitimately from places like Walmart and Seven Eleven. Then he marks them up and resells them for a profit."

"But, why would people pay more from him when they can buy the phone at Walmart for less?"

"Because those stores have surveillance cameras, Lisa. And the people who buy from Larry don't want to be seen."

"Oh I get it," Lisa replied, "you buy from Larry, pay cash, and nobody knows who you are. No questions asked. Very smart."

"Yes. I guess you could say it's smart. But I suspect that most of the people who do this are up to no good."

"Like planning a murder!" Lisa said, "anything else, Sheels?"

"Oh yes," Sheila said, "Every call made to Bobby James from the burner phone was made from within Riverside Estates!"

"Really?"

"Well," Sheila replied, "they came through a tower located right in back of the estates. You can't get any closer than that!"

"Wow!"

Lisa returned to her desk and called Joe O'Hara's cell phone.

"Joey, where are you buddy?"

"I'm at Chicken Delight," Joe replied, "want me to bring you some nuggets?"

"No thanks. I've got plans for lunch. You coming back soon?"

"I'll be there in ten minutes. Why? What do you need?"

"I need to know where Len Bates was on January 27th."

"I'm on it," Joe replied.

Dan Torres walked in the room.

"Care to join me for lunch at the Irish Pub, Danny?" Lisa asked.

"I just had lunch, Lisa."

"Too bad," Lisa joked, "I was gonna buy."

CHAPTER 24

FEBRUARY 27, 2018, 1:00 P.M.

IRISH PUB

Lisa and Dan entered the Pub and sat at the bar.

"Ever been here before?" Lisa asked.

"A few times," Dan replied.

"I hear the food sucks."

"Yes, I'd say that's a fair assessment," Dan replied, "most people don't come in here to eat."

"Too bad we're on duty," Lisa said, "I could use a cold one."

The bartender came over to them. He was large man with a bushy beard.

"What can I get you folks?" he asked.

Lisa showed the bartender her badge.

"We'd like to see the owner, please."

The bartender walked into the kitchen and two minutes later a small dark skinned man came out. He walked over to Lisa and Dan.

"I'm Rakesh Patel," he said.

"You the owner?" Lisa asked.

"Yes, that's true. I'm the owner."

"You own an Irish Pub?" Dan asked.

"Yes." The owner replied. "My real name is Shamus Mulrooney!" He let out a bellowing laugh. "What can I do for you, officers?"

"We're detectives," Lisa corrected him, "do you have security cameras in here?"

"Yes. We have one outside and one overlooking the cash register."

"That makes sense," Danny said.

"How long do you keep the videos?"

"They erase automatically after thirty days. Why? What are you looking for?"

"We need to see the outside video from February 15th," Lisa said, "can you get it for us?"

Rakesh Patel reached into his pocket and removed a cell phone. "I can do better than that!" he said with a grin.

He pulled up an app on his phone, pressed a few buttons, and handed the phone to Lisa.

"There you go," he said, "knock yourselves out."

"Thanks." Lisa said as she began to watch the video.

As Rakesh walked back toward the kitchen he turned to Lisa and said, "Let me know when you're finished. If you find what you're looking for I can make you a copy. And don't steal my phone!"

Lisa and Dan retreated from the bar and sat at an obscure table in the far corner of the restaurant. Together they watched the video footage from the front of the restaurant.

"Wow," Lisa said as they watched video of people entering the Pub that day, "this place has quite a collection of misfits!"

"Just then, on the video, a huge man came up to the door in a leather, sleeveless vest covering a white, sleeveless tee shirt. His body was covered with grotesque tattoos and he had a ring through his nose. His hair was cut in a Mohawk.

"How'd you like Lexie to bring this one home to meet the parents?" Dan asked with a laugh.

"Hey, mom and dad," Lisa said, "meet my new boyfriend, Moose!"

"He's studying to be a brain surgeon!" Dan added gleefully.

They both laughed and continued to watch until suddenly they saw exactly what they were looking for.

There, at time stamp of 12:14 p.m., was none other than Bobby James entering the Irish Pub.

"It looks like he's coming from the direction of the dumpster," Dan said.

"I think so," Lisa agreed, "the camera doesn't pan far enough to catch the dumpster but I think we've got exactly what we came here for!"

"I'll get us a copy."

"Okay, ask Shamus for it!" Lisa smiled.

• • • • •

Lisa returned to the office where she was met by detective Beth Danelo.

"How are you doing, Beth?" Lisa asked quietly, she held her friend's hand.

"I guess I'm doing okay, Lise," Beth replied, "I'm trying to keep busy but every time I do something I think about Lonny, and what he would say if he was there."

Tears welled up in Beth's eyes.

"I know how it feels to lose a partner, honey," Lisa said.

"You lost a partner?" Beth replied, "I never knew that?"

"Yes," Lisa responded, "it was back when I was on patrol. My partner was shot and killed during a bank robbery."

"Oh, I didn't know that."

"The truth is, I've never forgiven myself," Lisa said, a small tear running down her cheek matched the tear on Beth's face, "I still think I coulda saved him."

"I'm sure you did everything you could."

"I still have nightmares about that day."

"And I have nightmares about Lonny."

"I'm afraid it never ends, honey."

The two friends hugged.

"Listen," Beth said as she pulled away from the hug, "I talked to Michael Studdard."

"Who?"

"Michael Studdard. He's the other guy whose DNA was on the murder weapon."

"Oh yes. So what did he say?"

"He's the club Pickleball pro," Beth explained, "he said he puts new grips on everybody's paddles so you can find his prints and DNA on the grip of just about every paddle at the club."

"Does he have an alibi?"

"Rock solid," Beth replied, "he was in Vero all day at a coaches' clinic. I checked it out. He's clean."

"Okay good," Lisa said, "that's one more name we can take off the board."

"So where are we on the handyman?" Beth asked.

"It looks like he's ready to confess, but he's looking for a deal."

"Wow! Okay let me know if you need anything else."

"Honey, you need to get away and relax," Lisa said, "tell that boyfriend of yours you need a little getaway to Marco Island."

"Sounds great, Lise," Beth replied, " thanks for being such a good friend."

CHAPTER 25

FEBRUARY 27, 2018, 5:30 P.M.

THE HOME OF LISA AND RICK MARCH

Lisa stepped through the front door and heard her husband making noise in the kitchen. She walked into the kitchen and there was Rick, standing over the stove frying something.

"What are you fixing for dinner tonight, Emeril?" she joked.

Rick turned towards his wife. He was holding a spatula, wearing a chef's hat, and an apron that said "KISS THE COOK".

"Tonight we're having your favorite, honey!"

"What? Tuna casserole again?" she joked.

"Nope! Tonight we're having home made lasagna."

"And you're making it in a frying pan?" Lisa asked, "I never heard of frying pan lasagna."

"I looked it up on YouTube, babe. Trust me, it's gonna be delicious!"

"Okay," Lisa said, "let me take a bath and then we can enjoy your frying pan lasagna."

Lisa enjoyed the bathtub after work. It gave her a few minutes to relax and soak in the warm water. As much as she loved to free her mind of everything at work, this was a day she just couldn't do it.

Talking to Beth Danelo today brought back memories that she had tried, for fifteen years, to forget.

It was August 10, 2003, a blazing hot day. She and her partner had been on patrol when they got word that a bank robbery was in progress on Federal Highway. They were the first officers on the scene.

When they had arrived at the bank Lisa could see that the robbery was still going on. Bank customers were lying on the ground with their hands over their heads. It appeared that two gunmen were standing guard, and she assumed that at least one more was busy in the bank vault.

Lisa had called for backup but before anyone else arrived she thought she heard shots fired inside the bank.

She and her partner, Josh Gray, rushed to the front door and opened it. She yelled "Police! Put your weapons down now!"

"Both gunmen, who appeared to be very young, dropped their weapons to the ground and put their hands up. Lisa and Josh immediately placed each of them in handcuffs.

Suddenly, a third gunman emerged from the bank vault and fired a shot, striking Josh in the head. He died instantly.

Lisa returned fire, killing the third gunman.

Over and over Lisa played the image in her head. What could I have done differently? Why didn't I take precautions against a possible third gunman? Why didn't I wait for backup? I was the senior partner. It was my responsibility to take care of my partner and I failed him. And even though she probably saved the lives of some bank patrons and staff she was put on desk duty for a month following the incident. The sight of her partner lying on the ground, dead, had haunted her every day since.

Lisa cried. She cried for Josh Gray and she cried for Lonny Carter. Why did we choose this terrible line of work?

She soaked in the tub for several minutes until she smelled something burning.

"Rick, are you okay?" she yelled.

"Everything's under control, honey," Rick replied, "take your time in there."

“Lisa continued to soak in the tub for twenty more minutes. She heard the doorbell ring and wondered who would be calling on them at dinner time. She threw on some clothes and walked into the kitchen.

“Who was at the door, Rick?”

“Are you ready for dinner, madam?” Rick asked.

“It smells like something was burning in here, Rick.”

“Oh yeah, well, “Rick said with a grin, “I sort of overcooked the lasagna so I ordered a pizza for dinner.”

As she sat down to enjoy the pizza Lisa was interrupted by her cellphone. She could see that it was Prosecutor Megan Harris.

“Hey Megan, what’s up?”

“It’s Bates, Lisa,” Megan said abruptly.

“Huh?”

“Just like we thought. It was Bates that hired Bobby to kill his wife.”

“You made a deal?”

The DA only agreed to murder 1 with a life sentence but with the possibility of parole.”

“Okay, that sounds good. Not much of a concession,” Lisa replied, “so what did you get in exchange from Bobby?”

“Bobby says that Bates told him he was gonna get a life insurance payout and he promised to give Bobby a hundred grand if he killed Diane.”

“So it was Bates on the burner phone?”

“That’s what Bobby says,” Megan replied, “but it sure would help if we can put that phone in Bates’ hand.”

“We’re working on it right now.”

CHAPTER 26

FEBRUARY 28, 2018, 9:00 A.M.

PORT ST. LUCIE POLICE DEPARTMENT

When Lisa arrived at the office, detective Joe O'Hara was waiting at her desk. He had a big grin on his face. Joe was a new detective, just finishing his first year on the job. And while he was still wet behind the ears, he always showed good instincts and a willingness to do whatever it took to close a case.

"You got good news for me, Joey?" Lisa asked.

"Better than good!" Joe replied, "guess where Doctor Leonard Bates was on January 27th?"

"I'm hoping you're gonna say....

"The Villages!"

"Woohoo!"

"He was at the Villages for a Pickleball tournament that day."

"Anybody go with him?"

"Yup, his partner slash girlfriend, Abby Jenkins!"

"Wait a minute. Didn't they break up, and she moved away from Riverside?"

"She definitely moved away, to Fort Pierce," Joe replied, "but I'm not sure about the breakup thing."

"Sounds for sure that they didn't break up as Pickleball partners."

"At least not for tournaments away from this area."

"We need to get this Abby Jenkins in here."

"I'm way ahead of you," Joe said, "she's due in at two today."

"You're awesome, Joey!"

"Tell me something I don't already know!" Joe said with a grin.

Lisa worked on paperwork, went home for lunch with Rick, and came back in time for her two o'clock interview with Abby Jenkins.

Dan Torres walked into the interview room with Abby Jenkins. Lisa was taken aback by how young she looked. Not much older than me, Lisa thought. What the hell is she doing with an old guy like Len Bates? He must be twenty-five years older than her. And a married old guy!

Dan directed Abby to a chair at the table and then he sat next to Lisa on the opposite side.

"Good morning, Mrs. Jenkins," Lisa began, "my name is Detective Lisa March, and you have already met my partner, Dan Torres."

"Yes," Abby replied.

"Mrs. Jenkins," Lisa continued, "we truly appreciate you coming here today. It was very kind of you to help us."

"No problem," Abby replied, "but I'm not sure how I can help you."

"As you can see, Mrs. Jenkins...would you prefer that we call you that?"

"Abby is fine."

"As you can see, Abby, this interview is being recorded. You are here of your own volition and you can terminate this interview at any time. Do you understand that Abby?"

"Yes."

"Good. Now, for the record, would you please state your full name and address."

"My name is Abigail Bernadette Wharton Jenkins. I live at 3454 Sunset Road in Fort Pierce."

That's a lot of names, Lisa thought. I bet there's a good story behind all those names.

"Mrs. Jenkins, er, Abby," Lisa began, "do you remember playing in a Pickleball tournament in the Villages on January 27th of this year?"

Abby checked the calendar on her cell phone, "Yes, I was there."

"And who did you go to the tournament with?"

Abby hesitated, "it was Len. I mean Doctor Bates."

"You drove with him?"

"Yes. Doctor Bates picked me up on his way. We were partners in the Central Florida Pickleball tournament."

"How did you do?" Lisa asked with the smile. She could see that Abby was very nervous so she wanted to break the tension.

"We made it to the semis of the 3.5 group!" Abby replied, "that's a huge tournament so we had to win four matches to make it as far as we did."

Lisa had no idea what Abby was talking about. What on earth is a 3.5 group? She chose not to ask.

"Well done," Lisa said, "so you drove up and back the same day?"

"Yes, Len picked me up at 7:00. It's about a two and half hour drive so we got there about 9:30.

"And what time was your first game?"

"I think around 10:15 or 10:30. I'm not sure."

"Did you stop anywhere on the way?"

"No."

"What time did your last match end?" Dan asked.

"I'm not one hundred percent sure, but I guess it was around 2:30."

"Did you go out for lunch?'

"No, they gave us lunch right there at the courts."

Lisa stared at Abby for a few seconds. "This is a very important question, Abby," she said, "at any point during the day were you and Doctor Bates separated for any length of time?"

"No," Abby responded quickly, "only for bathroom breaks, and those were pretty short."

"When the tournament ended, did you stop anywhere on the way home?"

Again Abby pondered before she spoke. "Why are you asking me all these questions?"

"Abby, it is very important that you tell us everything that happened that day," Lisa said sternly, "we will find out from you or from another source, and you need to know that lying to us can land you in jail."

"He drove me home right after the tournament,",came Abby's quick response.

"Okay then, what time did you get back to your place in Fort Pierce?"

"I dunno, I guess around five o'clock."

"Can anyone verify the time of your arrival back home?"

"No. My husband was working the evening shift and he didn't get home until midnight," Abby said, "and by then I was already home and sound asleep."

"Now, Abby," Lisa leaned forward and said, "this is extremely important. We have reason to believe that while he was in The Villages Doctor Bates stopped at a barber shop and made a purchase. We need you to tell us if that happened."

"I certainly don't remember anything like that."

"You don't remember, or it didn't happen? "Dan asked, "those are two different things, Abby."

Abby paused again before she spoke, "I say it never happened."

"One last thing, Abby," Lisa said, "did Doctor Bates ever tell you that he was going to divorce his wife and be with you?"

Abby sat still for a moment, then raised up in her chair. Lisa could see she was uncomfortable with this question. She took a deep breath and said, "no, he never said that to me."

Lisa handed her card to Abby. "Okay, thank you very much for coming in here today. If you think of anything else that happened that day please give me a call."

Dan escorted Abby Jenkins out of the building and returned to meet Lisa at her desk.

"What do you think, Danny?"

"I think she's protecting him."

"Me too."

"He better continue being really good to her!"

"So, what's next, Lisa?"

"Well, partner, I think you and I are gonna take a little field trip."

"To The Villages?"

"Oh yes."

"That's out of our jurisdiction."

"I know it is." Lisa said, "I'll get the captain to arrange someone from BCI to join us."

"BCI?" Dan asked, "never heard of it."

"It stands for Bureau of Criminal Investigations." Lisa replied. "It's the Florida state version of the FBI."

"You know," Dan said, "it's hard to believe that a woman her age would fall for a man so much older than her."

"That's exactly what I was thinking, Danny."

"It kind of reminds me of the eighty year old man who took up with a twenty-five year old woman."

"Huh?"

"Yeah," Dan continued, "so he goes to the doctor, and the doctor asks him if he's having sex with her."

"Oh!"

"And the old man said yes, every day, sometimes twice a day!"

"Wow!"

"Yeah, so the doctor says that could be very dangerous."

"I bet!"

"Yeah, and the guy says I know doc, but if she dies she dies!"

Lisa laughed. "I didn't know you were such a good joke teller Danny!"

"There's a lot you don't know about me, partner!" Dan replied with a grin.

CHAPTER 27

FEBRUARY 28, 2018, 1:00 P.M.

THE VILLAGES, FLORIDA

After driving two and a half hours, Dan noticed a very large sign that said 'WELCOME TO THE VILLAGES'.

"We made it," he said, as he pulled the car into the community.

"You know what they say about this place?" Lisa asked with a grin.

"Can't say as I do."

"They say it's the party capital of Florida!"

"Really?"

"Yup, a wild and crazy place!"

"You're kidding, right?"

"Not kidding," Lisa said, "I guess these senior citizens have a lot of free time on their hands and they do a lot of fun things."

Dan laughed, "We're gonna get there some day, Lisa," he said, "you sooner than me!"

"Ouch!" Lisa recoiled, "thanks for reminding me!"

"Where are we meeting the BCI guy?" Dan asked.

"He said he'd be waiting at the Sunset Pointe welcome sign."

After navigating for several minutes Dan pulled the car up to the sign. Waiting for them was a black sedan. Inside sat the BCI agent. As they parked behind the car the agent stepped out and came over to them. He was tall, well dressed, and adorned with aviator sunglasses. Exactly what a BCI agent should look like, Lisa thought.

"Hello." The agent said, "I'm Bob Elliott of the BCI. You must be the detectives from Port St. Lucie."

"I'm Dan Torres, and this is my partner, Lisa March."

"Okay then, follow me."

They drove behind Agent Elliott for five minutes until he stopped in front of a barber shop. A small sign above the door said LARRY'S. Next to the sign was a small red, white, and blue spinning barber pole. In the window was a sign that said OPEN.

Agent Elliott led Lisa and Dan into the shop. It was empty except for one middle aged barber. As soon as he entered, Agent Elliott grabbed the OPEN sign and turned it around so that now it said CLOSED.

"Hey, what the hell are you doing?" the barber said loudly.

Agent Elliott flashed his ID at the barber and said, "sit down. We have some questions for you."

The barber immediately complied. I like the way this guy operates, Lisa thought.

"I assume you are Larry?" Agent Elliott said.

"Yes, I'm Larry Hunsucker," the barber replied sheepishly, "what do you want?"

"I'm Agent Robert Elliott from the Florida Bureau of Criminal Investigations."

"Criminal?" The barber replied, "I'm not a criminal."

Agent Elliott ignored the comment. "This is Detective Torres and Detective March from the Port St. Lucie police department," he said, "they have a few questions to ask you."

Lisa removed two photos from a folder she was carrying. One was a photo of Len Bates, the other was Abby Jenkins.

"Have you ever seen either of these two people in your shop?" she asked calmly.

Larry examined the photos carefully.

"No," he replied, "can't say as I have."

"You haven't seen them or you can't say if you've seen them?" Lisa replied in a stern voice, "there's a difference."

Larry looked at the photos again. "Nope," he said, "I never saw either one of them."

"Listen," Agent Elliott interjected, "we know that you sell burner phones in this shop."

"There's nothing illegal about that!" Larry shot back.

"That's correct," Lisa responded quickly, "but helping someone to commit a crime is illegal. You understand that, don't you?"

"Of course I do," Larry answered, "what crime are you talking about?

"Murder," Dan replied.

"Murder?" Larry said, "I don't know anything about a murder!"

"Mr. Hunsucker," Lisa said, "On January 27th a burner phone was purchased from this barber shop and it was used to commit murder."

Larry answered, "I'm telling you I don't know anything about a murder!"

"Do you have any surveillance cameras?" Dan asked.

"Surveillance cameras? No. Of course not," Larry replied, "this is a barber shop. We don't need that kind of stuff. It's too expensive."

"Yeah, yeah, yeah," Agent Elliott said, "we get it."

Elliott walked very close to Larry, clearly in Larry's 'space', and said, "Let me make one thing clear, Mr. Hunsucker. If we find out that you in any way shape or form aided and abetted this crime, and especially if we find that you were less than totally honest with us, you'll be cutting hair in prison for a long time!"

With that, Agent Elliott returned the sign to its OPEN position and walked out the door.

Just before she left Lisa handed Larry her card.

"If you think of anything that you might not have remembered today give me a call."

Lisa thanked Agent Elliott for his help as she and Dan returned to their car for the long ride back to Port St. Lucie.

As Dan pulled away from The Villages he spoke to Lisa.

"I think old Larry the Barber is full of shit!"

"Oh yeah," Lisa replied, "but he's a businessman, and if he revealed who bought a phone from him that would be the end of his business."

"I was hoping maybe the BCI would scare him into revealing the truth."

"Me too, Danny, that agent was quite impressive," Lisa replied. "if I was gonna make a movie and I needed someone to play the role of an FBI agent...."

"He'd be your guy, huh?

"Oh yeah!"

As their car entered the Florida turnpike, Lisa called Rick.

"Hi honey, I'm on my way home."

"How about an ETA?"

"Let's see, it's 2:30 now so I figure I should be home by 5:30."

"Great. I'll be waiting for you with a big glass of Kendall Jackson,"

"Super, Rick. What's for dinner?"

"Your favorite, honey!" came Rick's quick reply.

"So what're you having?" Dan asked.

"Pizza!" Lisa replied, "you know, sometimes I feel like I live with the Teenage Mutant Ninja Turtles!"

CHAPTER 28

MARCH 14, 2018, 1:00 P.M.

OFFICE OF PROSECUTOR MEGAN HARRIS

Lisa was happy to once again be moving forward on the Diane Bates murder case. It had been a frustrating two weeks, with no new evidence to arrest Leonard Bates. They had been able to clear the son-in-law Dave Messenger, the drug cartel, and every other person of interest. This left only Len Bates in their sights.

She walked into Megan's tiny office and sat down across the desk.

"Anything new, Meg?"

"Bobby James pled guilty to first degree murder yesterday."

"Okay, that's good news."

"Based on the plea deal he was sentenced to life with the possibility of parole."

"We expected that," Lisa said, "did you get a statement from him yet?"

"I did," Megan replied, "that's why I asked you to meet me today."

"I'm dying to hear what he had to say."

"He fingered Len Bates as the one who offered to pay him to kill Diane Bates."

“We expected that,” Lisa replied calmly, “so now do we have enough to arrest Bates?”

“I’m afraid not,” Megan replied.

“No? Why not?”

“The way I see it, there are some big holes in our case against Len Bates..

“Huh?”

“Number one, the calls were made from a burner phone, and even though we can show that Bates was in The Villages the same day the phone was purchased we still can’t put the phone in his hand.”

“Didn’t Bobby recognize his voice?”

“He said he recognized the voice because of the Boston accent,” Megan replied, “I asked him if he had spoken to Len Bates in the past and he said many times.”

“So that should give him credibility on that issue. Huh?”

“That leads me to number two,” Megan continued, “Bobby James has little credibility, I’m afraid. He lied to us several times and it can easily be argued that he gave up Len Bates just to get a better plea deal.”

“Okay.”

“And here’s number three, Len Bates never paid Bobby anything.”

“Nothing?”

“Nada. Bobby says Bates told him he was gonna collect his wife’s insurance and that’s when he would pay Bobby.”

“And Bobby took that deal?” Lisa said, “what a shmuck!”

“Not the brightest bulb on the tree, for sure,“ Megan responded, “but the offer was pretty high.”

“How much?”

“A hundred thousand.”

“What about the drugs in the wife’s body?” Lisa asked, “did Bobby say that Bates told him he was gonna drug her to make it easier to kill her?”

“I asked him about that,” Megan replied, “no dice.”

"Okay but how about the murder weapon? Did Bates leave the paddle there for Bobby?"

"According to Bobby he was supposed to strangle her with a garrote," Megan said, "the first two times he went over to the house he had the garrote in his hands but he got cold feet. But then he says Bates called him and told him if he didn't kill Diane then Bates would ruin him. He'd make sure Bobby never set foot in Riverside again.

"So he finally went back to do the deed, but he forgot to bring the garrote. Rather than go back for it he saw the paddle in the room, so he grabbed it and whacked her with it."

"I bet Bates was surprised to see how she was killed," Lisa said.

"None of this matters unless we can put that burner phone in Bates' hand," Megan said emphatically.

"Okay then," Lisa said grimly, "I've gotta lean on Larry The Barber until he breaks."

"I think I can help you with that, Lise."

"Is there anything we can charge Larry with, you know, to put some pressure on him?"

"Actually there is," Megan replied, checking her notes," I spoke to an old friend of mine in the Sumter County DA's office."

"And…?"

"He says that Larry hasn't been paying state sales tax on the burner phones he sells."

"Really?"

"Yep. Then I called a friend in the Florida Department of Revenue and she was delighted to help us!"

"We just need Larry to ID Len or his girlfriend, Abby Jenkins."

"She knows that, Lise," Megan said, "and she expects to have something for us in a few days."

"If we can get a positive ID on either one of them I can use it to squeeze the truth out of Abby Jenkins."

"And, if she fingers Bates, he's toast."

"Oh, I can hardly wait to put the cuffs on Doctor Leonard Bates, that pompous ass!"

"Don't get ahead of yourself, Lise. Let's see what they come up with."

As Lisa was about to leave she called her partner, Dan Torres.

"Hey Danny, can you do me a favor?"

"Anything, Lise."

"I need you to contact the organizers of that Pickleball tournament in The Villages."

"Sure Lisa. What do you need from them?"

"Abby told us that she and Len made it to the semi-finals, so I'm hoping that there was a photo taken of them at the end."

"I'll call them now," Dan replied, "but I'm curious. Why do you need that?"

"We showed Larry The Barber a picture of Len from the crime scene and the photo of Abby was from her Facebook page."

"That's true."

"So, I was thinking that it might help jog Larry's memory if he could see what they were wearing the day they bought the burner phone."

"I thought Larry wasn't gonna cooperate with us?" Dan said, "what changed his mind?"

"I think we got him by the short hairs, partner."

CHAPTER 29

MARCH 21, 2018, 9:00 A.M.

PORT ST. LUCIE POLICE DEPARTMENT

Captain Davis called the meeting to order. All of the detectives were once again seated around the table.

"Folks," he began, "I've good news to report today.

"In a few minutes I'll be headed over to the Mayor's office to inform her that we now have an arrest warrant for Doctor Leonard Bates. Megan?"

"We will be charging Doctor Bates with the murder of his wife Diane Bates." Megan said softly.

"What happened?" JoJo asked.

"Yesterday we got a call from a lawyer representing Mr. Larry Hunsucker," Megan replied.

"Larry The Barber is the guy who sold the burner phone to Len Bates that was later used to contact Bobby James."

"Bates then offered Bobby James one hundred grand to kill Diane Bates."

"Did the barber identify Bates as the guy who bought the burner phone?" Beth Danelo asked.

"Actually, no," Lisa replied, "he identified Abby Jenkins."

“Abby was Len’s partner at the Pickleball tournament in The Villages,” Dan continued, “and after the matches she stopped by the barber shop and purchased the phone.”

“Larry described the woman who bought the phone. He said she was wearing bright orange neon sneakers, big white sequined sunglasses, and a white hat with sequins on it.”

“Take a look at this photo,” Lisa said, as she passed around a color photo print. “This was taken at the Pickleball tournament and look what Abby Jenkins was wearing!”

The photo was passed around the room and everyone mumbled as they saw that Abby Jenkins was wearing bright orange neon sneakers, big white sequined sunglasses, and a sequined white hat.

“We got him!” Lisa said.

“I want to thank all of you for your effort in this case,” Captain Davis said, “no doubt Megan will need our help as she puts together her case, so I’m asking each of you to do whatever she needs you to do.”

A collective head nod came from around the table as they all got up to leave.

As Meghan was about to leave she received a call on her cell phone.”-Just a minute,” she whispered as she looked at the caller ID on her cell phone, “it’s JD Treem.”

“I wonder what he wants?”

“Mr. Treem!” Megan said, “how nice to hear from you.”

Lisa heard only Megan’s side of the call.

“Uh huh, okay, no Problem, I understand, okay, I’ll let them know.”

As Megan hung up the phone she said, “son of a bitch!”

“What’s up, Meg? What did he want?”

“JD Treem has a new client….Abby Jenkins!” Megan said, “and I am to instruct you that any further questions you have for her should come through him.”

“I can’t believe it!” Lisa yelled.

“Oh you can believe it, alright.” Megan replied.

"How the hell did he know?"

"JD Treem has a lot more contacts in this state than I do!"

"Are you gonna charge Abby Jenkins?"

"If that's what it takes to get her to talk!"

CHAPTER 30

MARCH 21, 2018, 6:00 P.M.

THE HOME OF LISA AND RICK MARCH

Lisa was excited to see Rick. This was his first full day back to work and she wanted to hear everything about it. She had stopped on the way home to pick up Chinese food, all of his favorites, egg drop soup, egg rolls, spare ribs, and shrimp lo mein.

As she entered the house she called Rick's name, but was surprised not to hear a reply. Rick's car was in the garage so he must be home, she thought. Maybe he went next door to have a beer with his pal, Jason.

She dialed Rick's cell phone. It rang several times before giving her a voice mail message. Once again she called Rick's name. No answer.

Lisa placed the food on the kitchen counter and walked into the bedroom. No Rick. She then walked into the master bathroom and that's where she found him. Rick was unconscious on the floor.

"Rick!" she cried, "oh God, Rickey!"

Her police training immediately kicked in. She bent down and felt Rick's pulse, It was faint, but he was alive. She grabbed her cell phone and called 911.

"I need an ambulance right now!" she yelled, "1536 Southwest Magnolia Lane. It's in Coventry."

"Okay ma'am, we have an ambulance on the way."

"Please hurry, my husband is dying!"

"An ambulance will be there in three minutes, ma'am. Can you tell if your husband is breathing?"

"Yes! I'm a police officer. I'm doing CPR."

"Okay officer. I'll stay on with you until the ambulance gets there."

Lisa was franticly doing CPR. "Come on Rickey," she pleaded, "stay with me Rickey!" Stay with me!"

In two minutes the ambulance arrived. Battalion Chief Ron Hazelton and two other EMT's rushed into the house and took over for Lisa. "Please save him, Ronnie!" Lisa cried, "please save my husband!"

The crew worked over Rick for several minutes before taking him on a gurney to the ambulance.

"Where are you taking him?" Lisa asked.

"St. Lucie West Hospital, in Tradition," Ron replied as they closed the ambulance door and sped away.

By then Lisa's neighbor, Jason Tomlinson, was outside. "What happened, Lisa?" he asked.

"Oh God!" Lisa cried, "it's Rick! I gotta go to St. Lucie West Hospital!"

Jason grabbed Lisa's arm as she started towards her car. "I'll drive you."

Ten minutes later Lisa was at the emergency room of the St. Lucie West Hospital. She ran up to the admitting desk where she was greeted by a young woman.

"My husband, Rick March just came in," Lisa said, "where is he?"

"He's in triage ma'am," the young woman replied.

"I wanna see him!"

"Ma'am we can't let you in there yet. The doctors will speak with you as soon as they can."

Lisa was frantic. "I'm a cop!" she screamed, "I want to see him now!"

Just then, Ron Hazelton came into the waiting room.

"Lisa." he said.

"What happened, Ronnie?" Lisa cried, "is Rick alive?"

Ron led Lisa to a couch in the waiting room, sat her down, and parked himself right next to her.

"He's alive, Lisa," he said calmly, "that's all I know for sure right now."

"But what happened?" Lisa replied, "was it his heart?"

"I think so, but we need to wait until the doctor tells us."

Lisa's cell phone buzzed. She could see that the call was from her daughter.

"Mom!" came Lexie's frantic voice, "Jason called me and he said Dad was taken away in an ambulance. Is he okay?"

Lisa realized that now was the time for her to regain her composure and be strong for her crying daughter.

"They say that daddy's alive, honey. That's all I know right now."

"What does that mean, mom? Was it his heart again? Is he gonna die?"

"I just don't know, Lex. But as soon as they tell me I'll call you."

"I'm coming home, mom!"

"Okay honey, but just wait until I call you before you do anything, okay?"

"I'm leaving now. Daddy needs both of us, mom."

Just as the call ended a tall young man in scrubs entered the waiting room.

"Mrs. March?"

"Yes, I'm Mrs. March."

"I'm Doctor Jonathan Granger. Your husband had a massive heart attack."

"How bad is it, doctor?"

"It's very serious."

"Where is he? Can I see him?"

"We've called in an ambulance to transport him to Lawnwood Hospital for surgery."

"Lawnwood? Why?"

"Mrs. March, " Doctor Granger said quietly, "your husband is in grave danger. We were able to stabilize him but he will need very delicate surgery."

"No!"

"I'm afraid so. Several of the area's top surgeons and surgical teams are in the Lawnwood Hospital," Granger said, "and they'll be waiting for your husband as soon as the ambulance gets there."

Lisa took a deep breath.

"Thank you, Doctor," Lisa said softly, "when will I be able to see him?"

"They're just about to move him now. You can walk with them to the ambulance, but then you'll have to leave."

"Okay, thanks."

"And, by the way," the doctor added, "you saved your husband's life tonight."

"How's that?"

"Another few minutes and he would have died before he got here."

Doctor Granger escorted Lisa through the Emergency Room doors and they waited near the transportation door. Within a minute, a team of doctors and nurses were pulling Rick on a gurney to the awaiting ambulance.

Rick was barely visible underneath the tubes and breathing equipment that was keeping him alive. His eyes were closed.

Lisa had only a few second to speak to her husband as they rolled by.

"Rickey," she said, in her bravest voice, "it's me, Lisa. You're gonna make it, Rickey. I know you're gonna make it. I love you, Rickey! Lexie and I need you to come home to us."

In an instant the gurney was loaded into the ambulance and Lisa was ushered back into the waiting room. She was so overcome with emotion that she couldn't talk.

She weeped for a few minutes until she saw her neighbor waiting for her.

"It's very serious, Jason," she said, "thanks for everything. They're taking him to Lawnwood, so that's where I'll be going, too."

"I'll take you there, Lisa."

"No, no, it's okay," Lisa replied, "you need to go home to your family. I'll get a ride to Lawnwood."

"But, how will you get there?"

"I don't know, but I'll figure it out."

"Okay, Lisa," Jason replied. "Please let me know how Rick is doing and don't hesitate to call me if you need anything."

"Thanks, Jason."

Lisa grabbed her cell phone and called her daughter.

"Lex…" is all she could day before she began to sob again.

"Mom, mom?" Lexie screamed. "Did daddy die?"

Lisa composed herself long enough to reply to her daughter. "No, honey," she said, "they're taking him to another hospital for emergency surgery."

"I'm coming home right now, mom!"

"Listen to me, Lexie, neither one of us is in any condition to drive right now." Lisa said sternly, "I'm gonna find a way to get over to the other hospital and I'll call you as soon as I know anything."

"Okay, mom." Lexie replied.

"Promise me you won't drive, Lex!"

"I promise, mom." Lexie said, "I love you!"

In a few seconds Lisa called her partner, Dan Torres.

"Danny," she cried, "I need you!"

"I'll take you there, Elsa."

CHAPTER 31

APRIL 23, 2018, 9:00 A.M.

PORT ST. LUCIE POLICE DEPARTMENT

Captain Davis began the meeting with all of the detectives present except Lisa March, who was on temporary leave of absence.

"Listen up, everyone," he said in his typical booming voice, "Megan Harris is here to give us an update on the Bates murder case. It's all your's, Megan."

"Good morning, everyone," Megan began, "first, I'd like to introduce you all to my second chair in the trial of Leonard Bates."

A young woman stood behind Megan.

"This is Deandra Glick."

Rumblings of "Hello Deandra" could be heard from the assembled group.

"Deandra is new to our team but she is an experienced prosecutor who came to us from Houston, Texas. She looks young but she's had a lot if experience and I feel very fortunate to have her on my team."

At Megan's nod of approval Deandra stood up and addressed the group.

"As you know, Doctor Leonard Bates was arrested at his home on March 27th," she explained, "he was charged with murdering his wife, Diane Bates."

“Bates was arraigned and a hearing was held before Judge Jose Velez to determine bail.”

Megan continued, “we asked for Doctor Bates to be held without bail and, of course, his attorney argued for his client to be released.”

“Released with no bail?” Dan Torres asked.

“Yes, of course,” Megan responded, “pillar of the community, no flight risk, the usual BS.”

“The judge set bail at five hundred thousand dollars,” Deandra added, “and Doctor Bates is currently out of jail, awaiting trial.”

“Yesterday, Bates’ lawyer, JD Treem, filed what is called a ‘Demand for Speedy Trial’. In Florida that means the trial must begin no later than sixty days after the filing date.”

“In addition,” Deandra said, “Mr. Treem has filed over thirty separate motions that we must respond to.”

“What kind of motions?” Dan asked.

“Well, for example,” Megan replied, “he wants to suppress the use of Bates’ prints and DNA because they came from a water bottle found in Bates’ car, He claims the police violated his client’s fourth amendment rights by searching Bates’ car.”

“It’s called fruit of the forbidden tree,” Megan added.

“But I heard Lisa ask Bates if we could search the house,” Dan said, “and I heard him say yes!”

“Well,” Megan replied, “his lawyer says that didn’t include the car.”

“But it was sitting in his garage when we got there!” Dan said, “doesn’t that make the car part of the house?”

“We certainly will argue that, but ultimately Judge Velez will decide.”

“What else is JD Treem asking for?” Captain Davis asked.

“Lots and lots!” Megan replied, “basically, he wants to suppress any and all evidence that could possibly be used to convict his client.”

“That’s bullshit!” Dan said.

“Actually,” Megan replied, “it’s what I call being a good defense attorney.”

"You see," Deandra continued, "Treem demands a speedy trial and then ties us up answering motion after motion so we don't have time to prepare our case."

"But doesn't that also tie him up while he's preparing the defense?" Sheila asked.

"You'd think so," Megan replied, "but Treem's got an army of paralegals who just love writing this kind of stuff."

"So," Beth Danelo asked, "is it gonna work?"

"Not a chance, Beth!" Megan responded, "w e're on top of everything, and we'll be ready to go to trial in June."

"So what can we do to help?" Captain Davis asked.

"I need each and every one of you to review your notes carefully," Deandra said, "make sure all your t's are crossed and all your i's are dotted."

"As we prepare the case we'll determine which of you will testify," Megan added, "as soon as we know, we'll tell you. And, as always, we'll help you prepare for your testimony."

"And we'll also help you prepare for Mr. JD Treem!" Deandra added.

"What about the girlfriend?" Beth asked, "Abby Jenkins?"

"She was arrested as an accessory before the fact."

"So, did she finally admit she bought the burner phone?" Dan asked.

"Nope!" Megan replied, "she claims it was a case of mistaken identity."

"Oh sure!" Dan said, "there must been a hundred women dressed just like her that walked into a barber shop and bought a phone that her boyfriend used to plan a murder."

"That's what she claims!"

Just as everyone was about to leave, a familiar person entered the room. It was Lisa March. A collective cheer came from the gathering.

Lisa smiled. She stood in front of the group and spoke from the heart.

"I just wanted to stop by and say thanks to every one of you for the love and support you've all shown me and my family over the past month."

"This has been the most difficult challenge I've ever faced and I want you to know, from the bottom of my heart, that I couldn't have made it without you."

"So what's the latest on Rick, Lisa?" Joe O'Hara asked.

"He's coming home tomorrow!"

A round of applause and whistles broke out as Lisa was hugged by everyone.

"And I'll be back to work Monday!"

Another round of applause filled the room.

CHAPTER 32

JUNE 14, 2018, 9:00 A.M.

ST. LUCIE COUNTY COURTHOUSE

"This is Mary McCambridge, reporting to you live from outside of the St. Lucie County Courthouse in Fort Pierce, where today we will hear opening arguments in the trial of Leonard Bates. Ever since Diane Bates was found dead in her Port St. Lucie mansion four months ago this case has been the most high profile case ever to hit the Treasure Coast."

"Judge Jose Velez will preside over this case, which now has a jury of six men and six women. Prosecutor Megan Harris is handling the case for the state and renowned defense attorney JD Treem represents the accused. A long and lively trial is expected by all the experts."

"So let's go live inside the courtroom for the opening arguments"

• • • • •

Megan was nervous. This was certainly not her first trial, or even her first murder trial, for that matter. But never had she gone up against anyone like the famous JD Treem. She had already seen a few of Treem's tricks and she was wondering what he might pull out of his sleeve next.

She looked up at the bench and was happy to see Judge Jose Velez sitting there.

Jose Velez was the longest tenured judge in the St. Lucie County system. He had certainly come a long way from the streets of Cuba, where he grew up. After arriving on the beach in Miami in a row boat as a young man he had gone on to become a successful lawyer and eventually a well respected judge. Jose was known as a judge who kept complete control of his courtroom and had zero tolerance for attorneys who played fast and loose with the rules.

Judge Velez was eagerly awaiting this high profile trial so he could show everyone that a county judge in little Fort Pierce, Florida could control the big boys from the south when they entered his courtroom. Even with his thick accent he was ready to run the show.

Megan looked around the court room. Sitting next to her was her second chair Deandra Glick. At the opposite table was JD Treem, Leonard Bates, and one of Treem's many colleagues.

As she stood up to present her opening argument, Megan couldn't help but notice the jury. They were very serious, and Megan could sense that they were well aware of the enormity of the task that was ahead of them. Most had pads of paper and pencils for note taking.

She put on her most solemn face, stepped up to the podium and glanced back at Deandra. That was Deandra's cue to play the recording.

The courtroom hushed as the recording began to play.

Female voice: "911 operator, how can I help you?"

Male voice (calmly): "Ah, yes, ah, my name is Doctor Leonard Bates. My wife has been murdered. We need the police and a coroner to come and check out the crime scene."

Female voice: "Excuse me sir, did you just say that your wife was murdered?"

Male voice (calmly): "Yes, she was bludgeoned to death. I found her here a few minutes ago and I checked her pulse. She's dead. It appears that she was killed about three to four hours ago."

As the recording ended Megan addressed the jury. She made eye contact with each of the twelve jurors as she said loudly.

"Ladies and gentleman, what you have just heard is the voice of a stone cold killer!"

"Notice the voice in this call. Not an ounce of sadness or compassion for the woman who had shared his bed for eight years."

Megan walked from behind the podium and approached the jury, stopping about six feet from the jury box.

"No, ladies and gentlemen, this was not the voice of a grieving husband. This is the voice of a man who diabolically planned the murder of Diane Bates."

"Did Leonard Bates strike the blows that killed Diane Bates? No he did not. Instead he planned and hired someone to do the dirty work for him."

"In this trial we will systematically show you that Leonard Bates carefully planned the murder of his wife. We will show you how he did it, and why he did it."

"And in the end, I know that you will help me bring justice for Diane Bates and her loving family by finding the defendant, Leonard Bates, guilty of murder."

Megan stood in front of the jury and stared at them for several seconds before she walked back to her table and sat down.

And now it was JD Treem's turn.

JD was dressed in his signature suit with red suspenders. Today he sported a bright red bowtie.

Treem slowly stood up from his chair and walked directly over to the jury. He smiled.

"Good morning, friends!" he said.

Most of the jurors mumbled "good morning" back to JD.

"My name is JD Treem. The JD actually stands for John David, but nobody ever calls me that. Even my mom always called me JD, which made me wonder why she even bothered to add all those other letters to my name."

As several of the jurors chuckled Megan could see that JD was warming up the jury. He was a master at that.

"Folks, my mom was not very well educated. She dropped out of high school in the tenth grade so she could go to work and support her family.

And then years later when she had me and my sister she kept working day and night just to give us the education that she missed out on."

"You see folks, Gertie Treem wasn't well educated. But she was a very smart lady!"

"I remember, when I was young and would do something bad, which wasn't too often, but it did happen, I'd come home and mom was ready to hear me out before she gave me my punishment. Of course I would give mom a line of BS a mile long, trying to fool her into blaming my sister, or someone else, for whatever it was I had done wrong."

"But you see folks, mom would never buy what I was trying to sell her. No, she was just too smart for that. She had a sixth sense about her that allowed her to cut through the smoke and mirrors and get to the facts."

"Folks, I learned a lot from my mom, may she rest in peace, and I carry her photo in my wallet every day to remind me of the things she taught me."

"I'll never forget what she told me when I became a lawyer. She said JD, when you get in front of a jury you always tell them the truth! She said jurors are intelligent people who understand that facts matter, not speculation or a bunch of smoke and mirrors."

"Ladies and gentlemen." JD said as his voice lowered. "I've been defending people for over forty years and it's always the same. The prosecutor will stop at nothing to win the case, get a guilty verdict out of the jury, and put another notch on their belt. But my job, folks, is to not let them get away with it. My job is to help you find the smoke and mirrors in their case, and point every one of them out to you."

"And folks," JD raised his voice, "I've looked at this case over and over again, and I can tell you that it is nothing but smoke and mirrors!"

He then pointed at Leonard Bates. "Ladies and gentleman, I want to introduce you to Doctor Leonard Bates, an innocent man falsely accused by a prosecutor who wants another notch on her belt."

"Together you and I won't let her get away with it."

As JD walked back to his seat the room fell silent. Even Megan was taken aback by the power of Treem's opening.

Judge Velez pounded his gavel and said "We'll see everyone back here tomorrow morning at 9:00."

• • • • •

Megan and Deandra stopped at the Three Nines tavern for lunch. They sat down at a table occupied by Lisa March and Dan Torres.

"How's Rick, Lisa?" Megan began.

"He's doing better every day," Lisa replied with a smile, "he's starting to drive me crazy again, so that's a very good thing! Last night he dropped a jar of mustard and it shattered all over the floor. My first reaction was to yell at him for being so careless but then I realized how lucky I was to have him. We came very close to losing him, Meg."

"Is he still fixing dinner for you every night?"

"Well, let's just say he tries," Lisa answered, "most nights we have pizza."

"Wow," Megan replied, "I want a Rick!"

"Me too!" Deandra added.

"I do rent him out!" Lisa joked.

"So what did you think of the opening?" Megan asked.

"I think you were very strong, Meg. Very strong!"

"Me too," Dan added. "Playing that 911 recording was smart."

"I remember when we first heard it," Lisa added, "right away, my first thought was, this guy killed his wife!"

"How did you like Treem's opening?" Deandra asked.

"Now I understand why JD Treem has the reputation." Lisa replied.

"He blew me away, didn't he?" Megan said sheepishly.

"No!" Lisa said, "I don't think that at all."

"My momma told me to always tell the truth!" Megan said, imitating Treem's dialect. "What a crock! That son of a bitch would lie through his teeth to win a case. Talk about your smoke ands mirrors. He invented that!"

"And you don't think the jury understands that?" Dan asked.

"I don't know, Dan," Megan replied, "he had a jury consultant help him find just the right kind of people for this jury, and then he set things up as though it was him and the jury against me, the mean prosecutor who only wants another notch on my belt." She paused for a moment and said, "I don't even wear a belt, for God's sake!"

"Don't worry about that, Meg," Lisa said, "you've got a solid case and that's what really matters."

"Yeah, I suppose so," Megan replied softly, "you know, I've had to rehabilitate many witnesses before, but this is the first time I've ever had to rehabilitate myself!"

• • • • •

"This is Mary McCambridge, channel 12 court reporter. I'm joined this evening by Palm Beach defense attorney Steven Cohen. Mr. Cohen, what were you thoughts about the opening statements today?"

"Well, Mary, I thought prosecutor Megan Harris came out flat. She tried to grab the jury's attention by playing the 911 tape and pointing out the lack of emotion from Leonard Bates, but I don't think it worked."

"And how about JD Treem?"

"Mary, JD Treem is the gold standard when it comes to criminal defense attorneys. I've watched him for years and I was always grateful that I never had to face him in court."

"What was it that impressed you the most about his opening?"

"Treem was able to establish a rapport with the jury, something the prosecutor failed to do. This is very important because it allows you to speak directly to the jury throughout the trial even though your words are directed at the witnesses."

"Okay, thanks Steve. We're looking forward to hearing from the first prosecution witness tomorrow. This is Mary McCambridge. Now back to the newsroom."

CHAPTER 33

JUNE 15, 2018, 6:00 P.M.

THE HOME OF LISA AND RICK MARCH

This had been a very difficult day for Lisa. As the second witness for the prosecution, she knew how important she was to the case. She had to be sharp and effective.

Her first objective was to describe her meeting with Len Bates at the murder scene. Then she explained how she led the detective team through the investigation that resulted in Bobby James' confession and, ultimately, the arrest of Len Bates.

Megan had prepared her perfectly for her two and half hours of direct testimony, carefully describing the methodical steps that were taken to rule out all other possible suspects.

She felt great when Megan finished, but she was totally blindsided by the cross examination of JD Treem.

She walked in the house, kicked off her shoes, and was happy to be greeted by her daughter, Lexie.

Lexie was a clone of her mother, exactly the same face with dark curly hair. She was two inches taller than her mother, but most people thought they were sisters rather than mother and daughter.

"Daddy burned dinner again," she said matter-of-factly, "I thought you were the pizza delivery guy."

Oh well, Lisa thought, a perfect ending to a miserable day.

"Are you gonna join us for dinner, Lex?"

"No, mom, I have a date tonight."

"A date?" Lisa said with a grin. "Anybody we know?"

"Actually, you do know him," Lisa replied, "we were good friends in high school. Andrew Wilson."

"Andrew Wilson? The son of Mayor Wilson?"

"Yep, that's him. We met last week at the Ale House. I hadn't seen him in two years so we decided to catch up on old times."

"So, nothing serious then?"

"Come on mom, every time I have a date you think I'm gonna end up marrying the guy!"

"Well," Lisa joked, "he was your boyfriend in high school."

"He wasn't my boyfriend, mom. He was just a friend!"

"So he was a boy, and he was a friend, but not a boyfriend. I get it!"

"He remembers you guys, too. Says he'd like to stop by and see how dad's doing."

"Wow, that's really nice of Andrew," Lisa said, "so, when his mother becomes the governor, that will make you the first daughter-in-law."

Lexi rolled her eyes and answered the door for the pizza delivery.

"Lise," Rick shouted from the family room, "come quick. They're talking about the trial today on the news."

Lisa hurried into the family room and sat down. "Can you rewind it?"

Rick carefully rewound the program back to the beginning.

• • • • •

"Good evening, this is Brian Reagan, TV 12 evening news. Today's top story is the high profile murder for hire trial taking place in Fort Pierce. For more on that let's go to our legal correspondent Mary McCambridge."

"Thanks, Brian. I'm here once again with noted Palm Beach defense attorney Steven Cohen. So Steve, what are the big takeaways from today's testimony?"

"Well Mary, the prosecution began by calling coroner Stephanie Rogers. She's a veteran coroner who clearly has testified many times in the past. She was precise and to the point as she showed the jury the murder weapon and described the exact method of death of Mrs. Bates."

"She showed a lot of photos too."

"Yes, she showed the jury over fifty photos from the crime scene and the autopsy. Most of them are too graphic to show here on TV. But in fact they were projected on a large monitor in the courtroom so everyone, especially the jury, could see them."

"So why show the jury so many gruesome photos, Steve?"

"This is done to make the jury angry. Once they see these photos they often picture one of their loved ones and they begin to appreciate how devastating this must be for the victim's family."

"So they really do get angry?"

"Yes. That's the point. The prosecution wants the jury to be really angry so they will be determined to punish someone for this horrible crime."

"This is a tactic that's been used for years, hasn't it Steve?"

"You bet Mary, but of course JD Treem was fully prepared to use the photos to his advantage."

"How so?"

"Let's watch as he cross examines the coroner."

• • • • •

JD Treem stepped up to the witness box. On his way he smiled and nodded to the jury.

"Good morning, Doctor Rogers," he said politely.

Stephanie did not return the sentiment.

"Doctor Rogers, I was certainly impressed to learn about your credentials and I'm sure that our jury was too. Thirty years is a long time to be doing this."

"Yes it is," Stephanie replied cautiously.

• • • • •

"He's setting her up for something!" Rick said.

"Shhh!" came Lisa's quick retort.

• • • • •

"So, Doctor Rogers," JD continued, "you said you've done how many autopsies in the past?"

"Over three hundred," Stephanie proudly replied.

"Over three hundred," JD said as he looked at the jury, "that's also very impressive."

No response from Stephanie.

"So tell me Doctor Rogers. In all of the three hundred autopsies you've done, how many of the murder victims had been beaten to death by a Pickleball paddle?"

"Um... this is the first time."

"The first time?" Treem replied. "So you've seen gunshots?"

"Yes."

"Stabbings?"

"Of course."

"Strangling?"

"Yes, that too."

"But never a Pickleball paddle."

"Objection!" Megan yelled, "asked and answered!"

"Sustained," Judge Velez replied, "come on Mr. Treem, move it along."

Treem walked toward the jury and asked his next question of Stephanie.

"Doctor Rogers, you said that the first blow from the Pickleball paddle most likely was enough to kill Mrs. Bates. Is that correct?"

"I said that, yes."

"And yet the killer hit Mrs. Bates two more times with equally forceful blows. Is that correct?"

"Yes it is."

"Now, there's a term that's often used when a murderer, for example, with a knife, stabs the victim over and over again far beyond what would be necessary to kill them. Do you know that term?"

"Yes."

"And what is that term?"

"It's called overkill."

"Overkill!" Bates repeated in a very loud voice. As he said the word he made sure to look straight at the jury.

"And when there is overkill, Doctor Rogers, is it fair to say that you often call the murder a crime of passion?"

"Objection!" Megan screamed, "calls for speculation."

"Your honor," Treem said softly, "isn't that what coroners do? Don't they often speculate based on their findings?"

"Overruled." Judge Velez said, "please answer the question, doctor."

"Yes we do say that, but…"

"Thank you Doctor, no further questions."

"Redirect, Ms. Harris?" Velez asked.

Megan rose from her chair. "Doctor Rogers, do you have any reason not to believe that the person who murdered Mrs. Bates could have been paid to do it?"

"No, I do not."

"So then, nothing you have found precludes the possibility that this was a murder for hire? Is that correct?"

"That's correct."

"Thank you, Doctor Rogers."

• • • • •

"As you can see, Mary, JD Treem was able to put doubt in the jury's mind about the whole murder for hire scheme involving his client. Obviously, if this was a crime of passion, then it leaves a serious question as to whether there even was a murder for hire plot."

"I'm told that next week the jury will hear from Bobby James, the handyman who has confessed to the murder, but now claims he was hired by Leonard Bates to kill Diane Bates."

"That testimony should light up this courtroom, Mary!"

"So then, after lunch today ,we heard the testimony of Lisa March."

"Yes, Mary. Lisa March was the lead detective who investigated this case from the day of the murder."

"And what was her role in the trial?"

"I think Lisa March's most important task was to show the jury that the investigation which led to the arrest of Leonard Bates was a thorough one that ruled out all other possible suspects, and led to the obvious conclusion that Leonard Bates was guilty of hiring Bobby James to murder Diane Bates."

"And she also testified about Doctor Bates' demeanor, didn't she?"

"Yes, Detective Marsh conducted an interview with Doctor Bates at the house shortly after he had discovered his wife's body, and she testified that he showed no emotion or grief during their interview."

"Overall, how did Lisa March do?"

"Her direct testimony was rock solid Mary. You could tell that she was an excellent detective who knows her stuff."

• • • • •

"That's my girl!" Rick said.

"Shhhh!" Came Lisa's reply.

• • • • •

"But then, along came JD Treem."

"Yes, that's exactly right, and Treem took Lisa March to a place she clearly was not prepared to go. Let's watch."

Once again JD Treem stepped up close to the witness box and once again he turned to the jury, nodded, and smiled.

"Hello, Detective March."

Lisa nodded.

"Would you say that you did a professional job in your investigation of the Diane Bates murder?"

"Yes, I would."

"I expected that. And would you say that you were the best and most qualified detective to lead this investigation?"

"Objection!" Megan shouted.

"Sustained," Velez responded.

"I'll withdraw the question, your honor," Treem replied, "so let me ask you this. You said that Doctor Bates showed very little emotion when you first interviewed him, is that correct?"

"Yes, that's correct."

"So, that was your judgment of Doctor Bates, was it not?"

"Yes, it was my professional judgment."

"Detective Marsh, would you say that, as a detective, you often rely on your professional judgment to take you along certain paths toward solving a crime?"

"Yes, of course."

"Every good detective does that, correct?"

"Yes, I believe so."

"So then, Detective March, is there any reason that this jury should question your professional judgment?"

"Objection!" Megan screamed, "your honor, this is ridiculous!"

"Overruled," Judge Velez said, "please answer the question, Detective March."

• • • • •

"Where the hell is he going with this, Lise?" Rick asked.

"Shhhhh!"

• • • • •

"I've been a detective for several years, and I've investigated several murders."

"So then, there is no reason for this jury to question your judgment?" Treem asked, as he looked at the jury.

"I don't believe there is," Lisa replied with confidence.

JD Treem walked over to his table and grabbed a photo. He calmly walked back to Lisa, once again stopping to smile at the jury.

He handed her the photo and said, "could you please tell the court who this person is?"

As Lisa looked at the photo she glanced up and saw that the same photo was also projected on the huge TV monitor in the courtroom. She was stunned as she looked at the photo. It was her former partner, Josh Gray.

"I object!" Megan yelled, "what does this have to do with this case?"

"I'll get to that your honor, if you'll let me continue."

"Alright, Mr. Treem," the judge said, "but I'll stop you cold if you cross the line here. Please answer the question, Detective March."

"His name was Joshua Gray." Lisa said stoically. "He was my partner many years ago."

"I see," Treem responded, "and Joshua Gray was killed in the line of duty, I understand?"

"Yes, that is correct."

"And you were the senior officer at the time?"

"Yes, I was."

"And was there a subsequent investigation into his death by Internal Affairs?"

"Yes, there was."

Treem again went to his desk and removed a piece of paper. He walked back to the witness stand and handed the paper to Lisa. At the same time a copy of the paper was projected on the TV monitor.

"Detective March," he said calmly, "this is the finding of the Internal Affairs Department on October 15, 2003. I've highlighted one sentence. Would you kindly read that sentence to the court?"

Megan started to object but stopped. She knew that her objection would appear to the jury as though there was something to hide. Lisa looked at Megan for approval and then read the sentence aloud.

"Officer March exhibited bad judgment by entering the bank without proper backup."

"And the death of your partner, Josh Gray, was the direct result of your bad judgment, was it not Detective March?"

Lisa didn't reply.

"And now, detective March, you want this jury to rely on your judgment to determine whether or not Leonard Bates' life is ruined."

"But..."

"No further questions."

As Treem walked back to his seat Megan jumped to her feet and approached Lisa. Lisa was visibly shaken, so Megan waited before she asked a question.

"Detective March," she said quietly, "that was a very difficult time for you, wasn't it?"

"Yes, it was. Josh was my partner and my friend, and I think about him even today."

"So what was the result of the investigation?"

"I was placed on desk duty for one month."

"That's all?"

"That's all."

"So, you continued to serve as a Port St. Lucie police officer?"

"Yes"

"And that was fifteen years ago?"

"Yes."

"And since then you have been promoted to detective, yes?"

"Yes, in 2010."

"So, you've been a detective for eight years?"

"It will be eight years in October."

"And, for the record, Detective March. How many times in your career have you been reprimanded for on the job activity?"

"Just that one time."

"Just that one time, fifteen years ago?"

"Yes."

"And how many times have you received commendations for exemplary work and service beyond the call of duty?"

"Five times."

"Thank you for your service, Detective March. No further questions, your honor."

Judge Velez banged his gavel and said, "We'll meet back here Monday morning, 9:00 a.m. sharp!

• • • • •

"So, on balance Steve, how would you say Detective Lisa March fared today?"

"On balance, I think she came out of this in very good shape. I think JD Treem laid an egg when he brought up a tragic incident from fifteen years ago. And Megan Harris did an outstanding job on redirect.'

"I agree."

"And I believe the net result was that Lisa March came across as a sympathetic and highly competent police officer. Score one for the prosecution Mary."

• • • • •

"Way to go Lisa." Rick yelled.

"Okay, now you can talk." Lisa replied with a grin. "And I'll take another Kendall Jackson!"

CHAPTER 34

JUNE 16, 2018, 2:00 P.M.

JENSEN BEACH, FLORIDA

Jensen Beach had always been one of Lisa's favorite places on earth. She loved the soft sand and the rippling ocean water fueled by the Atlantic tides and the occasional boats passing by. The beach was especially wonderful in the summer months after all the snowbirds had gone back up north, leaving plenty of space for the locals, like herself, to spread out on the beach.

It had been just about three months since Rick's heart attack and Lisa was delighted that he was now well enough to join her for a walk along the beach. She and Rick had been coming to Jensen Beach most weekends since they first met twenty-three years ago. And she would never forget that special day in 1996 when Rick proposed to her. He had insisted that he take a photo of her looking out at the water, and when she turned back around, there he was on one knee with a beautiful engagement ring.

But today was simply a day for rest and relaxation. They set their chairs out several yards away from the water and held hands as they talked about how lucky they were to be alive.

When Lisa's phone buzzed she knew instantly it was Lexie.

"Hey, Lex!"

"Hi Mom. I hope you got my text last night."

"I did, honey."

"It was late, and I didn't want to alarm you with a phone call. I spent the night at Shelby's house."

"So, how is Shelby?"

"She's great, mom. She said to say hi."

"And her folks?'

"Oh, they're great too. They also sent their regards and they asked how daddy was doing."

"I heard their dog died."

"Ah, yes, they were all sad about that."

"And how's Shelby's little sister, Debbie? I heard she broke her arm when she fell off her bike."

"Ah, yes, she still has a cast on it."

"Lexie?"

"What, mom?"

"You know I'm a detective, don't you honey."

"Uh huh."

"So you should know that I made up all that stuff about the dog and the broken arm."

"Oops!"

"And I also know that Mayor Wilson and her husband were at a fund-raiser event in Tallahassee last night."

"Okay."

"So my conclusion is that you spent the night with Andrew. Am I correct?"

"Why did I have to have a detective for a mother?"

Lisa chuckled. "It's fine with me, honey. You're twenty years old and that makes you a grown woman in the eyes of the law."

"But not in the eyes of daddy. So let's not tell him about it, okay?"

"He's sitting right next to me, Lex." Lisa replied. "But fortunately for you he just put his earphones in and he's listening to his favorite music."

“Thanks mom.” Lexie replied. “Oh by the way, I invited Andrew over for dinner tonight.”

“You did what?”

“Don’t worry, I’m gonna cook.”

“You? Honey, you went to the Rick March culinary school. How about if I pick up Chinese?”

“No thanks, mom. I’m gonna do salad and chicken parm, all by myself.”

“Where did you learn to make chicken parm?”

“YouTube, mom!”

“Oh lord! Good luck to us!”

“I’ll stop at Publix and pick up all the ingredients.”

“You have money?”

“I found some in the emergency money jar.”

“You know about that jar?”

“Come on, mom, I’m the daughter of a detective, remember?”

Rick removed his earphones.

“What’s up with Lexie?” he asked.

“We’re having her new boyfriend over for dinner tonight.”

Lisa and Rick sat quietly in their beach chairs, with Lisa reading a Danielle Steel novel and Rick playing games on his Iphone.

It wasn’t long before Lisa’s cell phone buzzed again. This time it was Megan Harris calling.

“Hey Megan, what’s up?”

“I just got a call from JD Treem,” Megan said.

Lisa sensed a measure of panic in her voice.

“He wants to quit the case?” she replied sarcastically.

“I wish!” Megan responded, “If only!”

“So what did the con man want this time, Meg?”

“You won’t believe it, Lise. He says he talked with Bobby James in prison.”

"That was like three weeks ago, wasn't it?"

"Yes it was," Megan replied, "but he waited until the last minute to tell me about it."

"Tell you about what?"

"Are you ready for this, Lisa?" Megan said, "Treem says that Bobby told him the names of every woman that he slept with in Riverside."

"Every woman?"

"Every single one!" Megan said.

"Does that include who I think it includes?"

"Oh yes!"

"Shit!"

"But wait. It gets worse."

"Worse?"

"Treem says when Bobby testifies he's gonna do the cross and ask Bobby to list under oath every single woman he slept with in the community."

"Can't you object and stop that?"

"That's what I told Treem but he says that every one of those women could possibly have seen Diane Bates as their rival and so they might have a jealousy motive to want her dead."

"You gotta be kidding me, Meg!"

"Treem says he needs to do that to show that your investigation wasn't thorough and that you zeroed in on Len Bates to the exclusion of all those women."

"So, he's willing to ruin the reputation of all those women including the next governor of Florida, just to win his case?"

"Not only that," Megan replied, "he says he's gonna subpoena each one of them to testify, including Mayor Wilson!"

"Well, I can guarantee you one thing." Lisa said.

"What's that?"

"If Treem goes through with this I guarantee you that Candace Wilson with not be the next governor of Florida."

"She couldn't get elected dog catcher after that."

"So what's your next move, Meg?"

"I dunno. I've got a call in to the D.A. to get his advice."

"Are you gonna put Bobby on the stand Monday?"

"Not a chance," Megan replied, "I'm gonna go with Diane Bates' daughter Jennifer on Monday, and then hopefully figure out how to stop JD Treem from destroying a lot of peoples' lives."

"You know, Meg," Lisa said, "we heard that JD Treem was nasty, and he's proving it!"

"You're right about that, Lisa," Megan said, "and I suspect he wants something from us in order to stop him from pursuing his tell all plan."

"Wants something?" Lisa asked," like what?"

"Treem knows that, without Bobby's testimony, we have no case." Megan replied, "so I'm guessing he wants a plea deal, or even worse he wants us to drop the charge against Len Bates."

"He's a snake!"

"Yep," Megan chuckled, "and that's what makes him a great lawyer!"

"Okay, Meg. Just let me know if I can help."

"I'm thinking I might need to put you back on the stand."

"Anything, Meg. You know that."

As Lisa ended the call, Rick was curious about what had just taken place.

"Did I just hear what I think I heard?" he asked .

"I'm afraid so, honey."

"And we've got the mayor's son coming over for dinner tonight. How bizarre is that?"

"So let's just talk about the weather tonight." Lisa replied.

CHAPTER 35

JUNE 18, 2018, 5:00 P.M.
CARINO'S ITALIAN BISTRO
FORT PIERCE, FLORIDA

Carino's was the most popular restaurant and bar among lawyers who tried cases in the St. Lucie County Court House. Quite frequently, lawyers who fought battles all day long in the courtrooms, would eat and drink together when the day was done. 'No hard feelings' was the toast they always made as they tipped a glass together.

This evening Lisa joined Megan at the bar. She was curious to hear about how the day went.

"You'll never guess who had dinner at my house Saturday night," Lisa said.

"Not JD Treem, I hope!" Megan joked.

"No, but close," Lisa said, "it was Andrew Wilson, the son of Mayor Candace Wilson!"

"Oh geez, how did that happen?"

"It looks like he's now officially dating my Lexie," Lisa replied.

"Good luck, Lisa," Megan said, "This could get very tricky for you, and for Lexie too."

"Believe me, I know," Lisa replied, "I spent the whole evening trying to avoid any mention of his mother!"

"Hey!" Megan said as she glanced up at the television screen above the bar, "they're ready to analyze how we did today."

"Do you really care what the so-called experts say?"

"I'd love to say I don't give a damn what they say Lise, but the truth is I do! I guess it's an ego thing."

• • • • •

"Good evening. This is Brian Reagan, TV 12 evening news. Today's top story is the high profile murder for hire trial taking place at the St. Lucie County Courthouse. For more on the trial, let's once again go to our legal correspondent, Mary McCambridge."

"Thanks, Brian. I'm here again this evening with Palm Beach defense attorney Steven Cohen. So, Steve, weren't we supposed to see our star witness today?"

"That's right, Mary. Everyone was braced for what was supposed to be the explosive testimony of Bobby James. You'll recall that James was the handyman who admitted to killing Diane Bates and then later, in a plea deal, accused Diane's husband, Doctor Leonard Bates, of planning the murder and offering to pay him to kill Diane Bates.

"But he was a no show today Steve. Do we know why?"

"My sources say that the prosecution just needed a couple more days to prepare for Bobby James' testimony, so they opted instead to put two other witnesses on today."

"So what did we see today?"

"The first witness was from the Universal Insurance Company. She simply confirmed that Leonard Bates was the sole beneficiary of a two million dollar life insurance policy on Diane Bates, life."

"And, of course, that is significant."

"Absolutely Mary. This establishes a clear motive for Len Bates to want his wife dead."

"So how did JD Treem handle his cross examination?"

"As usual, Treem was the maestro out there conducting the band. Let's watch just a few snippets."

• • • • •

JD was once again wearing his signature suit, suspenders, and red bowtie, He smiled at the jury and walked up close to the witness. Her name was Temperance Greenlaw, a fifty-six year old woman who looked much older.

"Good morning Ms. Greenlaw. My name is JD Treem, and I represent Doctor Leonard Bates."

Treem never missed an opportunity to refer to Len Bates as DOCTOR Bates.

"Ms. Greenlaw, approximately how many life insurance policies does your company write each year?"

Ms. Greenlaw paused or a moment, "I can't say for certain."

"Well then, would you say it's in the thousands?"

"Oh yes."

"Tens of thousands?"

"All over the country? Yes, I would say so."

"And how many times each year does your company pay out benefits because the insured passed away?"

"Again…"

"I know I'm asking you a question you weren't prepared to answer," Treem said with a warm smile, "and I sincerely apologize for that. But would you venture to give us an educated guess?"

"Well, I would say about a thousand or so."

"So every year your company pays out a thousand claims to the beneficiaries of someone who died."

"Yes that's right."

"And I'm sorry again Ms. Greenlaw. I know you said this at the beginning, but how many years have you been with the company?

"Twenty-two," Ms. Greenlaw replied.

"Well, congratulations on that!"

"Thank you."

"Okay now, let me see," he turned to the jury and said, "folks I'm not really good at numbers. I shoulda paid more attention in Miss Rubio's math class."

Several in the gallery chuckled, as did a few jurors.

"Let me see now. Shoot, this one's pretty simple! Twenty-two years, one thousand claims each year. That comes out to twenty-two thousand claims paid over your career at Universal. Is that a pretty good estimate?"

"Yes."

"So now let me ask you this Mrs. Greenlaw, in those twenty two thousand claims how often did the beneficiary kill the person that was insured?"

"Objection!" Megan screamed.

"Your honor." JD said sheepishly. "I was just trying to show the court that being a beneficiary doesn't make you a murderer! But I'll withdraw the question if you want me to."

Judge Velez pounded the gavel. "Mr. Treem," he said in a stern voice, "these antics of yours may work in Palm Beach County, but they won't be tolerated in my courtroom!"

"The jury shall disregard this entire line of questioning," Velez added, with a pounding of his gavel.

• • • • •

"Well, Steve, there he goes again!"

"You're right Mary. JD Treem is the master of making his points even when the judge tells the jury to disregard them. We all know they'll remember it."

"Score another one for JD Treem?

"I'd say so, Mary. And later he had the witness confirm that Doctor Bates also applied for a two million dollar life insurance policy with same company."

"A policy that named Diane Bates as the beneficiary."

"Yes, that's right, Mary, but Bates' application was denied because of his age and medical history."

"So then, Steve, this afternoon we saw a very significant witness for the prosecution."

"Yes. That was Jennifer Messenger, Diane Bates' daughter."

"And how did she do?"

"You know, I give a lot of credit to prosecutor Megan Harris. She does a great job preparing her witnesses."

"How so?"

"Jennifer was clear, succinct, and strong. She got emotional when she described her relationship with her mother, which is something the jury wants to see from a loved one.

"And that's exactly what they didn't hear from Leonard Bates when he made the 911 call."

"True, and Jennifer got even more emotional when she talked about the volatile relationship between Diane and Len Bates."

"She got interrupted a lot."

"Yes she did. Frequently, JD Treem would object to something prosecutor Harris asked. Most of his objections were overruled by Judge Velez, but it was obvious that he was trying to throw off the rhythm of Jennifer's testimony."

"Did it work?"

"To some extent yes, I think it did."

"So what were the most important facts gleaned from Jennifer Messenger's testimony?"

"I think the most powerful testimony we got from Jennifer Messenger was that her mother was deathly afraid of Len Bates, and that she even predicted he would try to kill her."

"She also talked about his internet searches of how to get away with murder."

"Yes, she did, Mary. And JD Treem tried vociferously and repeatedly to stop that from coming in. But Judge Velez was having none of that. He allowed it all to come in."

"Possible grounds for appeal?"

"Possible."

"Anything else?"

"Yes. Jennifer also talked about the prenuptial agreement Len Bates signed before he married Diane."

"Which left him with nothing if he and Diane got a divorce."

"Absolutely nothing!"

"Well, that's it for now. We'll all be back here on Wednesday for more on what has been dubbed The Pickleball Murder Trial. Back to you, Brian."

• • • • •

Lisa finally sipped her Kendall Jackson Chardonnay.

"I think you did well today, Meg."

"Thanks Lise. It's so hard to judge when you're right there in the middle of the battle, but I feel pretty good about how things went today."

"Me too."

Megan's phone buzzed. She said hello, and then quickly walked outside the restaurant to finish the conversation.

Lisa sat by herself and sipped her wine. Since she wasn't a lawyer she didn't know any of the other patrons.

Within a few seconds a young, well dressed gentleman walked over and sat next to Lisa at the bar.

"You're new here," he said with a smile.

"Yes, I am."

"It's not often that we get new people as pretty as you."

"Okay."

"So can I buy you a refill on your wine."

"No, thanks."

The young man then placed his hand on Lisa's arm and squeezed. "Come on now," he said, "we're all really friendly in here. We don't bite."

Lisa looked at the man's hand on her arm. Then she looked him right in the eye.

"There are four things you should know about me," she said quietly.

"Oh really?" The man laughed, still gripping Lisa's arm, "what four things are those?"

"Number one," Lisa said calmly, "I'm a cop."

"Number two, I have a gun under my jacket that is pointed directly at your crotch."

"Number three, I know how to use my gun."

"And finally, number four. If you don't take your hand off my arm you'll be singing soprano in the girl's choir!"

With that the hand and the man both disappeared fast.

Megan opened the restaurant door and signaled Lisa to come outside. Lisa paid for the drinks and headed outside to Megan's awaiting car.

"I didn't want to talk about it in there," Megan said, "too many big ears and big mouths."

"Big hands, too!" Lisa added.

"Huh?

"Never mind. Tell me about the call."

"It was from my boss."

"The D.A.?"

"Yes, it looks like we can put Bobby James on the stand without a problem."

"What happened?"

"It seems that the D.A. spoke privately with the Mayor late yesterday afternoon. He told her exactly what JD Treem threatened to do."

"Really?" Lisa said, "what was her reaction?"

"Actually, he said she was very calm," Megan replied, "she asked who knew about this and he told her I did."

"Did he mention me?"

"No, because I never told him that you knew."

"So, then what happened?"

"Then the Mayor thanked him for telling her and she said she would handle it. And then he left."

"So, that was yesterday afternoon?"

"Yes, right after she got back from Tallahassee."

"So, what happened next?"

"You won't believe it. About thirty minutes ago the D.A. got a call from JD Treem."

"Oh, wow!"

"Treem said he changed his mind about naming all of Bobby's conquests and that he was gonna pursue a different approach to his cross examination."

"No!"

"Yes!"

"So, they got to him, huh?"

"I would say so!"

"So, you think JD Treem is gonna be the next Attorney General of Florida?"

"I don't think he would take the pay cut!"

"Well," Lisa said, "they must have offered him something."

"Or maybe they had something on him!"

"Politics is a nasty game."

"It sure is!"

CHAPTER 36

JUNE 20, 2018, 6:00 P.M.

THE HOME OF LISA AND RICK MARCH

Lisa walked into the house, dropped her purse in the foyer and headed directly to family room. She had run a little late today, and she was afraid she might miss the six o'clock news. Earlier today Bobby James had testified, and she was dying to find out how it went.

When she entered the family room, she was surprised to see Rick sitting on the sofa with Lexi and her new boyfriend, Andrew Wilson. I hope Mayor Wilson's name never came up today, she thought.

Rick muted the TV to say hello to his wife but immediately turned the sound back on when anchorman Brian Reagan appeared on the screen.

• • • • •

"Good evening, this is Brian Reagan, TV 12 evening news. After a one day adjournment, the Pickleball murder for hire trial of Doctor Leonard Bates resumed again today in Fort Pierce. Here's our legal correspondent, Mary McCambridge."

"Thank you, Brian. Well, today was the most anticipated day of the trial and it certainly didn't disappoint. I'm joined, once again, by defense attorney Steven Cohen,

"Steve, quite a spectacle today, huh?"

"Spectacle is exactly the word I'd use to describe it, Mary. Bobby James, the admitted killer of Diane Bates, took to the witness stand to accuse Doctor Leonard Bates of hiring him to carry out the murder."

"So, how did he do?"

„Well, Mary, once again Prosecutor Megan Harris had her witness well prepared to give testimony. As you recall James was originally scheduled to testify on Monday but this was delayed until today."

"And the delay paid off?"

"Yes. James gave a detailed and coherent description of the murder scene and also the phone calls he received from Doctor Bates."

"Alleged phone calls."

"Of course, the alleged phone calls, in which he claims that Doctor Bates offered to pay him one hundred thousand dollars if he killed Diane Bates."

"There were a number of calls."

"Yes, he and Doctor Bates allegedly spoke several times prior to the murder, including on the dat the murder took place. James claims that Doctor Bates called him on February 15th and threatened him if he didn't follow through and kill Diane."

"It's interesting that they never met face to face to talk about the murder plan, only by phone."

"Yes, and this left an opening for JD Treem to pounce later on in his cross examination."

"Treem did a strange thing, reenacting the crime scene."

"That's true, Mary. He had a bed just like the one in the Bates' bedroom set up right in the courthouse. And he even had a mannequin in the bed to simulate Diane Bates. "

"Yes, and how he used it left everyone speechless. "

"But first, JD attacked the credibility of Bobby James. Let's watch a bit of that now."

• • • • •

The jury had just come back from lunch after three hours of detailed testimony from Bobby James. They were surprised to see a king sized bed sitting in the middle of the court room, It was covered with a blanket and it appeared to have a mannequin under the blanket.The gallery, as well as several jurors were murmuring as Judge Velez entered the courtroom.

He pounded his gavel and said, "you may proceed, Mr. Treem."

JD Treem, dressed in his signature outfit, began his cross examination of tattooed handyman Bobby James. He walked up to the witness stand with a look of disdain for the man sitting there. JD made sure that everyone on the jury knew how much he disliked Bobby James.

"Now, Mr. James, when the police first confronted you about this murder you told them that you didn't even know where the Bates family lived, isn't that right.?"

Bobby James nodded his head

"Mr. James," Treem said with disgust, "when I ask you a question you need to answer with your mouth, not with your head, so the jury can hear you. So let me ask you again if that is what you told the police?"

"Yes."

"And that was a bald faced lie. Was it not?"

Bobby nodded, then said, "yes."

Up on the large TV monitor came the words.

LIE #1- I DIDN'T KNOW WHERE THE BATES FAMILY LIVED

"Okay now, Mr. James," JD continued, "when the police asked you why your truck was parked three doors away from the Bates house, you told them you'd been hired to power wash the pool deck of that house. Now that was lie too was it not?"

"Yes."

Up on the large TV monitor came the words.

LIE #1- I DIDN'T KNOW WHERE THE BATES FAMILY LIVED

LIE #2- I WAS HIRED TO WORK BY THE NEIGHBORS

"Alright now, Mr. James, when the police asked you if you went to the Bates' house that morning you said no. And that was a lie too, was it not?

"Yes."

Up on the large TV monitor came the words.

LIE #1- I DIDN'T KNOW WHERE THE BATES FAMILY LIVED

LIE #2- I WAS HIRED TO WORK BY THE NEIGHBORS

LIE #3- I NEVER WENT TO THE BATES' HOUSE THAT DAY

JD Treem looked at the jury each time the TV monitor was updated. He wanted them to know that he was doing all of this for them.

"Okay now, Mr.James, let's continue. When you finally admitted that you went to the Bates' house that morning you said you went there to have sex with Diane Bates. Now, that wasn't true, was it, Mr. James?"

"No."

Up on the large TV monitor came the words.

LIE #1- I DIDN'T KNOW WHERE THE BATES FAMILY LIVED

LIE #2- I WAS HIRED TO WORK BY THE NEIGHBORS

LIE #3- I NEVER WENT TO THE BATES' HOUSE THAT DAY

LIE #4- I WENT THERE TO HAVE SEX

"And then, Mr. James, you told the police that Diane Bates was already dead when you got there, another lie?"

"Yes."

Up on the large TV monitor came the words.

LIE #1- I DIDN'T KNOW WHERE THE BATES FAMILY LIVED

LIE #2- I WAS HIRED TO WORK BY THE NEIGHBORS

LIE #3- I NEVER WENT TO THE BATES' HOUSE THAT DAY

LIE #4- I WENT THERE TO HAVE SEX

LIE #5- SHE WAS ALREADY DEAD

"Look at the screen please, Mr. James," JD said, as he turned toward the jury, "five lies, yes?"

James nodded.

"Uh, uh," Treem scolded, "what did I tell you about how this jury needs to hear words from your mouth?"

"Yes."

"Now Mr. James, are you ready to see lie number six?"

Up on the large TV monitor came the words.

LIE #1- I DIDN'T KNOW WHERE THE BATES FAMILY LIVED

LIE #2- I WAS HIRED TO WORK BY THE NEIGHBORS

LIE #3- I NEVER WENT TO THE BATES' HOUSE THAT DAY

LIE #4- I WENT THERE TO HAVE SEX

LIE #5- SHE WAS ALREADY DEAD

LIE #6- DOCTOR BATES HIRED ME TO DO IT

"Here's lie number six, Mr. James. When you said Doctor James hired you to kill his wife that was your final lie, wasn't it Mr. James?"

"No, that's the truth!" Bobby shouted.

"You see, Mr. James, when I was a young man my mom, Gertie Treem, always told me to tell the truth. Often times she would repeat a little ditty that she'd heard when she was little girl. It goes like this:

"'Oh what a tangled web we weave when first we practice to deceive.' Did you ever hear that little ditty Mr, James?"

"Objection!" Megan yelled, "counsel is badgering the witness."

"Sustained," Judge Velez said quietly.

"Okay then, Mr. James, let's talk about the alleged phone calls you got. You claim that all of these calls came from Doctor Bates. Is that right?"

"Yes."

"And you said you recognized his voice because he had, what you called, a Boston accent."

"That's right."

"Mr. James, I want you to take a guess at how many men in this country have a Boston accent."

"Objection!"

"Sustained."

"Okay then, Mr. James, you said in your testimony that Doctor Bates offered to pay you one hundred thousand dollars if you killed his wife. Is that correct?"

"Yes."

"I'm curious. What did you do with the money after you got it."

"Um, I never got it."

"You never got it?" Treem said loudly, "why, I'm shocked! You were promised one hundred thousand dollars and you never got it? Why not."

"He said he had to wait for the life insurance payment."

"Oh really? Well then, how about a little up front money, a downpayment, did you at least get that?"

"No."

"So, not a penny?"

"No."

"So, you claim that you were hired to kill Diane Bates, but you were never paid a penny?"

"Yes."

"Mr. James, do you expect me, and all the intelligent people on this jury, to believe that you murdered a woman for money, but didn't get it?"

"That's what happened."

"You know what that makes you, Mr. James? You are either the dumbest criminal on the planet or the biggest liar. And I think we all know which one you are!"

" Objection!" Megan shouted, "Counsel is badgering the witness."

"Sustained," Judge Velez said, "the jury will disregard Mr. Treem's last remark."

"I'm so sorry, your honor."

"Yeah, I'm sure you're very sorry," Judge Velez said with derision, "move on, Mr. Treem."

"Now, Mr. James," JD continued, "occasionally, you were having sex with Diane Bates, were you not?"

"Yes."

"And how often, let's say, over the past year, had you engaged in sex with Diane Bates?"

"About twenty times, I guess."

"Twenty? And she paid you for your, ahem, services to her?"

"Yes, a hundred each time."

"Now, Mr. James, how many other woman in the Riverside Estates do you have a similar arrangement with?"

"I'd say about a dozen."

"A dozen women, you say? That was quite a lucrative side career you had going on there, wasn't it Mr. James?"

"I guess you could say that."

"Mr. James, you and Diane Bates sent a lot of text messages to each other, did you not?"

"Yes, we did."

"And included in these text messages were some very close up shots of your private parts, true?"

"True."

"And, on several occasions, Diane Bates texted you about anther woman on your list of, shall we say, clients. Correct?"

"Yes."

"And, Diane Bates told you that she wanted you to stop seeing one particular woman who lives in Riverside. Yes?"

"Yes."

"Why did you think she did that, Mr. James?"

"She said they had a few arguments and they don't like each other."

"Arguments on the Pickleball courts?'

"That's what she told me."

"And Diane Bates wanted you all to herself didn't she, Mr. James?"

"She never said that."

"Did she know about all the other women?"

"I'm not sure."

"So, clearly she saw this particular woman as her rival. Yes?"

"I guess so."

"Now, Mr. James, in your earlier testimony you claimed that Doctor Bates, in one of his numerous alleged phone calls to you, threatened that if you didn't kill his wife he would, let me see what you said…"

Treem paused and looked at his notes.

"You said he would, quote, ruin me and see to it that I never set foot in Riverside Estates again, unquote. Is that what you testified to earlier?"

"Yes, that's what he said to me."

"But, it wasn't Doctor Bates who said those words to you, was it, Mr. James?"

"Yes, it was!"

"No, Mr. James, it was Diane Bates who threatened you. She threatened that if you continued having sex with all those other women she would see to it that you never stepped foot in Riverside Estates again. That's what really happened! She wanted you all to herself!"

By now Treem was right next to Bobby, pointing and screaming at him.

"No! It was him!" Bobby yelled, pointing toward Len Bates.

"Nice try, Mr. James," Treem said, as he looked at the jury, "but we're not buying your sixth lie any more than we bought your first five lies."

Bobby sat silently on the witness stand. He looked totally defeated.

"You know why we're all so sure of this, Mr. James? It's because it's so obvious that you killed Diane Bates out of anger. Just like the coroner told us, this was a crime of passion!"

With that JD jumped on top of the mannequin in the bed and began furiously beating her head three times with the edge of his hand. "You can't ruin me Diane!" Treem screamed as he delivered the three blows, "I won't let you do it to me!"

As soon as Megan saw the theatrics begin she started to yell, "objection! Your honor, you have to stop this!"

Judge Velez had heard and seen enough. He pounded his gavel over and over. Treem continued screaming and pounding until he was finished with his demonstration.

"Mr. Treem," Judge Velez said in a loud firm voice. "You will not make a mockery of this courtroom! The jury will disregard that demonstration by Mr. Treem. Mr. Treem, I am fining you a thousand dollars for contempt of court, and I'm warning you if there is another display like that you'll end up behind bars. Do you understand me?"

"Yes, your honor. I'm sorry. I just got carried away."

Velez pounded his gavel again. "This court is adjourned until tomorrow at 9:00 a.m. Now get that damned bed out of my courtroom!"

• • • • •

"Wow, Steve. That's all I can say. Wow!"

"Mary, today we saw the JD Treem that everybody's been waiting for, and he certainly didn't disappoint."

"True, but did the jury buy his theory of a crime of passion?"

"I'm not so sure, Mary. When Treem jumped up on that bed at first everyone was shocked. But after that it almost looked to me like some of the jurors were laughing."

"I guess we'll find out how they felt about it come verdict time, Steve."

"And there's a lot more to come before we get to that, Mary."

"It will be interesting to see if either Treem or Megan Harris wants Bobby James back on the witness stand tomorrow."

"And we'll all be watching to see how that contentious relationship between JD Treem and Judge Jose Velez plays out.

" A lot to look forward to in this Pickleball murder trial. Back to you, Brian."

• • • • •

"Do you believe this guy?" Lisa said, as Rick turned off the TV.

"He's a piece of work," Rick replied, "that's for sure."

"I know that guy, Bobby, the handyman," Andrew said, "he was at my house a lot!"

"Oh, really?" Lisa asked, "why was that?"

"He did a lot of projects for us," Andrew replied calmly, "mom said he was great at what he did, and she even joked that she wanted to take him to the statehouse with us!"

Lisa looked at Rick. They each rolled their eyes as far back as they could go.

CHAPTER 37

JUNE 21, 2018, 5:00 P.M.
CARINO'S ITALIAN BISTRO
FORT PIERCE, FLORIDA

Lisa was sitting at the bar waiting for Megan to arrive. At one point she looked around and saw her young suitor from three days ago. He noticed Lisa and quickly made his way to the far corner of the restaurant.

When Megan walked in, Lisa already had a drink waiting for her friend.

"So tell me," Lisa asked quietly, "How did it go today?"

"Much calmer than yesterday," Megan replied, "that's for sure!"

"Here comes the news!"

• • • • •

"Good evening, this is Brian Regan coming to you from the TV 12 newsroom. Our top story, as it has been for a week now, is the Pickleball Murder trial in Fort Pierce. So once again, here is our legal correspondent, Mary McCambridge, live on the scene."

"Hello again everyone. This Mary McCambridge, joined by our expert legal analyst, Steve Cohen. Well, Steve, not quite the fireworks we saw yesterday, but still a lot of excitement today.

"Mary, any trial that includes JD Treem will never be dull."

"So, what are the highlights of today's session, Steve?"

"First of all, both sides decided not to bring back Bobby James, the confessed murderer and main accuser of the defendant, Doctor Leonard Bates."

"I guess they both figured they'd gotten what they wanted from him."

"Right. So today began quietly with the prosecution calling a woman named Kim Klatsky from the Central Florida Pickleball Association. That's the group that ran the tournament in The Villages that Doctor Bates played in on January 27th."

"What was significant about that, Steve?"

"January 27th is the date that a burner phone was purchased from a barber shop in The Villages, and this burner phone was the one used to make several phone calls to Bobby James, allegedly to plan the murder of Diane Bates."

"What was the prosecution going for here?"

"It's critical for the prosecution to put that burner phone in the hand of Len Bates. That's the only way to prove that he was the one who made the calls to Bobby James."

"Did they succeed?"

"Well, Kim Klatsky was important because showed a photo of Doctor Bates with his Pickleball partner Abby Jenkins, right after they competed in the tournament at The Villages on January 27th. Abby Jenkins was wearing a very distinctive set of Pickleball clothing that became important later."

"She also verified what time Doctor Bates' last game ended."

"Yes, and that was important because the last game ended at 2:15, they took photos after that, and the burner phone was purchased nearby at 2:45, according to the man who sold the phone."

"So, that would create a plausible timeline linking the burner phone to Bates."

"Absolutely!"

"Was JD Treem able to score any points here?"

"In my opinion no, not really. He was able to get Mrs. Klatsky to concede that there might have been other woman at the tournament who wore

similar clothing, but frankly I don't think he succeeded in convincing the jury of that."

"Okay then, Steve, what happened next?"

"Next came a little Treem fireworks. You'll see them when the prosecution called a gentleman named Larry Hunsucker, the owner of the barber shop where the burner phone was purchased. Let's watch what happened."

• • • • •

Megan approached Larry Hunsucker with a smile.

"Good morning, sir, and thank you for coming today."

Larry nodded.

"Now Mr. Hunsucker, you are the owner of Larry's Barber Shop in The Villages, correct?"

"Yes, I am."

"And do you also occasionally sell used cell phones in your store?"

"Yes, I do."

"And these phones are not connected with any service that can be traced. They're called burner phones, right?"

"Yes," Larry responded, "some people like to remain anonymous when they make calls. There's nothing illegal about that."

"Of course not," Megan said calmly, "now, Mr. Hunsucker, did you sell one of your burner phones to a woman on January 27th of this year?"

"Yes, I did."

Megan nodded to her second chair Deandra and instantly the TV monitor showed the photo that Kim Klatsky had used to identify Len Bates and Abby Jenkins.

"Mr. Hunsucker, do you recognize either of the people in this photo?"

"Yes, the woman in the photo is the one who bought the burner phone from me on January 27th."

"And you're sure she was the woman in this photo, right?"

"As sure as I can possibly be."

"This woman has been identified as Abby Jenkins. That's who you sold the burner phone to?"

"Yes, I'm sure of it."

"What makes you so sure?"

"I remember those orange neon shoes she was wearing, and the white sequined hat, and the big white sequined sunglasses. That's something you just don't see around here."

"So, just to be sure, Mr. Hunsucker, it was Abby Jenkins, the Pickleball partner of the defendant, who purchased the burner phone that was later used to make calls to Bobby James. Is that your testimony today?"

"Yes, it is."

"Approximately what time did she come in to your shop?"

"It was at 2:45."

"That was approximately thirty minutes after the last game Doctor Bates and Abby Jenkins played that day. How can you be so sure of the date and the time, Mr. Hunsucker?"

"Well, I remember it was the day of the big Pickleball Tournament," Hunsucker replied with confidence, "and I remember the time because she left my shop just as my three o'clock appointment walked into the shop. He looked at her and, after she left the shop, he couldn't stop talking about how sexy she looked!"

"Thank you, Mr. Hunsucker. No further questions."

And now it was Treem's turn to cross examine. He made sure to walk past the jury and smile before he approached Larry Hunsucker.

He gently draped his arm over the railing and said, "Mr. Hunsucker, in the testimony you just gave were you describing a person or were you describing clothing? Because I didn't hear one word about the person wearing those clothes. Was she tall, short, blonde, brunette. Can you help me out with that?"

"I guess she was average height."

"You guess? I thought you said you were certain!"

"Yes, I'm certain."

"Blonde or brunette?"

"Her hair was tucked under her hat, so I couldn't tell."

"Okay, fair enough. How old would you guess this woman was?"

"Objection!"

"Overruled."

"I dunno, maybe thirties or forties."

"With all due respect, Mr. Hunsucker, it seems to me like you have no idea who that woman was."

"Objection!"

"Sustained," Judge Velez said, "The jury will disregard Mr. Treem's last remark."

Treem looked back at his assistant and, in a flash, a large photo of a woman wearing orange neon sneakers, a white sequined hat and white wrap around sequined sunglasses came on the TV monitor.

"Mr. Hunsucker," Treem asked, "could this have been the woman who purchased the phone from you on January 27th?" Treem looked at the jury box.

"Who is that?" Hunsucker said.

"Objection!" Megan shouted.

Instantly, a second photo of another woman wearing exactly the same clothing came up on the monitor.

"How about this one, Mr. Hunsucker?" Treem yelled as the courtroom erupted.

Megan was on her feet screaming, "Objection! Who are these women?"

"These are my two daughters, your honor," Treem said, "Jill Treem Sirota and Amy Treem Leonard."

Judge Velez was furious. "Approach the bench, both of you. Now!"

"Mr. Treem," the judge said sternly, "in my courtroom we have rules of evidence, and this doesn't fly here. You got that?"

"Yes, your honor."

"Ms. Harris," the judge asked "how would you like to handle this?"

"Just let me bring back my last witness your honor, if that's okay with you."

"Absolutely," Velez replied, "and you, Mr. Treem, are you finished with this witness?"

"Yes I am, your honor."

With that Larry Hunsucker was dismissed, and the court was adjourned for lunch.

Right after lunch Kim Klatsky from the Pickleball Association was recalled to the stand. Megan had only a few questions for her.

"Mrs. Klatsky, I'd like to ask you if either of these two names were participants in your Pickleball tournament on January 27th., Jill Treem Sirota or Amy Treem Leonard?"

Mrs. Klatsky opened her laptop and checked the roster.

"No, neither one was in our tournament."

"And, just to remind the court," Megan added, "was Abby Jenkins a participant that day?'

"Yes, she was."

"Thank you. No further questions."

• • • • •

"Okay Steve, so who won that battle?"

"Definitely a win for prosecutor Megan Harris, Mary. JD Treem tried to use a trick to force the barber to question his eyewitness account but Megan Harris was quick to poke a giant hole through it."

"So Steve, if this were a Pickleball game and you were keeping score what would the score be?"

"Sorry Mary, I don't play Pickleball, and I hear the scoring is very complicated, so I'll have to pass on that analogy."

"Okay, lets's go back to Brian Reagan in the TV 12 studio"

• • • • •

"I think you crushed him today!" Lisa said, sipping her wine.

"From your lips to God's ears!" Megan replied.

"Better yet, to the jury's ears!"

Both women laughed.

CHAPTER 38

JUNE 22, 2018, 11:00 P.M.

THE HOME OF LISA AND RICK MARCH

Lisa and Rick were relaxing on the sofa in front of the television screen. They had just finished watching a British detective show on Netflix.

"I wonder if the British detectives are really like that?" Lisa mused.

"Like what?" Rick asked.

"They're so damn polite, it's sickening!" Lisa laughed.

"I hear all Brits are like that, you know, super polite and proper."

"I guess, but that approach would never work for us in America."

"So they don't teach you to be polite in detective school?" Rick asked with a grin.

"Actually," Lisa replied, "I like the way Dalton, the bouncer, said it in the movie Roadhouse."

"You mean Patrick Swayze?"

"Yep. He said 'be polite, be very polite, until it's time to stop being polite'!'"

"Great movie, Roadhouse."

Just as Lisa and Rick were ready to go to bed the front door opened and Lexie walked in.

"Hey, Lex. How was your date with Andrew tonight?" Rick asked.

"You guys got a minute?" Lexie asked stoically.

Lisa could see that her daughter was troubled. Probably a break up, she thought. She and Rick returned to the sofa as Lexie sat down opposite them in an easy chair.

"What's up, honey?" Lisa asked, "is everything alright with you and Andrew?"

"I don't know, mom, something weird happened tonight."

"Weird?"

"Before I tell you anything, mom, you have to promise me that I'm talking to you as my mother and not as a cop."

"Okay, Lex, I'll give you my special mother daughter privilege," Lisa said with a grin, "so what happened?"

"Andrew and I were sitting around at his parents' house and he was telling me that he and his dad are going up to Durham this weekend to find him an apartment for next semester."

"He's at Duke, right?"

"Yes."

"He must be really smart," Rick said.

"Yeah well that's just it, dad. He's not that smart."

"Huh?"

"I hung out with him in high school, and I knew he wasn't that smart. He was an average student at best."

"So?"

"So, I asked him how he got into Duke and he told me a really crazy thing."

"What did he tell you, honey?"

"Andrew said that his mom knew a guy named Doctor Duke."

"Doctor Duke?"

"Yes, he was called that because he specialized in getting rich kids into Duke."

"Lexie, Duke is very selective in who they accept." Rick said.

"I know, dad. Andrew said they only accept less than one out of ten applicants, and most of those applicants are in the top one percent of their class in high school."

"So, how did Andrew get in?" Lisa asked.

"He said his mom paid this Doctor Duke guy twenty-five thousand dollars."

"Wow!" Lisa said, "what did he do for all that money?"

"This is where it gets scary, mom. I don't think Andrew was supposed to tell anybody. He said the guy changed his high school transcript and his SAT scores to get them up to Duke standards."

"No way he could do those things, Lexie!" Rick said.

"According to Andrew the guy did it, dad," Lexie replied, "and that's not all. He also made up extra curricular activities that Andrew never participated in. They even had fake photos of Andrew wearing varsity uniforms!"

"Holy crap!" Lisa shouted, "so that's how he got accepted at Duke?"

"That's what he said, mom."

"So how do you feel about all this, Lex?" Rick asked calmly.

"I feel like I don't want to date Andrew anymore," Lexie replied, "I mean, I really like him, maybe I even love him, but if he could lie like that to get into college then how could I ever trust him to be honest in our relationship?"

Lexie began to cry. Lisa quickly hugged her daughter and said nothing. She let the emotion her daughter was feeling play out. But as she sat with Lexie she couldn't help but wonder if this Doctor Duke guy was breaking the law. He must be, she thought.

Several minutes later Lexie calmed down and all of them went to bed. As Lisa joined her husband under the covers she said, "Rick, did you ever hear of anything like this before?"

"No I haven't," Rick replied, "but it just shows that there are two sets of rules in this world. One for the powerful and wealthy and one for the rest of us."

CHAPTER 39

JUNE 23, 2018, 7:00 P.M.
SAILOR'S RETREAT RESTAURANT
STUART, FLORIDA

Lisa had been looking forward to this dinner for a week. Ever since Megan told her about the engagement she was excited to meet "Mr. Right." And for Megan, she thought, this evening would be a great escape from the rigors of the trial she had been dealing with for weeks.

Sailor's Retreat was the best Waterfront restaurant on the Treasure Coast. Reserving a water view, outdoor table, on a Saturday night was nearly impossible during the winter season. But now, with all of the snow birds safely up north, Lisa was able to get the best table on the terrace overlooking the yachts that were ceremoniously parked in the marina. Lisa always wore her most expensive dresses and jewelry to Sailor's Retreat and tonight was no exception.

Lisa and Rick arrived first and they were led to their table by a young woman who was also impeccably dressed. They sat down at the table and within a few minutes they were joined by Megan Harris and her fiancé, Ed Borden.

He was blonde and handsome, and Lisa was amused to see that his Hawaiian shirt exactly matched the color and pattern of Megan's dress.

"We're twins!" Megan laughed, as they sat down at the table.

"I think it's adorable," Lisa said, "and I'm delighted to meet you, Ed. I've heard so much about you."

"Only the good things I hope," Ed said with a smile, as he shook hands with Rick and Lisa, the rest we try to keep secret!"

After the drinks were ordered Lisa asked the inevitable question. "Where did you two meet?" It was a question she always asked of couples, and Rick always chastised for being so nosy.

"We met at a lawyer's conference in Tallahassee, run by the Attorney General's office," Megan replied.

"Oh, are you a lawyer too?" Rick asked.

"Yes," Ed said, "I work for the Attorney General, special investigations unit."

"Looks like I'm the only one here without a law degree!" Lisa said jokingly.

"You might as well have one, Lisa," Megan replied, "I think you know as much about the law as I do!"

As they waited for their drinks, Ed remarked about how wonderful the view was from their table.

"Just look at all those boats," Rick said, "I guessed one time that there must be at least five hundred million dollars tied up in all these big yachts."

"And we never see anybody ever use them!" Lisa added.

"It's amazing to see how many wealthy people there are that can afford to own boats like that," Ed said, as their drinks arrived.

Lisa lifted her glass and toasted. "Here's to all the rich boat people," she said, "may we all join them one day!"

"They say money can't buy happiness," Megan said, "but it sure can buy fun!"

"It can buy more than that," Rick replied.

"How so?" Ed asked.

Lisa kicked her husband under the table but he kept talking.

"We heard a story about a kid whose parents paid twenty-five grand to get him accepted at Duke?"

"Oh yeah," Ed replied, "I bet they used Doctor Duke."

"You've heard of Doctor Duke?" Lisa asked.

"Oh, yes," Ed responded, "his name is George Applegate. We've been chasing him for several months. We know he's bribing schools and even College Board people to change grades and scores, but we just haven't been able to find that smoking gun to nail him."

"What kind of smoking gun do you need?"

"We need one of his clients to testify against him. They have to admit that their kid's grades and scores were changed. Then we can follow the trail and nail everyone involved."

"So, what happens after that?" Lisa asked.

"Once we nail Doctor Duke it will cause a ripple effect that's gonna bring down every one of his clients."

"But if they just hired him and he did the illegal things does that make them culpable too?" Lisa asked.

"I think you know the answer to that, Lisa," Megan replied, "it's no different than Len Bates hiring the handyman."

"These clients knew he was up to no good," Ed added, "and there's no way they can get away with claiming they didn't."

"So this is really big," Lisa said.

"There are a number of these cases going on in California right now," Ed added. "You're gonna see some high profile Hollywood people going down real soon."

"Wow!" Rick said, "this could really explode around here too!"

"Yep," Ed replied, "you could be reading some big headlines really soon!"

The rest of the dinner went well with Megan insisting they not talk about the Pickleball murder trial.

As they drove home from the restaurant Rick said, "Lise, are you thinking what I'm thinking?"

"I'm thinking we have knowledge of a crime." Lisa said

“Honey,” Rick said, “you’re a police detective, and as a lawyer I’m considered an officer of the court. You know what that means.”

“It means we’re both obligated to report what we know.”

“Absolutely.”

“But I promised Lexie I wouldn’t.” Lisa said, “I even gave her mother-daughter privilege!”

“Oh yeah, try using that as a defense in court.”

“You realize, if we do this, we destroy the mayor,” Lisa said, “her career is toast.”

“You know, Lise, considering what we already know about Candace Wilson, maybe this is a good thing.”

“I know Rick, but our daughter will never forgive me if I betray her trust.”

CHAPTER 40

JUNE 25, 2018, 6:00 P.M.
CARINO'S ITALIAN BISTRO
FORT PIERCE, FLORIDA

Lisa sat at the bar, sipping her wine, holding Megan's cocktail as she awaited her friend's arrival.

Just then the six o'clock news began.

• • • • •

"Good evening everyone. This is Brian Reagan, TV 12 evening news. Once again our top story today, as it has been for almost two weeks now, is the high profile Pickleball murder trial of Doctor Leonard Bates."

"Standing by at the courthouse is our legal correspondent Mary McCambridge."

"Hello, Brian, and hello, everyone. Today I'm joined by former St. Lucie County prosecutor Beverly Mays. Beverly, you tried a number of cases right here in this courthouse."

"That's right, Mary. I tried over one hundred cases here, and several of those were before Judge Jose Velez."

"So, what's your take on how Judge Velez has handled the trial so far?"

"Mary, I'm giving Judge Velez an A plus for the way he has handled the antics of defense attorney JD Treem. Mr. Treem has repeatedly attempted to turn this trial into a circus and judge Velez has cut him off every time. I also give prosecutor Megan Harris an A rating for how she has stood toe to toe with Treem. She has given as well as she's taken."

"So tell us about today. What did we see today?"

"Mary, today was what I call 'trash the defendant' day. Every good prosecutor tries to make the defendant unlikeable to the jury, and Megan Harris did a great job of that today."

"How did she do it?"

"Ms. Harris brought in a parade of Pickleball players who each testified as to their relationship with Doctor Bates."

"Doctor Bates was unpopular with most of the players, wasn't he."

"Yes, Mary. Many of them said that Len Bates was very selective about who was allowed to play with or against him. If you didn't measure up to his standards you were frozen out of the game. This aggravated a lot of people who felt that Bates considered himself superior to them."

"But of course, being a nasty person does not necessarily make one a killer, now does it Beverly?"

"True, Mary. But each of the Pickleball players also spoke of the obvious animosity between Len and Diane Bates. The arguments on and off the courts, the shouting matches and insults hurled at one another. It was palpable, to say the least."

"Some of them mentioned Bates' girlfriend, too."

"Yes, Megan Harris asked each of the witnesses if they could relate what some of the arguing between the Bates' was all about and several mentioned that he had a girlfriend and his wife knew about it."

"And how did JD Treem cross examine these witnesses?"

"Treem hurled an endless stream of objections to each and every question Prosecutor Harris asked. Several times Judge Velez admonished Treem for what he called baseless objections but that didn't stop JD from doing it."

"Do you think that tactic was effective, Bev?"

"Actually I don't, Mary. I've had defense attorneys do that to me in the past and later I learned that it really annoyed the jurors. They wanted to hear what the witnesses had to say."

"How about Treem's cross examination?"

"Treem was very clever. He simply asked each witness if they had any information as to whether or not Doctor Bates was guilty or not guilty of the crime for which he is on trial."

"And of course, each one said No."

"That's right. And, as soon as they said no, Treem looked at the jury, put his palms up and shook his head. His message to the jury was that these witnesses were a waste of time."

"Effective?"

"I think so, Mary. While there's no doubt that the jury was left with the impression that Leonard Bates is a nasty man who had a bad marriage they certainly got no direct evidence from any of these witnesses that would help them determine his guilt or innocence."

"Beverly, my sources tell me that Diane Bates was disliked even more than her husband. Why do you think JD Treem didn't ask each witness what they thought of Diane Bates?"

"He was smart not to do that, Mary. Often when a defense attorney tries to attack the victim, especially a dead victim, it backfires."

"That makes sense. So what's next for the prosecution, Beverly?"

"I wouldn't be surprised if the prosecution rests tomorrow."

"Then we'll hear JD Treem's defense."

"Oh yes, and that should be something to see!"

"Thanks Beverly, Our regular analyst, Steve Cohen, was off today, but he'll be back tomorrow. Now back to Brian Reagan in the newsroom."

• • • • •

Lisa was glued to the TV screen, so much so that she never even noticed that Megan had sat down next to her shortly after the broadcast began.

"Good day, Meg?" Lisa asked.

“Not bad,” Megan replied, “I needed to rough up Bates, and I think my witnesses did a really good job of that.”

“Great, Meg. What’s next?”

“I think we’re done, Lisa,” Megan replied, “we’ve established that Leonard Bates is a cold, unlikeable guy with a terrible marriage, a girlfriend, and a two million dollar life insurance payout coming his way.”

“And I think the jury now believes that Bates was the guy on the other end of that burner phone hiring Bobby James to murder his wife.”

“I’m curious,” Lisa asked, “Why didn’t you put the girlfriend, Abby Jenkins, on the stand?”

“She’d be hard for me to work with, Lise. She denied everything and we haven’t been able to get her to crack, even with a sweet deal from the DA that would let her walk away free.”

“So, she could walk and she still wouldn’t throw Bates under the bus?”

“The problem is that JD Treem wrapped her up as a client for his firm. My guess is that he’s gonna put her on the stand to tell everyone that her boyfriend is innocent and that we tried to get her to lie.”

“Are you ready for her?”

“You bet I am. JD Treem isn’t the only one with a few tricks up his sleeve!”

“I can’t wait until tomorrow!” Lisa said as she sipped her wine.

“By the way, Lisa,” Megan said, “Ed really liked you guys and he said he hopes we can get together again real soon.”

“Thanks, Meg, I really like Ed, and so does Rick. We think you guys are perfect together,” Lisa smiled, “But Rick says you gotta lose those matching outfits!”

Megan laughed. “Believe it or not, it’s Ed who encourages it!”

“Okay. I guess he’ll get over it.”

“Hey, Lisa,” Megan said softly, “Ed and I were talking on the way home about that person you know that used Doctor Duke for their kid.”

“Oh, I didn’t say we knew them, Meg.”

"Ed was wondering if you have a name. That would really be helpful. He's so close to cracking this case he can taste it."

Lisa was taken aback by the question. She paused for a few seconds and replied. "I don't think we have a name for Ed, Meg. Let me check with Rick and see if he knows the name"

"Okay, thanks girlfriend."

"Good luck tomorrow, Meg!"

CHAPTER 41

JUNE 26, 2018, 6:00 P.M.

THE HOME OF LISA AND RICK MARCH

Lisa walked into the house, dropped her handbag, and moved directly toward the family room. Rick was sitting on the sofa watching the six o'clock news.

"Rewind, Rick, please," Lisa said, as she plopped herself down on the sofa next to her husband. A glass of wine was waiting for her on the coffee table.

Rick grabbed the remote and rewound it to the beginning of the news.

• • • • •

"Hello this Darcy Henson in the TV 12 newsroom. Brian Reagan is on assignment today. Our top story comes from Fort Pierce, where the murder for hire trial of Doctor Leonard Bates continues."

"Our correspondent May McCambridge is live just outside the courthouse."

"Hi Darcy. Well it was another eventful day here at the courthouse. Prosecutor Megan Harris rested her case against Doctor Bates, and Defense attorney JD Treem called his first witness."

"I'm joined this evening by Palm Beach defense attorney Steve Cohen. Welcome back, Steve."

"Thanks, Mary."

"So how did JD Treem start his defense today, Steve?"

"Mary, I thought JD Treem did a very smart thing. He called Leonard Bates' son Jeffrey to the stand as his first witness."

"So what was the purpose of this witness."

"Up until now the jury has heard only negative things about Doctor Bates- he's cold, he's nasty, he wasn't nice to his wife, he had an affair- all negative."

"When Jeffrey Bates took the stand he was able to paint a different picture of Len Bates- a man who loved his son, a grieving widower whose first wife, Jeffrey's mother, was a police officer, killed in the line of duty."

"So, how did the son do?"

"It was absolutely perfect. Jeffrey Bates was well coached and rehearsed by the Treem team. For example, he looked straight at the jury when he talked about how his dad would rush home from work so he could coach his son's Little League team."

"He looked longingly at his father when he told the jury that his dad taught him to always be kind to others."

"Sounds like a masterpiece, Steve."

"It was, as close as one could get to perfection, in my opinion."

"Did Megan Harris do a cross?"

"Yes she did. It was brief. She simply asked Jefferey if he knew where his father was born and raised. He replied, Boston. And then she asked if his father had a distinguishable Boston accent, to which he replied yes."

"She was confirming the voice on the burner phone, I guess."

"That's right, Mary, and I think Megan caught JD Treem off guard. It was obvious that Jeffrey Bates wasn't prepared for that line of questioning because he gave Megan Harris exactly what she needed."

"Score one for both sides?"

"Score one for both sides, Mary."

• • • • •

"You know, I testified about the Boston accent too." Lisa said, "I told them how he said his wife's CAH was in the garage when he came home. Do I sound like a Boston girl?"

"That's really good, Lise." Rick replied. "But you'll never be mistaken for a girl from HAHVID."

"Hey!" Lisa joked. "Maybe I could have gone to Harvard if my parents had paid twenty-five grand to Doctor Duke's PAHTNAH, DOCTAH HAHVID, to get me accepted!"

"Not funny, Lise!"

• • • • •

"So who was the next witness called by JD Treem, Steve?"

"Next, Treem called Abby Jenkins to the stand. If you recall Abby was Len Bates' Pickleball partner at the tournament in The Villages."

"And she was later identified by the barber as the woman who purchased the burner phone."

"That's right, Mary. In her direct testimony today she admitted being at the tournament but she absolutely denied purchasing that burner phone and JD Treem was very clever in the way he pursued that. Let's watch."

• • • • •

"Now Abby," Treem said. He called her Abby with every question, "Abby, you have categorically denied, under oath, that you purchased a burner phone from Larry, the barber, correct?"

"Yes, that's correct."

"And Abby, the prosecution wanted you to testify to the fact that you did, indeed, purchase that burner phone. Correct?"

"Yes, they did."

"And you've been charged with a crime relating to this case, yes?"

"Yes, I have. "

"And you currently await trial as an accessory to murder, don't you, Abby?"

"Yes, that's right."

"Now, Abby, isn't it true that the prosecutor offered to drop the charges against you if you would lie and say that you bought the burner phone and gave it to Doctor Bates?"

"Objection!" Megan screamed.

"Overruled."Judge Velez replied.

"So, let me ask you one more time Abby. Did you purchase that burner phone from Larry the Barber on January 27th?"

"No, I did not!"

"No further questions, your honor."

As JD walked back to his table he looked at the jury and nodded to them. It was if he was letting them know that this was an honest witness.

As soon as Treem sat down Megan slowly walked to to the witness stand and addressed Abby Jenkins.

"Mrs. Jenkins…it is misses Jenkins, is it not?"

"That's correct."

"So, you're married."

"Yes."

"Still married?"

"Yes."

"Okay, Mrs. Jenkins. You had a sexual relationship, an affair, with Doctor Bates last year, did you not?"

"Yes."

"And the two of you were caught going into a hotel room together in Boston, yes?"

"Yes."

"So, Mrs, Jenkins, after Doctor Bates was found cheating with you, you moved away from Riverside Estates. Correct?"

"Yes."

"You moved to Fort Pierce?"

"Yes."

Megan paused, "and was that the end of your affair with Leonard Bates."

"Um, yes it was."

"You never had sex with him again after that?"

"No."

"But you still played Pickleball together, right?"

"Yes, but only once in a while."

"So, how often did you play Pickleball with Leonard Bates?"

"Hmm, maybe once a month. We only played in tournaments."

"Like the one in The Villages on January 27th, right?"

"Yes."

"Now, Mrs. Jenkins, you told the police when you were interviewed, and you repeated again today, that after you left the Villages, Doctor Bates drove you right home. Correct?"

"Yes, we stopped once at a rest stop to use the bathroom, but that was all."

"And, from there, Doctor Bates drove straight to your house in Fort Pierce?"

"Yes, that's right."

"And you arrived at your house about what time?"

"About six."

Megan nodded toward her second chair Deandra Glick. In an instant the TV monitor screen was filled with the image of a receipt.

"Now, Mrs. Jenkins," Megan said loudly as she faced the jury. "I'd like you to look at the receipt up on the screen. Do you recognize that receipt, Mrs. Jenkins?"

"Objection!" Treem yelled. "I haven't seen this or verified that it's accurate!"

"Your honor, we just received this receipt and I haven't yet had time to show it to Mr. Treem. I will certainly give him time to review and challenge it if he wants to."

"Overruled." Judge Velez said, "please proceed, Ms. Harris."

"Now, Mrs. Jenkins," Megan continued." This receipt is from the Fairview Inn in Vero Beach. It shows that Doctor Leonard Bates checked into a room at that hotel on January 27, 2018 at 4:27 p.m."

"Objection!" Treem shouted, as he jumped to his feet.

"Overruled!" Judge Velez yelled, as he pounded his gavel. "Sit down, Mr. Treem."

"But, your honor?" Treem objected.

"Sit down, sir, or I'll hold you in contempt again!"

Megan continued her cross examination of Abby Jenkins. She nodded once again toward Deandra. Instantly came video footage on the TV monitor."

"Mrs. Jenkins," Megan said sternly as the video played. "This is video surveillance footage from the Fairview Inn on January 27th at 4:30, just three minutes after Doctor Bates checked in."

Abby squirmed in her chair. She looked over at JD Treem for support, but none came.

"As you can see, that is what appears to be Doctor Leonard Bates checking in, and less than one minute later, we see a woman walking toward the elevator. Can you identify that woman, Mrs. Jenkins?"

Once again Abby looked to JD Treem for help.

"It's me." Abby said sheepishly.

"Could you repeat that please, Mrs. Jenkins?"

"It was me."

"So, you lied to us when you said that Doctor Bates drove you right home after the Pickleball tournament, didn't you, Mrs. Jenkins?"

"Yes." Abby screamed. "But I never bought a phone at that barber shop! I swear that's the truth!"

"Sure it is, Mrs. Jenkins," Megan said sarcastically, "sure it is. No further questions, your honor."

"Redirect, Mr. Treem?" Judge Velez offered.

"No questions, your honor."

Velez pounded his gavel. "This court is adjourned until 9:00 a.m. tomorrow."

• • • • •

"She nailed him!" Lisa shouted gleefully as she danced around her family room, "Megan told me yesterday she had a surprise for old JD Treem, and she sure did!"

"She gave him a taste of his own medicine!" Rick replied.

"It's over now," Lisa said with glee, "Leonard Bates is going down!"

"Honey, you know what they say about counting your chickens," Rick said, " I won't be surprised if JD Treem has a few more tricks up his sleeve."

• • • • •

"Wow, Steve. We never saw that coming!"

"And neither did JD Treem, Mary. He was completely blindsided by the receipt and the video footage from the hotel."

"And obviously this was really damaging to Treem's case."

"Yes, it made Abby Jenkins' denial ring false, and dealt a devastating blow to the entire defense. Once again young prosecutor Megan Harris beat the old veteran JD Treem at his own game."

"But how about the way this evidence was presented. Could that be grounds for appeal?"

"I'm pretty certain JD Treem will look for every reason he can find to appeal if Doctor Bates is found guilty."

"So Steve, are you ready now to give this trial a Pickleball score?"

"Sorry Mary, I still haven't figured out how to keep score in Pickleball."

"Okay Steve. Now back to our studio and Darcy Henson."

Velez pounded his gavel. "The court is adjourned until 9:00 a.m. tomorrow."

CHAPTER 42

JUNE 27, 2018, 6:00 P.M.

THE HOME OF LISA AND RICK MARCH

Lisa walked into the house and kicked off her shoes. She had spent the entire day investigating a sexual assault claim on Hutchinson Island, and she was exhausted. As she entered the kitchen Rick and Lexie were desperately trying to salvage what looked like either a giant hamburger or a deflated meat loaf.

"Quick!" Lisa said, "turn on the TV!"

Rick jumped into the family room, grabbed the remote, and tuned to channel 12.

• • • • •

"Good evening, this is Brian Reagan in the channel 12 newsroom. Today, the Pickleball murder trial of Doctor Leonard Bates came to a screeching halt as Doctor Bates was transported to Lawnwood Hospital in Fort Pierce. For more news on this stunning chain of events let's go to our legal correspondent, Mary McCambridge."

"That's right, Brian, a startling development this morning just before the trial was about to reconvene. Defendant Leonard Bates suddenly grabbed his chest and began to pass out. He was administered to by the bailiff, a trained EMT, until an ambulance arrived a few minutes later to transport him to Lawnwood. "

"So what's the latest on Doctor Bates' condition, Mary?"

"Well Brian, the latest word we have is that the doctor is in stable condition, and a series of tests are being conducted to determine the extent of his illness and what the treatment plan will be."

"And how will all this affect the trial, Mary?"

"Brian, we have an unconfirmed report that Bates' attorney, JD Treem, has asked judge Jose Velez to declare a mistrial, but I expect to get more on that tomorrow."

"So there you have it folks. Just when you thought this Pickleball trial couldn't possibly get any more bizarre, it just did."

• • • • •

Lisa grabbed her cell phone and called Megan Harris.

"It's all a stunt, Lisa!" Megan yelled into the phone.

"Really?"

"Treem has done this a few times in the past," Megan replied, "when he thinks he's gonna lose he tries to get a mistrial."

"He asked the judge for that?"

"Oh yeah, no more than five minutes after they carted Bates away."

"That sleeze bag!" Lisa said, "so what did the judge say about the mistrial?"

"Judge Velez is no fool," Megan replied, "he said let's wait and see that happens at the hospital before he'll even consider a mistrial."

"Good."

"So we're definitely in recess until at least next Monday."

"Okay, Meg, have a great weekend, and I'll talk you soon."

"I heard that," Rick said, "this guy Treem is the lowest of the low!"

"Or," Lexie replied, "maybe this guy Len Bates is really sick. Maybe he's gonna die!"

"How are things between you and Andrew, Lex?" Rick asked.

"Hard to say, dad. We went out to dinner last night and we never talked about that Duke thing."

“So, you’re still gonna date him?” Lisa asked.

“We’ll see how it goes, mom,” Lexie replied, “in two months I go back to Tallahassee and he goes back to North Carolina so it probably won’t last after that anyway. Meanwhile, we’re having a lot of fun!”

“Yeah. But come next January his parents could be living right there in Tallahassee,” Rick said.

“Oh yeah, well I guess I’ll cross that bridge when I come to it.”

“Hey Lex,” Lisa said softly, “There’s something I need to talk to you about.”

“Sure mom, what?”

“It’s about Andrew and that Duke thing.”

“Yeah?”

“You know, Saturday night we went to dinner with Megan Harris and her fiancé.”

“Uh huh,”

“Turns out he works for the Attorney General of Florida.”

“Special Investigations unit,” Rick added.

“I’m not sure I like where this is going, you guys!” Lexi said.

“He told us about a guy they’re investigating for helping students get into college,” Lisa said, “he said the guy was called Doctor Duke!”

“You didn’t say anything, did you dad, mom? You promised me you wouldn’t say anything!”

“We didn’t say anything about Andrew, honey,” Lisa said, “but I think you should know that this is pretty close to exploding and it could get very nasty for Andrew and his parents.”

“Honey, we just don’t want you to get caught up in the middle of it.”

“Me?” Lexi shouted, “I didn’t do anything!”

“Yes that’s true Lex, but you know things,” Lisa said quietly, “Andrew told you things he shouldn’t have talked about and it’s possible that you could be questioned about what you know.”

“We just don’t want to see that happen to you, Lex,” Rick said.

"I've seen first hand how powerful Andrew's mother is," Lisa said, "and I don't want you to have to deal with her, especially if they get caught up in this Doctor Duke scandal."

"So, we think it's best if you put some space between you and Andrew, at least for a while," Rick added.

"You said you're probably gonna break up when the summer's over," Lisa said, "so why not just do it now?"

"Okay, Mom," Lexie said.

She grabbed her handbag and walked towards the door. "I'll take care of it."

After Lexie left Rick turned to Lisa. "So you think she's really gone break up with him?"

"Maybe," Lisa replied, "but I can guarantee you it will be on her time-table, not ours!"

"Like mother, like daughter!" Rick said with a smile.

CHAPTER 43

JULY 2, 2018, 6:00 P.M.
CARINO'S ITALIAN BISTRO
FORT PIERCE, FLORIDA

As Lisa entered the restaurant she was happy to see Megan sitting at the bar, and even happier to see a glass of Chardonnay waiting for her on the bar in front of the next stool.

"You drinking to celebrate or forget, Meg?" Lisa asked with a grin.

"A little of both, Lise," Megan replied.

Just then the TV monitor above the bar came to life.

• • • • •

"Good evening, this is Brian Reagan in the TV 12 newsroom. After a five day delay the murder trial of Doctor Leonard Bates began again today. You may recall last Wednesday Doctor Bates was taken to Lawnwood Hospital suffering from chest pains. "

"After a two night stay in Lawnwood, Doctor Bates was released to spend the weekend recuperating at home."

"Let's go to our legal correspondent Mary McCambridge for the highlights of todays action."

"Thanks once again, Brian, this is Mary McCambridge reporting to you live from the St. Lucie County Courthouse in Fort Pierce. As always, I'm joined by Palm Beach defense attorney, Steve Cohen. Steve, what was the takeaway from today?"

"Thanks Mary. Today marked the debut of what I call Leonard Bates two. Up until last week Doctor Bates appeared to be a very strong and healthy sixty-nine year old man."

"A Pickleball champion!"

"That's right, Mary. But today the jury was stunned by the man they saw enter the courtroom and sit at the defendant's table."

"How so, Steve?"

"Doctor Bates was seated in a wheel chair with oxygen tubes running into his nostrils. He looked as though he had aged ten years in only five days."

"Really?"

"And, to everyone's surprise, JD Treem called, as his first witness today, Doctor Bates himself."

"Wow! Most defense attorneys consider it risky to call the defendant in a murder trial."

"True, Mary. To me this was a clear indication that JD Treem feels that he's losing. I would call this a 'Hail Mary' testimony."

"Let's watch how it went."

• • • • •

Doctor Bates was helped up to the witness stand by two men dressed in hospital scrubs. They lifted Bates from his wheel chair and gently placed him in the witness chair, where he was administered the oath.

JD Treem slowly walked to the witness stand, smiled and said, "We're so glad to see you here, Doctor Bates. For a while there we thought we might lose you."

"Me too," Bates replied in a gravel voice.

"Doctor Bates, if at any time you feel that you need medical attention you just let me know and these fine gentlemen will come right up and help you."

"Thank you."

"Now Doctor Bates, we've heard from a lot of people about the relationship you had with your wife. How would you describe it?"

"I loved Diane," Bates said in this gruff voice, "she was my best friend in the world. Yes, we had our arguments, but what married couple doesn't?"

"And the infidelity?"

"That's something I'm not proud of," Bates replied, "Diane and I both strayed at times in our marriage, but we were always able to get through it. We loved each other and that's what mattered most."

"You had a two million dollar life insurance policy on Diane is that correct?"

"Yes that's right. We tried to get the same thing for me with Diane as the beneficiary, but I was rejected because of my medical history."

"So, they wouldn't insure you?"

"No."

"Doctor Bates, can you tell us what happened after the Pickleball tournament in The Villages on January 27th of this year?"

"Abby Jenkins and I finished playing around 2:30 and we left shortly after that."

"Then what happened?"

"As we drove by a barber shop Abby asked me if I would stop for a minute so she could buy hair gel for her husband. She said they only carried it in barber shops."

"So you stopped at Larry's Barber Shop?"

"Yes."

"And you waited in the car?"

"Objection!" Megan yelled, "counsel is testifying!"

"Sustained," Judge Velez said, "ask questions, Mr. Treem."

"Sorry, your honor." Treem replied. "So, Doctor Bates, what happened after you stopped at Larry's Barber Shop?"

"Abby went into the barber shop, and she came out a few minutes later."

"Was she carrying anything?"

"Just a small bag. I assumed it contained the hair gel for her husband."

"Doctor Bates," Treem said, as he leaned on the rail and looked straight at the jury, "at any time were you aware that Abby Jenkins had purchased a burner phone from the barber shop?"

"No, never."

"And at any time was that burner phone ever in your possession?"

"No, it was not."

"Doctor Bates, did you hire Bobby James to kill your wife?"

"No. Absolutely not!"

"Your witness." Treem said as he walked past Megan Harris.

Megan was loaded for bear. She had anticipated that Treem might put Bates on the stand today and she was prepared.

She quickly walked up to Bates and said, "Doctor Bates, where were you born?"

"Lexington, Massachusetts."

"And you went to high school there?'

"Yes."

"And where did you go to college?"

"I did my undergrad work at Boston University and then went to Tufts Medical School."

"Tufts is also in Boston, correct?"

"Yes it is."

"And then you lived and worked in the Boston area until when?"

"We moved to Florida eight years ago."

"So, Doctor Bates, is it fair to say that you spent the entire first sixty years of your life in the Boston area?"

"Yes."

Megan looked over at Deandra and, within seconds a recording played of excerpts from the first meeting between Lisa and Doctor Bates.

Megan then attacked. "Doctor Bates. Do you recognize the voices in this audio?"

"No."

"Well then, let me refresh your memory. The woman is Detective Lisa March, the interview took place in your home on the day of your wife's murder, and the other voice is yours."

"Okay."

"Let's listen to an excerpt shall we."

"We lock up when we go to bed at night but during the day we don't lock our dooahs. Sometimes we even fahget to lock up at night. This is a safe neighbahood.We've got a gahdhouse so nobody can get in heah without pahmission."

"No question where you come from in that interview, Doctor Bates, is there?"

"Objection!" JD Treem yelled.

"So where's the Boston accent today, Doctor Bates?"

"Objection!" Treem yelled.

"How convenient of you to pronounce all of your R's in front of this jury today!"

"Objection, your honor!"

"Sustained," Judge Velez said, "the jury shall disregard Ms. Harris' remarks."

"Okay. Doctor Bates. You said you had a warm loving relationship with your wife. You said the spats you had were typical of most married couples, yes?"

"Yes, that's right."

"I think you said that most married couples have these kinds of arguments. Is that what you said?"

"Yes."

"So tell me, Doctor, how many of those couples include a wife who tells her daughter that her husband was planning to kill her?"

"Objection!"

"Overruled."

"I never said I wanted to kill her!" Bates replied.

"But you checked out websites that tell people how to get away with murder, didn't you Doctor Bates?"

"I never did that!"

"Let's go back to the stop you made at Larry's Barber Shop on January 27th. You said that Abby Jenkins told you she was buying hair gel, right?"

"Yes."

"And you said she never told you that she was actually buying a burner phone that would be used to hire Bobby James to kill your wife. Is that right?"

"That's right."

"And you said that the burner phone never made it into your hands."

"Right."

"And you said you never used it to hire Bobby James, right?"

"I never did."

"So that means Abby Jenkins bought the burner phone and gave it to someone else other than you?"

"I guess so."

"Perhaps someone else she was having an affair with?"

"Perhaps."

"Perhaps someone else who stood to make two million dollars from Diane Bates' death?"

"I don't know!"

"And what an amazing coincidence that this mystery man has a Boston accent just like yours."

"Objection!"

"Sustained."

"So, Abby Jenkins spends the day with you, she plays in the Pickleball tournament with you, she buys the phone while you wait for her, she stops at a hotel and has sex with you, but she gives the phone to someone else, a mystery man. That's what you want this jury to believe, is it Doctor Bates?'

"Yes, it's the truth!"

"And she's protecting this mystery man even today?"

"Yes, I suppose she is."

"And now she faces not only accessory to murder charges, but also perjury charges for giving false testimony to this court, right?"

"Yes, I guess so."

"So then let me ask you this. If Abby Jenkins gave that burner phone to someone else, and she wanted to protect that person, then why wouldn't she simply say she bought it and gave it to you, so she could take the deal we offered her, and walk away scot-free?"

"I don't…"

"It's because the person she is protecting is you, Doctor Bates! You're the man she gave the burner phone to!"

"No!"

"You're the man with the thick Boston accent who used that phone to call Bobby James and hired him to kill your wife!"

"No!"

"Oh yes, Doctor Bates. It was you!"

"Objection!"

"Overruled."

"I'm finished here, your honor."

"Redirect, Mr. Treem?"

Treem once again stared at the jury as he asked this question. "Doctor Bates, did you hire Bobby James to kill your wife?"

"No!"

"That's all your honor." He then turned to the two men dressed in hospital scrubs. "Please help Doctor Bates back to his wheel chair."

"Okay then," Judge Velez announced, "we are adjourned until 9:00 a.m. on Thursday. In the meantime I hope everyone has a safe and happy July 4th holiday."

• • • • •

So who won today's battle Steve?"

"Well, Mary, I'll give JD Treem some credit for making his client look more sympathetic to the jury, but.."

"You think the wheelchair and oxygen were little over the top?"

"Look, I'm not a doctor so it's not for me to say how sick Len Bates is right now, but I'm not sure that at least some of the jurors didn't see this as manipulation on the part of JD Treem."

"Another trick up Treem's sleeve, huh?"

"Maybe, we'll see."

"And how did Megan Harris do on cross?"

"I thought her pointing out the lack of Boston accent was very smart. It's very likely that JD Treem was planning to play back Doctor Bates' testimony in closing to show the jury that he didn't have the accent that Bobby James heard in the phone calls."

"But Megan Harris took that tactic away from him!"

"Absolutely. And I also thought she did a great job of dismantling the story about Abby Jenkins buying the burner phone for someone else."

"Yes, that did seem like a bizarre theory."

"So, overall I feel like today JD Treem threw a Hail Mary pass that was intercepted by Megan Harris."

"A nice football analogy, Steve."

"Yes. Those are a lot more familiar to me than Pickleball."

"Back to you, Brian."

• • • • •

"Looks like you killed him again today, Meg," Lisa said, as she sipped the final drop of her wine.

"You never know what a jury is thinking, Lisa. I think I could have done a better job on cross."

"Don't look back, Meg. I'm sure you've got a killer closing argument for Thursday."

"I'm working on it, Lise. I'm working on it."

CHAPTER 44

JULY 5, 2018, 9:00 A.M.
ST. LUCIE COUNTY COURTHOUSE
FORT PIERCE, FLORIDA

Lisa was happy to sit in the gallery for the closing arguments. No longer eligible to be brought back as a rebuttal witness, she was as free to observe the trial as any other bystander.

JD Treem was wearing the same suit and bow tie that he had worn for his opening statement three weeks earlier.

He stood up and walked over to Len Bates, patted him on the shoulder as to show the jury that everything was going to be alright.

Then JD walked up to the jury box and spoke.

"Good morning!" He said with a big smile.

Several jurors mumbled greetings back to him.

"This has been a wild three weeks, hasn't it?'

Many heads nodded.

"My friends, when we first met three weeks ago I spoke to you about my dear mom, Gertie Treem." He stood directly in front of the jury box and leaned on the railing.

"I told you that Gertie Treem made me promise to always tell the truth to a jury,. I'm sure you remember that. But there was also something else Gertie taught me, and that was to deliver on my promises. She always said JD, if you say you're gonna do something you should darned well do it, and if you say you're not gonna do something you better not do it."

"I took my mother's advice to heart, ladies and gentlemen, and I've applied it to every trial and every jury I have ever worked with."

Treem walked back over to Leonard Bates and once again placed his hand on Bates' shoulder. "My friends, three weeks ago I told you that this was an innocent man and I'm telling you that again today.

"I told you that the prosecution's case was based on smoke and mirrors and that's exactly what their case turned out to be."

"So let's review." Treem motioned to his assistant, and quickly a slide appeared on the TV monitor."

BOBBY JAMES LITANY OF LIES

LIE #1- I DIDN'T KNOW WHERE THE BATES FAMILY LIVED

LIE #2- I WAS HIRED TO WORK BY THE NEIGHBORS

LIE #3- I NEVER WENT TO THE BATES' HOUSE THAT DAY

LIE #4- I WENT THERE TO HAVE SEX

LIE #5- SHE WAS ALREADY DEAD

LIE #6- DOCTOR BATES HIRED ME TO DO IT

"You all remember this don't you?" JD asked, as a few jurors nodded.

"The prosecution's entire case rested on the testimony of one man, Bobby James."

"So what do we know about this Bobby James? First of all, we know that he's serving a life sentence for murdering Diane Bates."

"Folks, justice was served in this case the moment Bobby James pled guilty to killing Diane Bates. But the prosecution wasn't satisfied with that. So they said 'Hey Bobby, we'll keep you off death row if you testify against Leonard Bates, because Leonard Bates is the husband! And we watch a lot of TV crime dramas. The husband always does it, right?"

"But you see, friends, the prosecution had a little problem with this strategy. Not only were they relying on the word of a murderer but also the word of a proven liar!"

"Look at these lies, folks. Every word out of that man's mouth was a lie. And the worst lie of all, oh yes the very worst lie of all was the last one. Because we know better. We know that Leonard Bates did not hire Bobby James to kill Diane Bates."

"How do we know?" There's an old adage that tells us to follow the money. I'm sure you've heard that. Follow the money! So let's do that, shall we? Bobby James says Leonard Bates hired him for one hundred thousand dollars."

"So how much did Leonard Bates pay Bobby James? You and I know the answer to that folks. The answer is nothing! Not one dime! And that's what they call a murder for hire plan? You know that's nonsense, my friends, and so do I."

"Now, let's talk about that infamous burner phone that the prosecution was so concerned about. They tried desperately to convince you that Leonard Bates used that phone, but where is it? Where are the finger prints? Where is the DNA?"

"Where is the eye witness who saw Len Bates with that phone? None of that exists, and you know why? Because it never happened! Len Bates never saw or touched that burner phone. Len Bates never called Bobby James, and Len Bates never hired him to kill Diane Bates."

"Len Bates is an innocent man, my friends and I need your help to let this poor, sick, widower go home and live out his remaining days in peace."

"Thank you, and may God bless each and every one of you with the wisdom to make the right decision."

With that JD Treem once again walked over to Leonard Bates' wheel chair, He placed both arms around Bates and embraced him, as if to say. "It's okay. I'll protect you from those evil prosecutors."

The entire court room fell silent for what seemed like several minutes.

Wow, this guy is good, Lisa thought. But she also knew that Megan Harris was up to the task.

After a short break it was Megan Harris' turn to close. She has practiced her presentation over and over, because this was the most important closing she had ever done.

Megan stood directly in front of the jury box, made eye contact with each of the twelve jurors, as she delivered her final message to them. He presentation was deliberate, calm, quiet, and powerful. The total opposite of JD Treem.

"Good afternoon. There's an old adage in trial law that says the following:"

"If the facts are on your side, pound the facts."

"If the law is on your side, pound the law."

"If neither the facts nor the law are on your side, pound the table!"

"Folks, you've been subjected to a lot of table pounding by the defense these last three weeks, and I think it's pretty obvious why."

"For the next few moments, I'd like to ask you to put aside all of the histrionics that we've witnessed in this courtroom, and simply use logic and common sense to guide you to a verdict. "

"This isn't a trial to determine whose mother gave the best advice. It is a trial to determine who was responsible for the death of Diane Bates."

"We owe it to the children, grandchildren, extended family and friends of Diane Bates to get to the truth. They deserve nothing less."

"For the last three weeks I've told you a story. It's the story of a man trapped in a terrible marriage. A man having an affair with a younger woman. A man unable to leave his marriage because his wife controlled all of the money. A man who could have divorced his wife, but would have to walk away with no house, no car, no money, no hope."

"This was unacceptable to a man like Leonard Bates, a man who had become very comfortable living the lifestyle his wealthy wife afforded him."

"Leonard Bates wanted to have his cake and eat it, too. He wanted to be free from Diane so he could be with a younger woman. And he wanted two million dollars that Diane's insurance policy would provide to help finance his new life."

"So what did Leonard Bates do? He searched on the internet for ways to kill his wife without getting caught. And then he found one. Get someone else to do it for you. That would be a very handy man to find."

"And oh, by the way, be sure to find a killer who is naive enough to do the deed and expect you to pay him after the fact."

"And when you hire that handyman, make sure you communicate only by a cell phone that can't be traced back to you "

"Sounds like the perfect murder to me. And it would have been, were it not for the handyman finally realizing that he'd been had."

"And in the end, this diabolical murder for hire plot was unraveled because a woman wore distinctive and memorable clothes to a Pickleball tournament."

"The defense team tells you that Bobby James is a liar. And this should come as a surprise to you? Folks, you know and I know that every criminal claims they are innocent until they're confronted with overwhelming proof of their guilt. It's happening right here in this courtroom!"

"But when criminals are finally confronted with overwhelming evidence of their guilt, that's when many of them start to tell the truth. You see, that impressive list of lies shown to you by Mr Treem had one glaring omission. It was the time when Bobby James finally admitted that he killed Diane Bates. Folks, that's when the lying stopped and the truth began."

"Bobby James testified that it was Leonard Bates who called him and offered him a hundred thousand dollars to kill Diane Bates. How did he know who was on the other end of that call? He recognized Leonard Bates' voice over the phone. And despite Mr. Bates best effort to fool you and conceal his Boston accent when he testified here, Bobby knew who he was. Bobby had spoken to Leonard Bates numerous times in the past, face to face, and he was very well aware of what Len Bates' voice and accent sounded like."

"And then, we have the barber shop. Larry the Barber clearly identified Len Bates' girlfriend, Abby Jenkins, as the woman who purchased the burner phone. The story conjured up by Len Bates to explain away that cell phone is preposterous. You know that."

"Ask yourself this question. If not Bates, then who? Who else had a motive to see Diane Bates murdered, and who else had a Boston accent, and who else had access to the burner phone?"

"The answer is nobody! Nobody but the defendant, Leonard Bates."

"So I ask you, who is the liar now?"

"I think you know that too."

"And that's why there's only one verdict that truly reflects the facts of this case. Only one verdict that will bring closure, justice, and peace to the daughters and grandchildren of Diane Bates. Those young grandchildren were robbed of their chance to grow up with their grandmother by the greed of Leonard Bates."

"So, I ask you to forget the table pounding and bring home the only verdict that is based on the facts of this case. That verdict is to find the defendant, Leonard Bates, guilty of the murder of Diane Bates."

"Thank you."

Silence engulfed the court room as Megan Harris walked slowly back to her seat. She had delivered the closing of her life.

After a few moments Judge Jose Velez gave his instructions to the jury and sent them off to deliberate.

CHAPTER 45

JULY 9, 2018, 4:00 P.M.

"Hello, this is Brian Reagan in the TV 12 newsroom. We just received word that the jury has reached a verdict in the trial of Dr. Leonard Bates. For more on this breaking news let's go to Mary McCambridge, live at the court house in Fort Pierce."

"That's right, Brian. I'm here in front of the St. Lucie County court house, where we have just been notified that a verdict was reached after four days of deliberation in this, the highest profile trial ever to hit the Treasure Coast. Many people have dubbed this The Pickleball Murder Trial because the Riverside Estates community, where the murder occurred, is well known as the Pickleball capital of south Florida."

"Twice the jury had told judge Jose Velez that they were deadlocked, but both times he refused to accept a hung jury and forced them back into deliberation."

"Doctor Leonard Bates was accused of planning the murder of his wife, Diane Bates, in February of this year. The tumultuous trial lasted three weeks before it was handed over to the jury, and soon we will learn whether this sixty-nine year old retired doctor will go home, or spend the rest of his life behind bars."

"You can see behind me that many people are now entering the courthouse and we expect to hear the verdict read within the hour."

"Thanks, Mary. As soon as the verdict is announced we'll break into our regularly scheduled programming to bring you back to Mary at the courthouse."

• • • • •

Lisa was in her office when she got the word that a verdict had been reached. She quickly jumped in her car and made the ten mile trip from Port St. Lucie to Fort Pierce. She did not want to miss the verdict, and at one point she propped her flashing light on top of her car and used the siren to get through a red light on Federal Highway.

She parked her car and walked into the courtroom just as Judge Velez entered the room. The jury box was empty.

"All rise," said the bailiff, as Judge Velez walked in. He slowly took his seat and watched as the others sat down.

"Ladies and gentlemen," the judge began, "this has been a very emotional trial, but in just a moment it will be over. We are about to hear the verdict, and when we do some of you will be supportive of this verdict, and others will be bitterly disappointed. But I'm telling each and every one of you that there will be no outbursts in my courtroom. I expect each of you to accept this verdict. If you feel that you cannot accept the verdict with dignity and respect for this process then I ask you to leave my courtroom now."

Nobody left. In fact, they were all riveted to their seats.

"Bailiff, bring in the jury please."

As the jury walked in, Lisa looked for signs of what their verdict might be. They all looked sullen and exhausted. Four days, she thought, there must have been a lot of arguing in that jury room.

The bailiff was handed a piece of paper by one of the jurors. He gave the paper to the judge, who read it, nodded, and handed it back to the bailiff.

The tension in the room was palpable as the jury foreman stood up.

"Please read the verdict," Judge Velez said.

The jury foreman, a distinguished looking man dressed in a business suit and tie, read the verdict. "We, the jury in the case of the state of Florida versus Doctor Leonard Stanley Bates, find the defendant guilty of the murder of Diane Bates."

With that the courtroom erupted. Judge Velez pounded his gavel a few times before everyone settled down. Diane Bates' two daughters hugged each other as Judge Velez concluded.

"Doctor Bates, you are hereby remanded to the St. Lucie County jail to await sentencing, which will occur on July 24th in this courtroom. The jury is now dismissed with the appreciation of the people of this community. I know this was not an easy case for you and I thank you all for successfully fulfilling your duties as citizens of the state of Florida."

Len Bates was handcuffed to his wheel chair and taken away to the jail house. "I didn't do it!" he cried, as he was led out of the courtroom.

JD Treem rushed to the courthouse steps to present himself before the awaiting press. Megan Harris packed up her papers and walked away quietly. She had done her job.

CHAPTER 46

JULY 28, 2018, 10:00 A.M.

VETERAN'S PARK, PORT ST LUCIE

Lisa was excited to learn the game of Pickleball. Ever since that first visit to Riverside Estates she was intrigued by this game. How had a game that nobody ever heard of taken off so fast in Florida, and all over the country?

"You've got some knobby knees, girlfriend!" Megan Harris joked as she walked toward the court where Lisa awaited.

Lisa looked down at her bare legs.

"Hey, you should just be happy that I shaved my legs today," she said, "otherwise that Pickleball might have got lost in there!" Both women laughed, as Pickleball pro, Michael Studdard approached with a large canvas bag.

"Hello ladies," Michael said with a smile, "It's nice to see you and not be a murder suspect!"

"We never seriously considered you a suspect," Megan mused.

"Well, maybe for a little while!" Lisa joked, "it's that damned DNA that gets us every time."

Michael reached into his bag and handed each of the women a Pickleball paddle.

"Here you go," he said, "my DNA is all over these paddles, and now yours is too!"

"Hey Michael," Megan laughed, "we came here to learn Pickleball, not to have a murder trial!"

"I heard that Doctor Bates got twenty-five years to life."

"Yes, he did," Megan replied, "that's pretty much a life sentence at his age."

"You know," Michael pondered, "I always thought it was Dave Messenger that did it. Nobody hated Diane Bates more than him"

"No," Lisa replied, "we cleared Dave Messenger. He had a solid alibi."

"Oh, okay then," Michael replied, "let me teach you this awesome game!

CHAPTER 47

SEPTEMBER 17, 2018, 10:00 A.M.
MARTIN PROFESSIONAL BUILDING
STUART, FLORIDA

As Lisa stepped out of her car in the parking lot she took her cell phone out of her purse and speed dialed her partner, Dan Torres.

"Hey Danny, I'm gonna be a little late this morning."

"What's up, Lisa?" Dan asked.

"Nothing big, Danny," Lisa replied, as she walked toward the steps of the large office building on Federal Highway, "Rick and I decided we need to have a will drawn up. You know, with him being sick and all, it was important that we get a will made."

"So where are you?"

"Believe it or not, I'm walking into Baker and Breem right now."

"Aren't those the guys that we met with about Diane Bates' will?"

"Yep. Rick says they're the best in town so I figured I'd visit them as a client this time."

"Okay, good luck," Dan said, "and make sure you spell my name right in the will!"

Lisa laughed, "I'm leaving you my gun!"

As Lisa entered the building she noticed that the elevator doors we just closing. What she did not notice was the occupant of the elevator, Dave Messenger. Dave was heading for Suite 223 and the law office of Jason Baron, one floor below Baker and Breem.

When the elevator arrived back at the ground floor Lisa entered and pushed the button for the third floor. She exited the elevator and walked a few steps into the office of Baker and Breem. She was now five minutes late for her appointment with Henry Droter, the law firm's will specialist.

SUITE 301

LAW OFFICES OF BAKER AND BREEM

Lisa sat in the waiting room for a minute and then was greeted by a young African American woman.

"Hi," the woman said, holding out her hand to shake with Lisa, "I'm Latoya Taylor. I'm Mr. Droter's assistant."

With that Lisa was led into a conference room where Henry Droter was waiting. He looked as frumpy as he had the last time she met him a few months earlier. But, Lisa thought, I'm hiring this guy to write my will, not for fashion advice.

After a few minutes of small talk, Lisa expressed her concern.

"Everything my husband and I own will go to our daughter Lexie," she said, "but the thing that worries me the most is that I don't want the same thing to happen to her as happened to Jennifer Messenger."

Droter looked surprised, so Lisa continued.

"Look, my daughter isn't married, and I certainly hope that when she does finally get married it's to a great guy. But I just don't want to take a risk that Lexie might end up giving half of what we leave her to a divorcing husband like Jennifer Messenger did."

"There's no problem. You can simply leave everything to your daughter and that money will be hers, and hers alone."

"Really?" Lisa replied, "I thought if you were married then it became the property of your spouse too."

"That only happens if you co-mingle the assets." Droter said.

"Co-mingle?"

"Yes. If your daughter, for example, placed the money she inherits in a joint bank account with her husband, then it becomes what's called a marital asset, and he's entitled to half of the money."

"Okay, that sounds easy, " Lisa said, "the key is to keep that money in her name only."

"Exactly!" Droter replied, "so let me run back to my office for one minute and get the paperwork we need to start your will. If you'd like a water or anything Latoya will be glad to get it for you."

SUITE 223

LAW OFFICE OF JASON BARON

"David, I can't believe I'm seeing you again for another divorce!" Attorney Jason Baron said to his childhood friend, "what's it been, two weeks since your last one?"

"Not funny, shit head!" Messenger replied, "Jennifer and I got divorced in April. That was five months ago."

"You're amazing, my friend! I've got the new divorce papers here from Baker and Breem."

"My current wife used to work there." Dave said.

"I know," Jason replied, "they're right upstairs in this same building."

"Well," Dave said, "maybe if I'd married a scientist like you did, it would have been happily ever after for me!"

"Oh yeah?" Jason replied, "I thought being married to a scientist would be great."

"Don't tell me!" Dave said with a grin, "you too?"

"Turns out she was way too smart for me," Jason replied, "she found another genius at her work, and that was the end of my marriage."

"Sorry, Jase. Maybe the third time will be a charm for me."

"So, tell me about this second wife," Baron said, "how did you meet her?"

"She came into my restaurant on a Sunday night last January and she was gorgeous, super model, drop dead gorgeous!"

"And she swept you off your feet?"

"Just about," Dave replied, "the place was packed because everyone was watching the Eagles and Vikings playoff game on the big screen. She walked in and every head turned towards her, even the women."

"A real looker, huh?"

"Yes. She musta had twenty guys offer to buy her a drink that night but she just kept turning them down."

"So how did she end up with you?"

"The game ended a little after ten and most people started to leave, but she stayed and we were talking while I cleaned up. She even helped me put things away!"

"I think I know where this is heading."

"Yeah. So when I was ready to lock up she asked if I would wait outside with her until her Uber arrived."

"And you said you would drive her home!"

"I did."

"And one thing led to another…"

"Yeah, it did," Dave said sheepishly, "I never left her place until two days later!"

"So that was January. When did you guys get married?"

"You know, my divorce came through in April, and we got married a week later."

"And I wasn't invited?" Jason feigned surprise.

"We got married by a justice of the peace, Jason. Nobody was invited."

"Okay, Davey Boy. So here we are five months later and now you're getting divorced."

"It turns out she was only after me for my money, Jase."

"What money is that?"

"I inherited some money when my mother-in-law died."

"Wait a minute. Didn't Diane Bates die in February?"

"Yes."

"Okay, I'm a little confused, but let's continue."

"So anyway, ten days ago my wife packed up and left. She told me she wants a divorce."

"Did she say why?"

"She said she just doesn't love me any more."

"Sounds like maybe she never did, Dave."

"I think you're right, Jase."

Jason reached into his desk and grabbed a pad of paper. "Okay let's talk about marital assets."

"We don't have any," Dave replied, "all I have is my inheritance and my restaurant."

"Okay, the restaurants is in your name only?"

"Yes."

"What about the inheritance?"

"My wife worked for a law firm and she arranged it so my inheritance was placed in a safe account."

"Is the account in both names?"

"I don't know, why?"

"Shit!"

"What do you mean, Jason?" Dave shouted.

SUITE 301

LAW OFFICES OF BAKER AND BREEM

As Lisa waited for Henry Droter to return she decided to make small talk with the young woman in the room.

"Latoya?" she said with a smile, "that's a beautiful name."

"Thanks!" Latoya replied, "my mom was a huge Michael Jackson fan."

"So was I," Lisa replied, "so sad to see him die so young."

"Yes. I feel the same way."

"Tell me, "Lisa continued, "what happened to the young woman who used to have your job?"

"You mean Kelly?"

"Yes, Kelly... what was her last name?"

"Messenger," Latoya replied, "Kelly Messenger. She quit last week."

Lisa was dumbfounded. "Are you sure it's Messenger? I thought it was Knowles, Kelly Knowles."

"No, I'm pretty sure it was Messenger."

As Henry Droter returned to the conference room Lisa politely asked Latoya to leave for a moment so she could talk privately to her boss.

"Is everything okay?" Droter asked.

"Henry," Lisa replied quietly, "you know that I'm a police detective, right?"

"Of course I do."

"So, as a police detective, when I see or hear things that surprise me, I become a little suspicious and determined to learn more about them."

"Huh?"

"Your former assistant, Kelly Knowles, did she recently get married?"

"Yes. I think it was in April."

"Who is she married to?"

"She married David Messenger."

"And that's the same David Messenger who inherited almost five million dollars, right?"

"The same."

"And he inherited that money because Mrs. Bates' will wasn't changed in time for her to sign it before she died, right?"

"Where are you going with this, Lisa?"

"I'm not sure, Henry," Lisa replied, "but wherever it takes me I'm gonna go."

SUITE 223

LAW OFFICE OF JASON BARON

"What's the problem?" Dave asked his old friend.

"Do you have access to that account?"

"I can go online and check it."

"Let's do that right now," Jason said, as he turned his computer monitor toward Dave.

Dave called up the bank website and entered his user name and password.

"What name is on the account, Dave?"

"It says David or Kelly Messenger."

"Okay, my friend," Jason said, "you're gonna have to take all the money out of that account right now!"

Dave hit several key strokes.

"Fuck!" Dave yelled.

"What happened?"

Dave turned the monitor back towards Jason.

"Where's the five million?" Jason asked.

"It's gone!" Dave replied, "that bitch took it all!"

SUITE 301

LAW OFFICES OF BAKER AND BREEM

"Henry," Lisa said firmly, "this is not gonna look good for your firm."

"What the hell are you taking about?" Henry shouted, "we didn't do anything wrong."

"Your law firm is responsible for the actions of your employees when they act as agents for the firm, are they not?"

"Of course, but what are you driving at."

"I'm not one hundred percent sure, Henry, but I'm gonna need your cooperation if you want to come out of this clean."

"Okay," Henry said sheepishly, "what do you need?"

"First of all, I need to know who handled the disbursement of funds from Mrs. Bates account to her beneficiaries?'

"Well, that was Kelly Knowles."

"And exactly when did that happen?"

Droter checked his cell phone and responded. "The will was read on May 9th. After everything was liquidated, the cash was distributed to the beneficiaries on August 28th."

"Okay, I'm gonna need the bank account numbers used for the beneficiaries."

"I'm not sure I can give you that," Henry said nervously.

"Look, if you prefer I can come back here in one hour with a warrant and I can assure you that the warrant will require you to give us a lot more that those account numbers!"

"I need to check with my boss," Henry said, as he headed out of the conference room, "I'll be right back."

SUITE 223

LAW OFFICE OF JASON BARON

"She took every dime that I inherited!" Dave screamed.

"Okay," Jason replied calmly, "let's not panic. We can go after her in court for your fair share of the money."

"We can't do that, Jase."

"What the hell are you talking about, Dave?'

"Let me ask you," Dave said quietly, "if I tell you some things, will it be covered by lawyer client privilege?"

"Of course it will, Dave," Jason replied, "anything you say to me will remain with me. Why do you ask?"

"But, what if I committed a crime?" Dave continued, "and I tell you about it, do you have to report me to the police?"

"No, Dave. I would never do that," Jason replied, "what the hell is going on?"

Dave took a deep breath.

SUITE 301
LAW OFFICES OF BAKER AND BREEM

After a five minute delay Henry Droter came back into the conference room and handed Lisa a list of account numbers.

"So which one of these was for David Messenger?" Lisa asked.

"The one at St. Lucie Bank and Trust," Droter replied.

"Exactly when did Kelly Messenger quit her job here?"

She gave notice on August 31st."

"So, that was three days after the wire transfer."

"Uh huh."

"And her last day was?"

"She stayed for one week after that to train her replacement."

"That would be Latoya?"

"Right."

"So' she left your office for the last time on September 7th, right?"

"Yes, that's right."

"Okay, do you have a cell phone number for Kelly Knowles Messenger?"

Droter removed his cell phone from his pocket, searched his contacts, and wrote down the number for Kelly Knowles. He handed it to Lisa.

"Thanks, Henry," Lisa said, as she stood up from her chair and began to leave, "I'll be in touch if we need anything else from you."

Droter stood up and said, "but what about your will?"

"I'm afraid that's gonna have to be put on a hold for a little while, Henry," Lisa replied, "I'll call you when I'm ready."

Droter looked stunned by what had just taken place.

As soon as Lisa exited the building she called her partner.

"Danny?"

"Did you get the will done, Lisa?"

"Never mind that. I need a meeting with you, me, Megan Harris, and Captain Davis. See how fast you can pull it together, okay?"

"What's up, Lise?"

"I'm not really sure, Danny," Lisa replied, "I'm really not sure."

SUITE 223
LAW OFFICE OF JASON BARON

"So, I told you how I met Kelly."

"Right, at your restaurant."

"Yes, on January 21st, a Sunday, and we spent all night Sunday and all day Monday together. My restaurant is closed on Mondays and she even called in sick from her work"

"Okay."

"So, after that we were inseparable, I thought. She worked all day but then she always came to the restaurant to be with me after work. Then we went home together, sometimes to my place, sometimes to hers."

"Okay," Jason said, "no crime in that."

"Sure thing." Dave said. He paused for a moment and continued, "you're sure about that client privilege thing, right?"

"Davey," Jason said, "I've known you since we were four years old. Do you think I would lie to you about something like that?"

"No, I don't."

"Then tell me what happened for God sakes!"

Dave took another deep breath.

"One night, after we'd been dating for a few days, Kelly showed me a copy of Diane Bates' will. She showed me that I was gonna inherit close to five million bucks!"

"You didn't know that?"

"No, why would I know? Nobody ever told me that," Dave said, "and for the life of me I couldn't figure out why that old hag would leave money to me. She hated my guts!"

"I know that, my friend. I remember the things she accused you of doing to your little girl. It was disgusting what she did to you."

"So anyway, Kelly said she worked for the law firm that drew up the will, and she said I was a beneficiary, as long as I was still married to Jennifer when her mother died.

"So why was Kelly telling you this?" Jason asked.

"Well, then she showed me a revised will that she was working on."

"Revised will?"

"Yes, and the new will was gonna cut me out completely."

"So, Dave, tell me this. Why do you think this strange woman would come to your restaurant, start having sex with you, and tell you about the wills. Weren't you a little suspicious of her?"

"Actually I was thankful, not suspicious."

"Sounds like you were thinking with the wrong head, my friend," Jason said, "so what happened next?

"So, a couple of days later Kelly and I are in bed, and she tells me that there is one way I could get that five million."

"And what way was that?"

"She said she could delay the signing of the new will until after Diane Bates died."

"What the fuck? How in hell was she gonna do that?" Jason asked.

Dave looked at his friend.

"Holy shit, Davey! Did you kill her?"

"No I didn't kill her, Jase. It wasn't me."

"Was it really that stupid handymen, or was it you, Davey?"

"I swear Jason, it wasn't me. It was Bobby James that killed Diane."

"Okay Dave, but how were you so lucky to have the murder take place before she signed the new will?"

"It wasn't luck, Jason."

"Well then, you must have convinced her husband to hire the handyman."

"No, Jase, listen to me!"

"I'm all ears, Davey."

"So, Kelly tells me that she's been talking with my wife, Jennifer…."

"What?" Jason screamed. "How the hell did she know Jennifer?"

"Because she worked for Baker and Breem, and they represented Diane Bates and her family in the will."

"Jeez Louise, Davey, that's conflict of interest 101!"

"Yeah I guess so, but anyway she knows a lot of things."

"Like what?"

"Like she knows that Diane and Len hated each other, and Diane was afraid Len was gonna kill her."

"Okay."

"And she knows that Diane was having an affair with the handyman, and Len was having an affair with Abby Jenkins."

"Geez, Davey, she knew a lot!"

"So, then she tells me she has a plan."

"Plan? What plan?"

Another deep breath from Dave Messenger.

"Okay, here goes, client privilege, right?"

"For Christ sakes, Davey, either tell me or don't tell me!"

"Kelly said we should hire Bobby James to kill Diane Bates before she signed the new will."

"How did you know he would do it?"

"She didn't, but she was hoping that we could offer him enough money to make the deal worth it for him."

"And he went for it, huh?"

"He said he owed money to some bad people," Dave replied.

"But he fingered Len Bates as the one who hired him, right?" Jason asked.

"That's right, and he said Bates used a burner phone."

"Right."

"And that phone was purchased in The Villages the same day Bates and his girlfriend went up there for a tournament.

"Yes it was." Dave responded, "you see, Kelly knew that Len and Abby were gonna play in a Pickleball tournament in the Villages on January 27th. She also knew that Abby always wears the same shoes, hat, and sun glasses every time she plays in a Pickleball tournament. It's her good luck outfit."

"Uh huh."

"And she said she looks enough like Abby that she could buy the phone and the seller would identify the buyer as Abby."

"Which he did."

"Yes, because Kelly watched the tournament until Len and Abby left. Then she put on the same color clothes Abby was wearing and went to the barber shop to buy the phone"

"I see," Jason said, "and if Abby was identified as the buyer that would tie the burner phone to Len Bates."

"And it did."

"Yeah, but the handyman identified Len Bates as the man who called him.

Dave began to imitate Len Bates' Boston accent.

"Bobby, this is LENAHD Bates. This is a HAHD call for me to make. I need you to be my PAHTNAH."

"It was you that made all the calls?" Jason said incredulously.

"Yes. It was me," Dave replied. "I went to school in Boston so I know how they talk up there. That's where I met Jennifer."

"So, after Diane was killed, you got your five million?"

"Close to five, it came at the end of August."

"By which time you were officially divorced from Jennifer."

"And married to Kelly, yes."

"So, was Kelly the one who set up the joint account for you, Dave?"

"Yes, and she was the one who got the money transferred from Diane"s account to mine…I mean ours."

"And then Kelly empties the account and puts the money, God knows where, probably in a Swiss bank account in her name only."

"I wish I knew, Jason."

"And now she wants to divorce you. How convenient," Jason said, "I wonder what took her so long?"

"So, what can I do now, Jase?"

"Davey, you're my oldest friend in the world," Jason said, as he grabbed Dave's arm, "so I'm gonna give it to you straight. If you don't want to end up in prison for the rest of your life the smartest thing you can do is sign the divorce papers and move on with your life."

"So, you're saying there's no way I can get my money?"

"Remember, Dave," Jason replied, "it wasn't supposed to be your money in the first place."

"That bitch," Dave shouted, "that conniving little bitch!"

Jason removed the divorce document from an envelope and turned it to the final page.

"Dave," he said quietly, "I know you're upset. You have every right to be. But I think the safest thing you can do right now is to sign this divorce document and put this whole thing behind you."

"What does it say?"

"It grants an uncontested divorce, and allows each of you to keep what you came into the marriage with. It means you get to keep the restaurant."

"But, what about the inheritance money?"

"Not mentioned, Dave." Jason explained. "And, based on what you just told me, you don't want it mentioned to anyone."

Dave picked up a pen from his friend's desk and signed the divorce document.

"I'll notarize it for you." Jason said, "and, for what it's worth, I think you did the right thing."

CHAPTER 48

SEPTEMBER 17, 2018, 1:00 P.M.

PORT ST. LUCIE POLICE DEPARTMENT

Lisa stood up in front of the conference table. In the room with her were Dan Torres, Megan Harris, and Captain Davis.

"I want to reopen the Diane Bates murder investigation," she said calmly.

"What?" Captain Davis shouted, "are you out of your mind, March?"

"We solved that case, Lisa," Dan added, "what's up?"

"Listen," Lisa replied, "I could be wrong about this, but there's a possibility that the wrong man is in prison for this murder."

"What makes you say that, Lisa?" Megan asked.

"I just found out that Kelly Knowles, you know, the woman who delayed Diane Bates' will until it was too late for her to sign it..."

"Cause she was already dead." Dan interjected.

"Yes," Lisa continued, "I just found out that Kelly Knowles married Dave Messenger, the same Dave Messenger who stood to gain five million bucks if the will didn't get signed before Diane Bates died."

"Okay, I get that," Megan said, "so maybe we go after them for fraud."

"But that ain't murder," Captain Davis added.

“Wait a minute,” Lisa said, “hear me out. Who were the only ones who benefited from Diane Bates dying on February 15th?

“How about Len Bates and the two million dollars in life insurance?” Megan replied.

“That’s true, Meg. But that life insurance payout wasn’t dependent on her dying that day. He would have gotten the money any time she died.”

“So what are you driving at, March?” Davis bellowed.

“I’m saying that there were two people who needed Diane Bates to die by February 15th in order to cash in big time, Dave Messenger and his soon to be wife Kelly Knowles.”

“Are you saying Messenger and Knowles are the ones who hired Bobby James?” Megan asked, “not Len Bates?”

“I’m saying it’s a possibility,” Lisa replied, “we eliminated Dave Messenger as a suspect because he had a solid alibi for the time of the murder. But we never fingered him as the guy who hired the handyman.”

“I don’t like this, Lisa!” Captain Davis said.

“Please, Captain, just give me a couple of days to walk this through,” Lisa pleaded, “Megan, will you support me on this?”

“Look Lisa,” Megan replied, “the last thing I want to see is Len Bates walking out of jail.”

“And he won’t, unless I can prove that he really didn’t do it.”

“Okay, March,” Captain Davis said, “two days, and then you’re moving on to another investigation. We’ve got a pile of cases on my desk.”

“Thanks, Captain,” Lisa replied, “Meg, I might need a couple of warrants from you.”

“Just let me know.”

As they left the meeting Lisa handed Dan the cell phone number that was given to her by Henry Droter.

“Danny, find out where this phone was on January 27th between 2:00 and 3:00 p.m.”

“I’m on it.”

Then Lisa called Detective Sheila Feeney.

"Sheels, it's Lise. I need a big favor."

"Anything Lise, what's up?"

"I've got an account number at St. Lucie Bank and Trust."

"Uh huh."

"I need you to tell me whose names are on the account."

"When do you need it Lisa?"

"Yesterday, Sheels."

"Got it."

"And one more thing."

"Sure."

"Can you find out what items Kelly Messenger ordered online between January 19th and 25th?"

"Easy peasy. What are you looking for?"

"I'm looking for neon orange sneakers, white sequined hat, and white sequined sunglasses."

"Check. I'll get warrants from Megan and get right on it."

Lisa went to her laptop and downloaded an audio file of her February 21st interview with Dave Messenger. She played a couple of minutes of it to make sure it was the right one, and then made the three hour drive to the Okeechobee Correctional Institute.

When she arrived at Okeechobee she was escorted to the interview room where Bobby James was waiting for her. Dressed in his prison clothes Bobby looked a lot less like a handyman gigolo than he once did.

Lisa sat opposite Bobby and placed her laptop on the table between them.

"Bobby," she said, "I appreciate your willingness to meet with me today. I'll only take a few minutes of your time."

"It's okay, honey," Bobby replied with a grin, "I got all the time in the world!"

Lisa smiled, "Bobby," she continued, "in Len Bates' trial you testified that you knew it was Doctor Bates' voice on the phone offering you a hundred thousand dollars if you killed Diane Bates."

"Yeah, that's right. It was him."

"I see, Bobby," Lisa said, "I'd like to play you a recording of a voice and I want to ask you to listen very carefully to it."

"Alright."

"And Bobby, I need you to think back to all those phone calls you got and ask yourself if it's at all possible that this was the voice you heard. Okay?'

"Play it."

"There's a few others, but I guess I'm the best!"

"I'm not sure. I used to play a lot of tennis so Pickleball just came naturally to me."

"Let me know when you want to start. I'd be happy to teach you."

"Lots of people. The place was packed, and I talked to a lot of people."

Several more excerpts from the February 21st interview with Dave Messenger were played. Bobby listened attentively. At first he made no response, but then he said, "play that again for me, will you?"

Lisa played the audio over and over again, at least ten times before Bobby said, "that's him."

"That's him?" Lisa replied.

"Yep, that's the guy who called me," Bobby said, "that's Doc Bates. I'd recognize his voice anywhere. I heard he deliberately lost the Boston accent when he testified in court so this must be what he sounded like on the witness stand."

Lisa was stunned by what she had just heard.

"Bobby," Lisa said sternly, "this is very important. Are you telling me that you're absolutely certain that this is the voice you heard in every one of the phone calls leading up to the murder of Diane Bates?"

"Yep, that's Doc Bates," Bobby said, "he told me who he was when he called me!"

"Okay now Bobby, I'm going to record you listening to this audio and telling me that this is Doctor Bates' voice.

“Sure, no problem,” Bobby said, “and make sure you tell that cheap bastard he still owes me a hundred grand!”

On the ride back to Port St Lucie, Lisa received a call from Dan Torres.

“You’ll never guess where Kelly Knowles’ cell phone was between 10:00 a.m. and 3:00 p.m. on January 27th?”

“Don’t screw with me, Danny!”

“The Villages!!”

“No!”

“Yes!”

“She is conniving bitch,” Lisa said, “and what’ll you bet that she put Dave Messenger’s inheritance into a joint bank account with her name on it, too?”

“Huh?”

“I’ll explain it tomorrow.”

CHAPTER 49

SEPTEMBER 17, 2018, 8:00 P.M.

THE HOME OF LISA AND RICK MARCH

Lisa was exhausted. She had driven more than six hours today, but the adrenaline rush from her visit with Bobby James was keeping her mind racing.

She was met at the door by her husband, Rick. He immediately handed her a glass of Kendall Jackson Chardonnay.

"Hungry?" he asked with a smile.

"Starved!" Lisa replied. In her excitement she had forgotten to eat all day. "What ya got for me, babe?"

Rick opened the oven door and removed a warm pizza box. "I've been keeping it fresh for you ever since you called."

"That was two hours ago!" Lisa said, "has it been sitting in the oven all that time?"

"Oops!" Rick replied sheepishly.

As they sat and ate the dried up pizza together. Lisa couldn't help but talk about the amazing events of the day. She rambled on for several minutes about her meeting at Baker and Breem, the discovery of the marriage between Kelly Knowles and Dave Messenger, her meeting with the Captain, and her visit with Bobby James.

"You really think Len Bates is innocent?" Rick asked.

"I'm not certain," Lisa replied, "but if I was a gambler I'd put my money on Dave Messenger as the guilty one."

"Lexie called today."

"She always calls you, not me!" Lisa said, "what's up at Florida State?"

"She finally broke it off with Andrew Wilson."

"Wow! That's a step in the right direction!" Lisa said, "I wonder what made her finally do it."

"Oh, you didn't hear the news?"

"News, what news?"

"I recorded it for you."

Rick grabbed the TV remote and turned it on. He found the recording and let it play.

• • • • •

"Hello everyone, this is Brian Reagan in the TV 12 newsroom. Our top story today is the college admissions scandal that has rocked the Treasure Coast. Port St. Lucie mayor Candace Wilson and her husband George have been indicted by a federal grand jury on charges of mail fraud and extortion. For more on this explosive story let's go to our legal correspondent Mary McCambridge."

"That's right Brian, today a Federal grand jury in Fort Pierce handed down indictments on twelve people, including Mayor Candace Wilson and her husband. The indictments charge that the Wilsons paid a college admissions consultant George Applegate to insure that their son would be accepted at Duke University in North Carolina. Allegedly, Mr. Applegate, who calls himself Doctor Duke, used bribes, fake transcripts, enhanced test scores, and created fake resumes that caused the students to bypass other, more qualified applicants and gain admission to the prestigious university. Applegate was charged with multiple counts of mail fraud and bribery."

"We contacted Mayor Wilson's office, and we were told that the Mayor, who is currently running for governor, will make a statement tomorrow. We'll cut into regular programming to bring you that statement as it happens.

"Now back to you, Brian."

• • • • •

"This was inevitable," Rick said.

"How's Lexi taking it?"

"She's okay," Rick replied, "she's really angry that the Wilsons would do something like that."

"I'm just glad that she broke up with Andrew."

Lisa's cell phone buzzed, and an unfamiliar number appeared on the screen.

"Who could be calling me this late?" she said, as she tapped the green answer button.

"Hello."

"Lisa, it's Sheila. Sorry to call you so late but you said you needed this information right away."

"Of course, Sheels, got something good for me?"

"I do. The account number you gave me at St. Lucie Bank and Trust was opened on May first of this year."

"Whose name is it under?"

"David or Kelly Messenger."

"Both names?"

"Yes."

"And was there a deposit of around five million made to the account?"

"Yep," Sheila replied, "on August 28th a wire transfer in the amount of four million, nine hundred and twelve thousand dollars was deposited into the account by the Baker and Breem law firm."

"Anything else?"

"Oh yeah," Sheila replied, "on September 7th that money was wire transferred to an account at the Cayman National Bank."

"That was the day she left her job," Lisa said.

"And I bet she was on her way to Grand Cayman that day or the next."

"No grass grows under her feet now, does it?" Lisa said with a grin, "any information on the Cayman account?"

“Nope,” Sheila replied, “that’s where the trail ends. At least for now.”

“You mean you can’t find it?”

“I can do it, but not without a name on the account and some high level support,” Sheila said, “we just can’t hack into foreign banks on our own.”

“Okay,” Lisa replied, “anything on the online orders?”

“Oh yeah!” Sheila replied, “Kelly Knowles is a huge Amazon fan!”

“So, what did she buy?”

“On January 22nd she ordered orange neon tennis shoes, a white sequined golf cap, and a pair of white sunglasses with sequins. Everything was delivered by Thursday, January 25th.”

“Bingo!” Lisa yelled, “thank you, thank you, thank you, Sheila! I owe you big time for this?”

“So, what’s my reward?”came Sheila’s fast response.

“You win my undying respect, Sheels!” Lisa replied, “how the hell did you get all this information so fast.”

“Lise, If I told you, I’d have to shoot you.”

“And you’d probably get away with it, too!” Lisa joked

As she ended the call, Lisa turned to her husband.

“Sheila Feeney is a genius,” she said, “I don’t know how she does it!”

“What did she say?” Rick asked.

“It all fits together, Rick, Kelly Knowles was the mastermind behind this whole thing.”

“You can’t be sure of that, Lise.”

“Look,” Lisa replied, “she knew about the will change and delayed it for almost a month until Diane Bates was dead. She went after Dave Messenger and married him. She put on clothes to look like Abby Jenkins, and bought the burner phone in The Villages. Then she got Messenger to use a fake Boston accent and make the call that hired Bobby James to kill Diane Bates. It was all her!”

“Her, and two clueless idiots who didn’t realize they were being used,” Rick added.

"And then, the best part." Lisa said, "she set up an account with her name on it, transferred the inheritance money into it, and then sent the money off to a Cayman bank account in her name only."

"Or whatever name she's using for that," Rick pondered.

"You know, you're right," Lisa replied, "I'm sure she isn't Kelly Knowles, or Kelly Messenger now."

"That's one smart chick!" Rick said with a grin, "I wonder if she's using the same name Kathleen Turner used in *Body Heat*?"

"What name was that?" Lisa asked.

"I've got no clue," Rick replied with a smile, "great movie, *Body Heat*."

Lisa grabbed her cell phone and called Captain Davis.

"Hey, Captain. It's Lisa. I need you to arrange for Dave Messenger to be arrested right away!"

CHAPTER 50

SEPTEMBER 18, 2018, 9:00 A.M.
PORT ST. LUCIE POLICE DEPARTMENT
INTERVIEW ROOM 1

Lisa sat and stared at Dave Messenger for what seemed like several minutes. She could see that he was nervous, so she waited even longer before she finally spoke. Megan Harris was siting next to her.

"Mr. Messenger," she said quietly. "You've been read your rights and you understand the you're under arrest for the murder of Diane Bates."

"You already convicted Len Bates for that!" Dave responded quickly, "why are you arresting me?"

"Mr. Messenger," Lisa responded, "we have sufficient evidence now to know that it was you who made the phone calls to Bobby James."

"It wasn't me!"

"I'm sorry, Mr. Messenger, but we know that it was you. And we also know that Kelly Knowles dressed up in clothes to look like Abby Jenkins, and she bought the burner phone in The Villages."

"What?"

"We also know that, after you received the inheritance money from Diane Bates' estate, Kelly, by then your wife, stole every penny of it from you and sent it to a foreign bank account in her name only."

Dave Messenger was fuming. He was unable to control his anger and frustration.

"She set me up for all of this!" he yelled.

"I believe you, Dave," Lisa said quietly, "I believe this was all her plan, and I believe that you were just a small part of it."

"We can help you, Dave," Megan interjected, "It's Kelly Knowles we're after, and the money she stole. And you can help us get to her."

"That's right, Dave," Lisa continued, "we need you to help us nail Kelly Knowles for what she did to you."

Messenger sat for a minute pondering his next move.

"I want to talk to my lawyer," he said.

"That's certainly your right, Dave," Megan said, "we can have a phone brought in here for you and we'll leave the room until you're ready to talk with us again."

The two women left the room as a phone was handed to Dave Messenger. He immediately called his friend, Jason Baron.

"I've been arrested, Jason, and I need you right away!"

"Jesus, Dave!" Jason replied, "I'm not a criminal defense attorney, you know that!"

"I don't care," Dave whispered, "they know everything, Jase."

"Everything?" Jason replied.

"Yes, and I don't know what to do."

"Okay, okay." Jason said, "do you want my advice?'

"Of course I do!"

"My advice is to come clean. The money's gone, so now the best thing you can do is cooperate. Just tell them how Kelly set you up and stole your inheritance."

"But if I do that I'll go to jail!"

"Dave, that ship has sailed," Jason said, "look, you're my best friend and I would never steer you wrong. You believe me, don't you?"

"Yes."

"Okay then, put me on the phone with them and let me try to make you a deal."

With that Dave signaled for Lisa and Megan to return.

"Put me on speaker phone, Dave," Jason said.

As soon as the two women sat down, Megan spoke. "Hello sir, this is Megan Harris, St. Lucie County prosecutor. Also here with me is Detective Lisa March."

"Good morning to you both," Jason said, "my name is Jason Baron. I represent David Messenger."

"Okay," Megan replied, "it's your dime."

"I want to know if, hypothetically, Mister Messenger were to admit that he hired the handyman to kill Diane Bates, and he'd be willing to testify that Kelly Knowles hatched the whole plan, what kind of plea deal might we be able to make?"

"What kind of plea deal were you looking for, Mr. Baron?"

"What's the best you can do?"

"Let's see," Megan pondered, "hiring someone to commit murder is considered as serious a crime as committing the murder."

"So what does that mean?"

"It means he could get the death penalty if he's convicted."

"Can you do better if he confesses?" Jason asked.

"I probably can get the D.A. to agree to twenty-five years to life." Megan replied.

"Uh huh."

"He'd be eligible for parole in twenty-five years. He would still be a relatively young man by then."

"David, it's totally up to you," Jason said, "but you could get a much worse sentence if you don't take this deal."

Dave Messenger sat stoically. He was about to agree to a deal that would land him in prison for at least twenty-five years.

"This offer expires in five minutes, David," Megan said forcefully, "If it goes to trial all bets are off, and I can assure you that you will be convicted."

“Then you’d be looking at spending the rest of your life in prison,” Lisa added, “maybe even the death penalty!”

“I need an answer from you now!” Megan said forcefully. She began to pack up her things as though she were ready to leave.

“I’ll take the deal!” Dave shouted.

“Okay then,” Megan replied, “I’ll get someone in here to record your confession. Goodbye Mr. Baron.”

As they left the interview room Lisa grabbed her cellphone and called her partner.

“Danny,” she said, “we nailed Messenger. Now we have to track down Kelly Knowles.”

CHAPTER 51

SEPTEMBER 18, 2018, 6:00 P.M.

THE HOME OF LISA AND RICK MARCH

Lisa walked into the foyer and Rick, as always, was waiting for her with a glass of Kendall Jackson Chardonnay.

"Big news today," he said, "did you see it?"

"I've been busy all day, hon. What did I miss?"

"I recorded it for you," Rick replied, "Mayor Wilson."

• • • • •

"Hi, this is Brian Regan in the TV 12 newsroom. Port St Lucie Mayor Candace Wilson appeared on the steps of City Hall late this afternoon to address the charges against her and her husband in what has become known as the Doctor Duke scandal. Let's listen to what the Mayor had to say.

"Good afternoon. By now I'm sure most everyone has heard about the charges leveled against my husband and me regarding our son's acceptance to Duke University."

"First, let me say that our son, Andrew, is a fine young man and an excellent student who deserves to be at Duke University."

"Last year my husband and I hired a consultant who had the reputation and experience of helping parents to understand and comply with the rigorous entrance requirements of Duke University."

"At no time did my husband, nor I ask this consultant to break any laws, and if he did we were totally unaware of that fact."

"As of now I am suspending my campaign for governor and I can assure you that my attorneys will vigorously challenge these false charges against me and my family. Thank you."

• • • • •

"You see, she didn't take any questions," Rick said, "she's a smooth politician, that's for sure."

"Did you see who was standing right beside her, Rick?" Lisa asked.

"Who?"

"None other than the man who, I assume, will be her attorney through this mess."

"I missed him. Who was it?"

"My old friend, JD Treem!" Lisa said with a belly laugh.

"Well, he must be happy to see Len Bates get out of jail."

"Of course," Lisa said, "once Dave Messenger confessed, both Len Bates and Abby Jenkins were off the hook."

"So Bates was innocent after all!" Rick said.

"That's how it turned out," Lisa replied, "and I be he paid JD Treem a ton of money to defend him."

"If Bates was innocent and Treem still lost his case, that doesn't say too much for the legendary Palm Beach lawyer, does it?"

"Yep, I guess Bates isn't too happy with JD Treem," Lisa replied. "Megan Harris kicked his butt in court!"

"The only reason Bates is a free man today is because of you, Lisa," Rick said, "he owes you big time!

"That's true, Rick, but I'm not expecting a thank you card. Remember, I'm the one who arrested him in the first place!"

"Bates must really be pissed at the lady who set him up like that!" Rick said, "but I guess he'll get over it after the insurance company finally releases the two million to him."

"I'm not so sure he'll ever get over it, Rick," Lisa responded, "the guy went through a tumultuous trial, had his reputation dragged through the mud, spent a couple of months in prison, saw his health deteriorate, and when he came out of prison his house and almost everything else he owned were gone!"

"Kelly Knowles didn't care how many lives she ruined in her quest for five million bucks, did she?" Rick said.

"We've got an all points bulletin out for the arrest of Kelly Knowles Messenger," Lisa said, "every police department in the country will be looking for her."

"How about Grand Cayman?"

"Yes, they've been notified, too."

"What about all that money Kelly Knowles stole?" Rick asked, "isn't there any way to get it back?"

"We're sure as hell gonna try!" Lisa replied, "If anybody can get to it, Sheila Feeney can!"

"This has been one helluva case for you, hasn't it, honey?" Rick said, "a case to remember."

"I'll never forget the Pickleball murder case!" Lisa said with a smile, "and I'm gonna learn to play that game if it's the last thing I do!"

"I'm not so sure he'll ever get over it," Lisa responded. "The guy [illegible]

[illegible]

CHAPTER 52

OCTOBER 23, 2018, 5:00 P.M.

THE HOME OF LISA AND RICK MARCH

Sheila Feeney walked into Lisa's house with a bottle of Prosecco in her hand. She was met there by Lisa, Rick, Megan, and Megan's fiancé, Ed Borden.

"We did it folks!" she cried, "we did it!"

"The money transferred already?" Lisa asked.

"I got the transfer in just before the bank closed so they couldn't possibly stop it," Sheila replied, "it hit our Swiss bank account ten minutes ago."

"Kelly Knowles, or Mary Ann Simpson, is gonna shit a brick when she finds out she's broke!" Rick said.

"Ooh, that will make it even sweeter!" Sheila said, as she popped the cork on the Prosecco, "I wish I could be a fly on the wall when she finds out she's got no money!"

"How much was in there?" Megan asked.

"We got four million, seven hundred fifty-two thousand, and change," Sheila said.

"Oh, so she didn't spend a whole lot. That's good!" Ed said.

“I was worried that we wouldn’t get it done in time, and she would spend all the money before we got to her,” Lisa said.

Sheila poured each of them a glass of Prosecco.

“This was a real team effort,” Megan said, “first, thanks to you, Rick, for successfully contesting Diane Bates’ will.”

“Not me, folks,” Rick replied, “the real thanks goes to Judge Velez for granting us a speedy hearing.”

“It’s not often a will gets contested after the money has already been dispersed!” Lisa chuckled.

“That’s for sure,” Rick continued, “but after Dave Messenger pleaded guilty to killing Diane Bates and we showed Judge Velez the new, unsigned will, it was easy for him to grant David’s share to Jennifer Messenger.”

“That’s who Diane wanted to get it in the first place,” Megan said, “so he respected her wishes.”

“But the hard part was getting permission to hack into the Cayman account,” Shiela said, “I could have done it once I had the name, but I needed air cover first.

“That was Eddie’s job,” Megan replied.

Ed took a sip of Prosecco, “I had to call in a lot of chips at the Attorney General’s office, but we finally got it done!”

“You know,” Lisa said, “the only way we were able to find out that Kelly Knowles became Mary Ann Simpson was because she got her fake passport from a local guy. She used a passport forger named Billy Wayland.

“Yes, and it turns out that Billy Wayland was a confidential informant for Lonny Carter,” Sheila added, “and once he heard that we were looking for Kelly Knowles, he phoned in a tip to Lonny’s old partner, Beth Danelo.”

“What a break that turned out to be!” Lisa said.

“Yep, and as soon as I had the name, the rest was easy!” Sheila said proudly.

“So, even after he died,” Lisa said, “Lonny helped us bring justice for Diane Bates’ family!”

Megan lifted her glass. "Here's to Lonny, may he rest in peace."

"To Lonny!" They all said in unison.

"I wonder what Kelly Knowles is gonna do now?" Lisa asked.

EPILOGUE

OCTOBER 26, 2018, 1:00 P.M.

THE GRAND HOTEL

GRAND CAYMAN ISLAND

"Another Bloody Mary, and make sure you put lots of celery and olives in it," Juanita, the young cocktail waitress, said to Nigel, the bartender, "that's the way the lady likes it."

"Okay," Nigel replied.

Since this was Juanita's first week on the job at the Grand Hotel she was eager to please her guests, especially this woman. She had been told that the lady was a very important visitor from the United States, and a big tipper, too. She also considered herself very fortunate to have landed a job in one of the fanciest hotels in the Cayman Islands.

Juanita delivered the drink and was surprised to see that a man had joined the woman at the table. The man ordered a gin and tonic, which Juanita quickly provided. The woman then asked Juanita to 'stay away for a while'.

"Hello, sir," the woman said calmly, "my name is Mary Ann Simpson."

"It's a pleasure to meet you, madam," the man replied, "I'm Arturo Everett with Cayman Realty. I understand that you're interested in buying a condominium here."

"Yes, I am," the woman replied, "I've decided to move here to Grand Cayman."

"A very wise choice, madam, this is a glorious place to live. We welcome you with open arms!" Mr. Everett said with a grin, as he sipped his gin and tonic.

Kelly Knowles stared into the eyes of Mr. Everett. Since her arrival in Grand Cayman seven weeks ago she had been suspicious of everyone with whom she had come into contact. She had been careful to keep a very low profile, secluding herself in the Grand Hotel, except for periodic excursions to look at possible sites for a permanent residence.

A fake U.S. passport had allowed Kelly to claim her new identity as Mary Ann Simpson. This new identity, coupled with dermal fillers for her face, blue contact lenses, and dark hair dye, had transformed and protected her up to this point, but caution was always prudent in a situation like this.

Grand Cayman was considered a safe haven for people like her, but it was better to be safe than sorry. Kelly had been smart enough to set up her bank account in the Cayman Bank six months ago, in anticipation of moving the inheritance money into it. For a long time she had planned to end up here.

"I have a beautiful, one bedroom villa on Seven Mile Beach for you to look at today," Mr. Everett told her.

In a few minutes they were inside a luxurious condominium. Kelly looked around and marveled at the details.

"This comes fully furnished," Everett said, as he opened a kitchen cabinet, "dishes and everything else included."

"Very nice," Kelly said.

"All you need to bring are your clothes and food!" Everett said, "and look at this magnificent view of the Caribbean from the balcony."

"I've looked at several properties here, but this one seems like it has real potential," Kelly said, "what's the price, again?"

"The owner purchased this condo for two point four million last year, but he is extremely motivated to sell it now," Everett said, "I think any offer above two million could make the deal. Would you be financing?"

"No, I'll pay cash," Kelly replied.

"Even better, madam!" Everett said, "a cash offer with a healthy deposit could seal the deal!"

"This is the nicest one I've seen so far," Kelly said, "tell me about the details, closing costs, homeowners association fees, insurance."

"Of course, madam," Everett replied, "I have all of the particulars and paperwork in my car. It'll just take me two minutes."

"Okay," Kelly replied, "I'll get the bank started on the deposit."

Everett closed the door behind him, leaving his briefcase on the kitchen counter.

Kelly immediately took out her cell phone and tapped on the Cayman Bank app. She used facial recognition to access her account.

"What the fuck?" she screamed.

Kelly exited the app and immediately called the Cayman Bank.

"Where the hell is my money?" she yelled.

"I'm sorry, madam," the Cayman Bank representative replied, "all the funds were withdrawn from this account."

"Withdrawn?" Kelly screamed, "by who?"

"By you, madam."

"By me? When?"

"A few days ago, madam. You requested a wire transfer to an account in Swiss Bank."

"What account in Swiss Bank? Who owns that account?"

"I'm sorry, madam, Swiss Bank won't give us that information. Perhaps you can call them."

Mr. Everett opened his car door and grabbed a remote controller. He carefully pressed one of the buttons and watched as his briefcase exploded inside the condo.

The force of the blast was so powerful that it blew the shattered windows all the way to the water's edge.

Everett picked up his cell phone and dialed a number in Port St. Lucie, Florida.

"My mission has been accomplished." he said, "you have my account number here."

On the other end of the phone, Doctor Leonard Bates said, "your payment is on its way."

CPSIA information can be obtained
at www.ICGtesting.com
Printed in the USA
BVHW032003301121
622895BV00006B/281

9 780578 794358